Loved Like That

Loved Like That

by Julie Wright

BONNEVILLE BOOKS™

ISBN: 1-55517-629-1
e.2

Published by Bonneville Books
Imprint of Cedar Fort Inc.
www.cedarfort.com

Distributed by:

Typeset by Kristin Nelson
Cover design by Nicole Mortensen

Printed in the United States of America
10 9 8 7 6 5 4 3 2 1

Printed on acid-free paper

Library of Congress Cataloging-in-Publication Data

Wright, Julie, 1972-
Loved like that / by Julie Wright.
p. cm.
ISBN 1-55517-629-1 (pbk. : alk. paper)
1. Near-death experiences--Fiction. 2. Accident victims--Fiction. 3. Police--Fiction. I. Title.
PS3623.R55 L68 2002
813'.6--dc21

2002012569

To Scott,

For laughing and crying in all the
right places. You are my greatest audience.

I love you härifrån til evighet.

A special thanks to Officer James Cowan
for your friendship and honor,
and to Annette for your amazing typing skills
and your Christ-like service.

Chapter 1

It had been raining for three days straight. The humidity was a relief in the dry air of Utah. The air was thick enough to taste with your fingertips when you stretched your arm out the window. Wind, rain, and dust blown up from the wind all backlit by lightning, brought the elements together in a way that made a man shiver.

Rain pelted James' arm while he was driving with it jutted out into the sky from his car window. His fingers folded into his palm and flexed out again, rotating his wrist so that every inch of skin was privileged to touch the droplets of water. He half closed his eyes wishing for the tenth time that he had taken the motorcycle. The headlights reflected off the water rushing to the windshield like the speed of light star-lines in a Star Wars movie.

The weather was perfect as far as James was concerned. The July heat melted into the rain. The humidity that came with it and adhered his shirt to his back didn't bother him like it did others; it actually did not bother him at all.

His hand shot out and his finger punched a preset button. The radio personality announced a nonstop '80s flashback weekend. James settled into the driver's seat.

He was on his way to Allen's house. Allen was his best friend from childhood, and as such, felt a personal responsibility in finding James a wife. James had been through countless of "perfect women for him" and had wanted to tell Allen to take a hike. He would too, were it not for the fact that the blind dates broke up the monotony of his nightlife. Allen's wife, Cindy, was also a great cook and it was hard not to want to eat whatever she may be fixing.

It was that thought alone that kept James going the direction of Allen's house in West Jordan instead of . . . well, anywhere else. His new blind date was with a girl from Cindy's work place. He arrived at the door a few minutes early but knew that his date was early too, from the strange car parked in the driveway.

Cindy opened the door and kissed his cheek after giving him a hug. Allen called up from the basement where he was setting up his new computer. He promised to be up in a minute to which Cindy rolled her eyes. "He will be way more than a minute," she laughed. "He has been down there all day installing new programs and will go back as soon as dinner is over."

Cindy turned to the woman who had trailed to the front door behind her. The woman had blonde hair wrapped tight in a twist at the back of her neck. She was thin and fair and gorgeous as far as looks went. He could have fallen for her green eyes alone. "James, this is Lydia." Cindy touched the woman's shoulder. Lydia flashed a dazzling smile and took the hand that James extended to her.

"Hello, James."

"Hey there, Lydia. It is really nice to meet you."

"It's nice to meet you too. So . . . where are you from?"

"Utah," he said, a bit puzzled by the question. Cindy had told him Lydia had just moved from Oregon, so maybe she was just in the mindset of people being transplanted instead of actually from the state.

She smiled thinly. "No, I mean originally."

James shrugged. "I've lived here all my life except when I went on my mission to Sweden. Other than that . . ."

"I mean your ancestry." Lydia had now taken the tone of lecturing as though she had to spell out to him every word she said. She very well may have needed to. James was entirely confused.

"Excuse me?" He could not keep the wonder out of his voice.

"Oh, yes, I just asked where you are from, originally, I mean. I just think it is so important to establish a person's origin immediately upon meeting them so as to understand them better." She barely paused. "I mean sure, you think you're merely Caucasian, but in truth you are probably German or Irish or Scandinavian or something."

His jaw tightened. *You have the right to remain silent,* he thought to himself. A low growl that was only audible to him, rumbled deep in his throat. "I am an American," he said. "Just like everyone else that lives in America."

He moved away from her to the kitchen where Cindy had gone to finish preparing dinner. Lydia, he thought that was what her name was, followed closely behind. Her perfume hung thick in the air, enough to feel smothering. It smelled herbal, instead of sweet, as he felt a perfume should. He wondered how rude exactly it would be if he just left now and saved them all a lot of misery in trying to find things to talk about.

"You only say . . ." She went on, barely breathing between words. "You only say that because you have been trained to think on a close-at-hand, selfish level. But you need to realize we live in a global world and need to think globally."

Had there been a door to the kitchen, he may have considered shutting it to keep her away from him. *Selfish?* His parents had taught him the concept of service and sharing and living globally for heaven's sake. The woman was insane! The most selfless people in the entire world had taught him and he carried his instruction of youth with pride. He liked to think the words, "I, James, having been born of goodly parents . . ." He was taught just fine and he was *not* selfish.

"I can think globally," he told her. "For instance, if I were Irish, I'd be living in Ireland. If I were Scandinavian, I would be living in Sweden, or Denmark or something. If I were Cuban, I would be living in Cuba or maybe doing an *I Love Lucy* show."

She didn't laugh at the joke he had attempted, although he heard Cindy chuckle to the side of him. He grinned at her, gratefully, and then stepped back to distance himself from the perfume. *Incense!* That was what she smelled like! A woodsy sort of incense was what was filling his nostrils.

"You know," James continued, "I know where all those places are on a map, too. I did great in geography." He smiled at her, hoping maybe she was really not so bad; after all he had just met her and impressions can always be wrong. He would give her a chance.

"Knowing where a place is and understanding its culture is not the same thing." Her eyes drooped in the bored way some women did when they were certain they were superior to the man they were addressing. He lost his resolve to give her a chance in less than a second.

"You haven't asked me about what cultures I understand so you may be surprised. I understand a whole lot of them, but it seems that you—"

Cindy stepped between them, cutting James off from the thrashing he was about to send to Lydia-the-Correct. "Lydia, could you help me get all of this to the table?" Cindy gestured to the counter filled with plates of various foods.

Lydia's lovely green eyes widened in surprise and dismay as she folded her arms across her chest. "Why is it you so naturally ask the female to do that? Isn't James capable of lifting a pan or a dish?"

Without saying anything, James clenched his jaw tighter against the words: *you have the right to remain silent*. He picked up two dishes and took them to the dining table. Cindy patted him empathetically on the shoulder and thanked him softly.

Lydia didn't end up taking anything to the table at all. She perched herself upon a chair and eyed the table disapprovingly. James wondered how so fair a face had become so sour internally.

Cindy called Allen to the table. They waited in silence for him to show up. When two minutes that felt like two hours had passed, Cindy stood up to get him herself. "You know how he is with his computers . . ." She smiled apologetically and trailed down the stairs to where he was.

James sat a moment longer and decided to give it another try. "So you work with Cindy?"

"Yes, I am in the investigations department."

"Investigations?" He perked up. That was at least a familiar word to him. Something they may have in common. "How does that work?"

"Since it is a bank, I deal with check kiting and people who close accounts after writing a lot of checks for high ticket items."

"That's pretty cool. I'm kind of in the same thing with my job—"

"You're finally here!" Lydia exclaimed impatiently, cutting James off, as Allen and Cindy came upstairs together. James stood up to greet them.

Allen pulled out Cindy's chair and helped her get settled before taking his own seat. James remained standing, trying to come up with a reason to stay. She had just totally interrupted him as well as looking as though Allen and Cindy had saved her from the absolute jaws of boredom by having to talk to him.

Allen's eyes widened as he jerked his head towards the seat James had decided not to occupy. James set his jaw stubbornly and shook his head slightly. Finally James let his good manners overtake him, yanked the chair out further and sat down hard, glaring all the while at Allen.

Cindy sighed in relief and Allen bowed his head to bless the food. The blessing was quick and to the point and once Amen had been chorused, the food was passed around the table. Allen very purposely did not look in James' direction.

"So, Lydia, have you settled into your new apartment?" Cindy passed the honeyed carrots to her.

"I guess so. The people next door listen to some really lousy '80s garbage and play it loud enough that everyone has to be tortured by it. "

"Like what kind of music?" James asked, genuinely intrigued by her use of the term "'80s garbage."

"Oh, you know that awful stuff we listened to when we thought we were cool . . . Depeche Mode, Pet Shop Boys, and Alphaville." She sighed as if contemplating a great tragedy.

"How can you not like '80s music?" James asked incredulously. "Everyone likes '80s music!"

"For the decade impaired people who cannot get out of the past, I can only say I pity them. Music is so much better now than it ever was then." She placed a forkful of carrots into her mouth and chewed thoughtfully.

James' jaw went slack. "It isn't decade-impaired to appreciate music from the past. It's like good literature; educated people would call them classics. The same is true for music, and that is not to say that just because you listen to older music that your tastes don't develop or change, but that there is a certain familiarity that comes from music from the past. I believe that music is timeless in all of its varieties, from Rachmaninov to the Beatles to . . . to any of the artists today."

Cindy chewed and swallowed quickly to interject, "James is a pianist and very involved musically." She said it as if to cover up or to excuse him in some way. But he was not the one behaving poorly! He scowled at her and stuffed a bite of roast into his mouth.

The conversation, if it could be called that, lulled into serious silence wide enough that a Mack Truck could drive through it. Allen concentrated on smothering his roast with A-1 sauce and then sawing away at it with zeal. He jumped suddenly. "Ow!" he barked, turning to Cindy. "What did you kick me for?" he demanded.

She smiled patiently. "You said you had something to ask James," she prompted; anything to help the conversation.

"What? Oh, oh yeah." He chewed his bite of roast too quickly and swallowed painfully. "I was wondering if you ever caught the kid that held up the pizza driver."

"Oh, yeah, funniest thing ever, his buddy turned him in! Dumb kid was bragging about making off with $42.00!" James snorted. "As if that kind of money was worth bragging about."

Lydia looked at them all as if they had left her out of the conversation. "Why are you hunting down petty thieves?" she asked.

"That's what I do. I'm a cop."

Lydia's eyes went wide with horror. "You're a cop?"

"Yeah, I am," James said with apprehension and more than a little pride.

She turned to Cindy. "You never said he was a cop," she flamed in accusation.

Cindy shrugged. "I didn't realize it made any difference."

Lydia wasn't listening, already reeling back to James. "Do you carry a gun?"

"Yes, I do." He wanted to say, "Duh!" but held it in.

"Do you have one on now?"

"Yes. I keep it in my fanny pack." He patted the bulge in the pack and then he grinned wickedly. "Wanna see it?"

Her eyes nearly popped out of her head. "NO! I certainly do not want to see it. I demand that you take that thing off and put it in another room for dinner."

"No thank you. I think it's fine right where it is."

"I can't eat knowing I am so close to such violence," she lamented, wringing her hands, and casting her eyes all about.

"It isn't like I plan on shooting anyone," James said sardonically.

"I just can't eat unless you take that thing off and put it somewhere else."

"Wow," James shrugged calmly. "That's a real shame you are going to have to go hungry like that. Hey, Cin-ful, would you pass the pepper?"

And from there the evening got worse. It went from bad to reason to commit suicide . . . or homicide as James saw it. She had been one female that he would've loved to take into the station kicking and screaming and hose her down. He had met some pretty wild ideas before but she was the pinnacle of disasters. He left before she did, only stopping long enough to kiss Cindy's cheek and tell her dinner was great. He whispered in her ear that he would be back later for leftovers. She smiled apologetically, but also gratefully. She knew by this statement that he wasn't mad at her or Allen for setting him up with someone so . . . unlike him.

For the hundredth time that night, James wished he had thought to take the bike instead of the car. He rolled down his window so he could feel the rain. Cupping his hand to catch a little, he pulled his arm into the car, rolled up the window, and scrubbed his wet hand over his face.

The cell phone at his side chirped. The temptation to not answer it was overwhelming. Sighing again, he picked it up and hit the "Send" button. "Yo . . . hello, Allen, my ex-best friend. Did the psycho go home? For Pete's sake, Allen, why wouldn't you have told her before that I was a cop?" He turned the radio down. "No, I am not picky. I just don't want to date a woman like her, especially since she treated me like a parasite when she found out I was a cop."

"No, I'm not looking for Miss Right, I'm looking for Miss right now!"

He rolled his eyes at the phone. "Yeah okay, yadda yadda yadda yadda. You just don't know what it's like; you're married to the girl of your dreams. I can't even find a girl that I can have a decent conversation with."

The rain stopped, and James flipped off the wipers. He exited I-215 from the 6200 South exit right behind a little red BMW Coupe. The BMW was going too fast and James thought if he had his patrol car he'd pull it over. Allen was rattling off about how James needed to put himself in better social situations to meet women.

James crossed Holladay Boulevard and slowed to take a curve in time to witness the BMW take the next curve without slowing at all.

The shout "Look out!" stuck in his throat and all moisture dried up in his hung open mouth. "I'll call you back!" he spurted into the phone and hung up.

The BMW had spun on the curve, then spun halfway around again before it rolled over, sliding on its top. The metal grated against the asphalt, throwing sparks and glass from the windshield like a violent fireworks display. He slammed on his brakes with a quick prayer that he would stop before becoming entangled into the mess unfolding in front of him. The brakes were now useless since his car had started hydroplaning. The BMW slid out of his way just in time for him to zoom through the wreckage of glass and metal.

Both cars came to a halt at nearly the same time. James' fingers fumbled over the seat belt buckle trying to get it undone as he reversed his car to the side of the road and out of the way of any traffic that might come by.

He grabbed his phone he'd thrown to the side and turned off the engine. He punched 911 as he ran to the BMW. The woman's clear voice responded, "911, what's your emergency?"

"This is Officer Hartman, 18-J-5. There has been a traffic accident with injuries by the Cotton Bottom in Holladay. Approximately 2500 East 6400 South."

The dispatcher's calm voice asked, "How many injuries? Do you know?"

The air smelled like the fresh rain, clean and earthy. He gulped deep breaths of it as he bent down to peer into the car. Through the tangled metal, he could see it was empty. The driver must have been thrown out.

"At least one, maybe more, but it looks bad."

"Medical personnel and officers are enroute."

"Thanks." He slid the phone into his jacket pocket.

Saying another quick prayer and fighting the desire to curse, he surveyed the wreckage trying to decide where the driver would have been thrown out.

He ran off to the right and found her.

Her body lay crumpled on the hard packed dirt like a doll discarded long after it was worn out. He bent over her and shook her gently to see if there was any reaction. He leaned his head down to check for breathing. There was none.

"No!" he whispered hoarsely and rolled her over gently to her back. He leaned back on his heels and stared for a moment. Her dark hair made a pillow framing her face and even through all the road rash, blood and bruises forming, she was easily the most perfect thing he'd ever seen.

Shaking himself, he placed his finger over the carotid artery in her neck to find a heartbeat—silence. He did curse this time. He ripped her shirt open, the buttons popping off neatly as he tore through it. Placing one hand over the other on her chest, he began compressions. "One, two, three, four . . ." He counted out loud to fifteen then tilted her head and lifted her chin. He pinched her nose and covered her mouth with his. Two breaths. He repeated this cycle four times. He placed his head back over her mouth and watched her chest for breathing and checked her neck again for a heartbeat. Nothing. Anxiety and the closest thing to panic he had ever felt threatened to clamp his heart closed.

"C'mon, beautiful, don't die on me," he cried out loud.

The trees rustled overhead as though there were a breeze, but he felt no pick up in the wind. "Do you know the last time anyone ever called me beautiful?" A female voice seemed to come from everywhere as though the voice itself surrounded him, but no one else was there. Confused, James looked down at the body he was hovered over. Her eyes were closed; the right side of her face was practically ripped off from skidding along the asphalt. Bits of gravel stuck into the bloodied flesh that hung from her chin. The body was still.

"It was when I got engaged to the guy I had been dating," the ethereal voice continued like a breeze around him. And then James saw her. She was standing next to him, looking down at her own body.

"He asked me to sleep with him, and actually thought I was stupid enough to fall for the old 'Well, we're going to get married anyway, what difference will it make?'" She let out a tiny laugh and shook her head.

James' eyes filled his entire face. She looked away from her crumpled body to stare at him. Her smile was soft and comforting despite the almost teasing tone of her voice.

"You said no, right?" he managed, not knowing what else he

could say to the spirit of the girl he was doing CPR on.

"Of course I said no, and that is why that was the last time anyone ever called me beautiful." She seemed to ponder James a moment before saying, "I'm very glad you're here. I think I would be afraid to be alone."

He drank in the sight of her. She didn't glow like he expected a spirit to, yet somehow seemed as bright as anything he could ever remember. And when she shook her head gently and the dark hair tumbled over her shoulders she seemed to shimmer like she was fading away and then back again.

"But you are beautiful," James heard himself say. "The most beautiful thing I've ever seen." He felt lame for having said the most sappy thing that had ever fallen from his lips, but he couldn't stop the words. Tears pricked at his eyes and he leaned closer to her, wanting to touch her but not daring to. "How does it feel?" he asked.

She looked down at herself as if aware for the first time of the shimmering essence she had become. She looked back at him, confused. "I don't know. It feels like nothing. No heat, no cold, no anything." She rubbed her hands together. "There isn't anything to feel like that but yet..."

"But . . . but what?" he prompted.

"You shouldn't stop." She motioned toward the body. Her body.

Startled back into the reality of the moment, James bent quickly to continue and started counting as he compressed his palms into her heart. "Sixteen, seventeen, eighteen."

He leaned over her mouth. Her voice from all around him whispered playfully as he breathed out, "After all, how will you ever get to know me if you let me die?" Her giggle sounded like chimes on a cool summer morning . . . chimes that surrounded him and filled his head.

He breathed into her and watched as her chest rose and fell

and then rose again. And then as he was about to start the compressions once more her chest rose and fell on its own.

He started to cry, not knowing why exactly. “You’re going to be all . . .” He looked over to where she had been standing but she wasn’t there any longer. Turning back to the now breathing body, he watched her eyelids flutter and open. “You’re going to be all right now,” he said softly and her eyes closed again.

Sirens filtered in from everywhere, screeching to a halt at the scene of the accident. He moved aside for the EMTs to take over and let the police question him about everything.

Through all the questions he tried to see her. What were they doing to her? Was she going to be okay? What was her name? He hadn’t asked her name.

Not like there was loads of time to ask questions, but he wished he knew the name of his dark haired angel. But the most important question in his mind was would she remember him when she woke?

Chapter 2

The hospital was busy and the emergency room was swamped. James sat on a pink and mauve checked chair wishing he could yank the arms off of a couple of chairs on the row to make a bed. It had been four and a half hours. Expectant mothers on their way to delivery seemed to trickle in on a steady flow of deep breathing and anxious glances at husbands. There had been a broken arm from a ten-year-old boy that jumped off his bunk bed and landed wrong, a drug overdose, and two cases of appendicitis.

The guys with the appendicitis screamed louder and whimpered longer than the women in labor. James wondered if that was due to level of pain or level of pain tolerance. He couldn't be sure and didn't want to find out firsthand either.

The worst pain he had ever felt had been a gunshot wound to his shoulder when he was 16 years old. His parents had been out of town and he had quickly mowed the lawn before they got back. He had finished his task early and gone to take a nap in his room until they finally got home. He awoke nearly an hour later to the sounds of rummaging in the hall closet.

Thinking it was his mom and dad, back from their trip, he swung open his bedroom door. The gun was level with his head held by a shaky hand. The wild eyes that met his from under the matted hair shifted around enough so as to appear to shake as violently as the gunman's hand.

His heart pounded, rushing blood in a roar past his ears. The wild-eyed man's finger twitched on the trigger and James thrust his arm out instinctively, knocking the gun from its aim between his eyes. It fired. The bullet found its mark in his shoulder. His mouth worked in a soundless scream as the bullet seared through his shoulder and burrowed down into his chest. The wild-eyed man yelled, pushed James back, dropped the gun, and fled the house.

James struggled to get up and accidentally bumped his shoulder on the doorframe. Knowing it should have hurt, he gritted his teeth, although he was so numb he barely noticed the jostling. He stumbled out the doorway left open by his assailant and onto the front lawn. The sun tore into his slitted eyes just as the bullet had through his shoulder. His legs buckled from under him and James lost consciousness.

He shivered now. That moment had been a catalyst that brought him to this point in his life. His desire to be a cop, his entrance to the military, everything he was, stemmed from the triangular scar on his shoulder and the occasional pain that spread from his lungs and heart, where bullet fragments were still lodged. Pain that was probably comparable to the dark haired angel's at this moment. James shifted in his seat with a grimace. What he would give to know her name!

There had been no ID in the car and the plates were registered to a Bradley Armstrong. That certainly wouldn't be her name, but maybe a father or a brother. He hoped it wasn't a boyfriend. She had mentioned a fiancé, but that had sounded very past tense. Anyway, he couldn't imagine a woman as beautiful and good as her staying with a guy like that.

The doctor, a slender woman in her forties with soft wrinkles barely forming around her eyes, stretched her neck as she approached him. There was blood on her scrubs and her eyes drooped in weariness or worry or both.

He stood quickly, the unread magazine falling unnoticed from his lap to the floor. "Is she all right?"

"She's going to be. It was some effort to reconstruct her arm and get the glass and asphalt out of her skin. She'll have to get the rest scraped out later."

The doctor shook her head. "She's lucky, very lucky you were right there to do CPR on her. If she had waited for the paramedics and survived it, who's to say what kind of brain damage she would have ended up with? As it is, nothing is certain."

The doctor spoke to him as a cop, not the concerned family member he felt like. She laid bare the truth as she saw it to him instead of coating it in comfort. Right then he wanted the comfort, needed it, but was glad for the naked truth. It meant the dark haired angel would be fine, eventually.

"Can I see her?" James' voice was surprisingly steady.

The doctor shrugged. "I don't see why not. No family has been found yet and so it isn't like you'll be in anyone's way. Stay quiet though. I don't know what difference it makes, but . . . you know the routine."

She passed a hand over her eyes. He looked again at the blood soaked into the doctors' scrubs and nodded at the directions to the room where she was.

The room was dimly lit. Monitors glowed with readings of various sorts; some blinking and beeping, others quietly humming away with numbers changing at regular intervals.

Most of her face was bandaged. Her lower lip was fat and dried out. James pulled a chair close to her bed. He wanted to take her hand in his, but didn't know how she'd feel about that if she were to wake up. No identification, no driver's license, nothing at all that would give him her name.

They had tried continually to contact the owner of the car without success. Voice mail answered the phone and no one was at the house when the police had been by. That meant no one was coming to see her. That thought made James feel better. He would be the one to protect her and hold vigil at her bedside. He would be the one she woke up to.

He pulled his cell phone from his fanny pack and dialed his parents' house. He wanted to give her a blessing and needed another priesthood holder. He needed his dad.

"Hi, Dad." James didn't take his eyes from her.

"James? Where are you? Are you all right?" The old mans voice quivered with sleep and worry.

"I'm fine. I'm at the hospital."

"The hospital?" His father's voice sounded wide awake now and very alarmed.

"I really am fine, Dad. Don't worry. Nothing happened to me. I'm here for someone else."

"You should never call a cop's dad in the middle of the night and say you are at the hospital! I thought you'd been hurt."

James smiled. "Nope. I'm fit as a fiddle, but I need a favor."

It took a few moments to assure his father that he really was fine and to explain all that had happened that led him to be hanging out at St. Mark's Hospital in the middle of the night. His dad agreed to come to help with the blessing.

When James' dad arrived, he was all business, removing the tiny flask of oil from his pocket and impatiently asking James what the girl's name was. Bishop Gerald Hartman was always business when it came to the priesthood.

James' eyes went wide. "Oh, no!" he groaned, nearly plopping down on the sleeping angel's bed before remembering what he was doing. "I don't know."

Gerald's lip twitched in a quick smile and then was as stone again. "You got me up in the middle of the night to give this girl a blessing, and you don't know her name?"

James pursed his lips. "Yeah, that sums it up pretty well, mmm-hmm." He shook his head and ran his hand over the velvet fine remains of his military haircut. "So now what? You gonna go home?"

Bishop Hartman smiled warmly. "Just because you don't know who she is doesn't mean her Heavenly Father doesn't know. I'll do the anointing." James simply nodded, trusting that his father always knew what was best.

The two men placed their hands on the dark hair that was matted with blood. "By the power of the Holy Melchizedek Priesthood . . ." Gerald's voice was clear and unwavering, ". . . we lay our hands upon this beloved sister's head whom we know that thou knowest well . . ."

James felt warmth explode in his chest and spread to his limbs. That had always happened when he was in close proximity to his father giving a blessing.

Every year on the first day of school, every time he was really sick, when he'd had his tonsils out, when he blew his knee out from his motorcycle wreck, just before he was set apart as a missionary, and again when he'd entered the police academy, the warmth was consuming and comforting. There was never a doubt in James' mind that his father was closer to God than any man he knew.

After the blessing had been given, his father picked up the umbrella he had leaned against the bed in preparation to go.

"Dad?" James wondered if he should start this conversation or not.

"Yes, son?"

"When . . ." He blew out a long breath and rubbed his suddenly sweaty palms over his jeans. "When I was doing CPR on her, I saw her in a way you don't normally see a person. Do you know what I'm saying?"

Gerald looked confused and then nodded in understanding. "James, it isn't bad what you did." He emphasized the word bad. "I mean, you've done CPR before. You know a person has to have their shirt off so you can do it properly . . ."

"Oh, Dad, no." James rolled his eyes. He could feel the heat from his face right into his ears. "I can't believe you'd think . . . no, that isn't what I mean. What I mean is, she was dead. I mean really dead and I saw her. I mean not just her body, but her. Her spirit was standing close enough I could've touched her and I think she was teasing me."

"Teasing you? And . . .?"

"And she was so beautiful I cried. I actually cried. Dad, I love her."

Gerald put his umbrella back down and took a seat by the bed at that last statement. "You love her?"

James shrugged. "I do. I'm going to marry her."

"James, you don't know her name. She might not be LDS. She might already be married."

"Oh, Dad, c'mon. I just had this great spiritual moment and you're bringing in practicalities?"

Gerald stood up and gave James a hug. "I'm your dad. I have to be practical. Look, James, I believe you really saw her. I believe it was a great confirmation of your testimony, but to love her as a sister in God's plan and to love her as a wife is different. If you want to love her like that, then you need to get to know her. Find out her favorite color, her hobbies, religious affiliation. Find out how she feels about you, about your profession. And then when you know all that and still look at her like she's the most beautiful woman in the world, then you can tell her that you love her."

"I know what you're saying, Dad. I really do and trust me, I'll be careful."

Gerald's face softened. "I'm not trying to burst your bubble, boy, but when you're dealing with love, you need to keep both eyes open and your hands on the wheel." He looked over to the sleeping figure on the bed. "And when your angel does wake up, chew her out for not wearing her seatbelt."

"How'd you know she . . ."

"You told me she'd been thrown out of the car." He started for the door and then turned around again. "And for Pete's sake, tell her to drive a little slower, would you?"

James smiled. "Sure, Dad. As soon as she wakes up." His dad let out a hearty laugh and left. James sat back down on the chair next to the bed and stared at her again. Even with the blood and bandages she still seemed radiant. He leaned back in his chair and closed his eyes. As uncomfortable as the position was, sleep came quickly.

The next thing he knew, he heard a man calling his name.

"James?"

"What?" he asked irritably.

"Wake up!"

His eyelids felt like they were glued together. It took every ounce of strength he had to force them apart. They focused somewhat on the form in front of him through a bleary haze.

"Jeff? What are you doing here?" James' mouth felt like cotton. He worked some spit around trying to keep his voice from sounding thick.

"Looking for you and it wasn't easy to find you either. I waited a half hour for you at the station, and then started asking around. We were going to play racquetball together and then go to the DARE class, remember?"

"What time is it?"

Jeff smirked. "Quarter to ten, Sleeping Beauty. Now get up and let's get going. We still can make it to the class if we hurry."

James stretched deeply and then gave a start. "I'm still in the hospital."

"Yeah, you're a regular hero, I hear."

"Did she wake up?" James looked frantically to the bed where the girl had not appeared to move at all.

Jeff also looked to the bed. "I don't think so. They still

haven't found any family, the nurses say. They think you're some kind of saint to stay with her like that. Saint James." Jeff smirked, looking him over. Then he grimaced. "You stink and you're wrinkled."

James almost told Jeff he couldn't go, that he had to stay. But stay to what? To listen to the monitors beep and nurses chatter in the hallway? He nodded reluctantly. He really wanted to go home and feel his pillow under his head.

The class. He'd forgotten about the class; forgotten everything really except her and her laughter. The way her hair had bounced over her shoulders as she shook her head made him shiver.

"I can't believe you are going to make us late for the class. The sarge is gonna kick your . . ." James tuned Jeff out. He was a great guy, the kind you wanted at your back when any danger was involved, but he cussed more than anyone James knew. Being around all the cursing and bad language made it very hard for James to keep his own language clean.

"We should go then," James said after Jeff was finished with his tirade.

"So move it, let's go."

James scrubbed a hand over his head and stared down at the girl. He licked his lips wishing he could say something to her, but with Jeff right there . . . . Well, what would he say anyway?

"Yeah, let's go." He stood heavily, not wanting to stand at all. His muscles ached from sitting in the hospital chairs all night. His spine cracked into place as he stretched. Shooting a last glance at his sleeping angel, he sighed in resignation and followed Jeff out the door.

"You need a ride?" Jeff asked once they were outside.

"No, I got my car. See you there. Thanks for coming to get me."

"Sure thing, pal. See you there."

The class they were teaching was a sixth grade DARE class. Today's class was going to be held at Butler Elementary School. He almost regretted going based on that fact alone. It was his old school in his old neighborhood filled with people who knew him and his parents.

The same people who had seen him baptized, sent him off with cheers on his mission to Sweden, applauded him when he came home, and then scowled when they realized his 30th birthday had passed and he wasn't any closer to being married now then he'd been when he got off the airplane from Sweden.

These were the people whose daughters he'd dated, sons he'd gone skateboarding with, people who now had many grandchildren by those same sons and daughters. Life was brutally unfair.

He pulled up in front of the red brick school building. He wasn't in uniform, but he kept one in the trunk for emergencies like this. He changed quickly in the restroom and followed the numbered doors down the hall to 113.

The kids were lined up sitting Indian style in the center of the pod. Jeff was already there, standing in front of the dry erase board. He flashed a grin and a wink at James. "And Officer Hartman is here to help you all understand the importance of daring to stay off drugs." James waved at the kids as he stepped up and Jeff stepped back.

A scrawny kid from the front raised his hand.

"Yes?" James said pointing the chalk at him.

"Are you a real cop?"

"Yes, I am." James turned to the board.

"Then why aren't you out catching bad guys?"

The words *"an ounce of prevention is worth a pound of cure"* crossed James' mind. "I am here today to teach all of you to look out for bad guys on your own and to help me out so my job isn't so big."

Chapter 3

"I don't know why you let that little punk bother you," Jeff scoffed.

"I just hate kids like that," James sputtered.

"To hear your mom tell it, you *were* a kid like that."

"Yeah, well, I grew up. That kid'll be lucky if I let him grow up."

"You coulda used the c.o. pouch on him."

James laughed. "I should have, rotten punk." The c.o. pouch was a pepper spray that he and every other cop carried on his belt.

James followed Jeff to the patrol car. They were riding together today. James would have to get his own car later. "You driving?" James asked.

"No way. It isn't my turn."

James arched a brow at him.

"It isn't!" he insisted.

"So what was up with that accident last night?" Jeff asked as he settled grudgingly behind the steering wheel.

"Oh man. I don't know," James sighed. "I was driving home from the worst date I've ever had . . ."

Jeff burst out laughing. "And that's saying something!" he hooted.

"Yeah, no kidding." James smiled in spite of himself. It really was saying something. The worst in a long line of really bad, and then he met the angel. Her voice had been warmth to him, her smile . . . his dad had to be wrong! He was in love and would ask her to marry him as soon as he knew her name.

"So about the accident . . ."

"What?" James looked quizzically at Jeff.

"About the accident, you were telling me what happened."

"Oh yeah, anyway this little red BMW came flying past me and then it just took the s-curve too fast. You know the one over by the Cotton Bottom." Jeff nodded. "Anyway the car rolled. You know it was raining and the roads were all wet and I can't believe I didn't get tangled in the mess, but when I went to check on everything, the girl was lying on the ground.

"No seatbelt, huh?"

James grunted. "That is *not* the point of this story."

"Hartman, the law is always the point of the story."

"Not in this one. Will you just let me finish?"

"Sure, go on."

"She was dead, and I did CPR on her and brought her back."

"So . . ."

"So, she's like the most beautiful, incredible woman I've ever seen!"

"How do you know she's incredible? You haven't spoken to her." James opened his mouth to explain when Jeff cursed and yelled, "Would you look at that!" James looked forward at the car in front of them. The license was expired. Jeff flipped on the overheads to pull the car to the side of the road and out of traffic and picked up the radio. "This is 18-J-7. I need a 1028 check."

"18-J-7 go ahead."

"451 echo bravo foxtrot."

Jeff got out of the car after dispatch had confirmed the expired registration and make of the car. He stayed just behind the driver's door as he accepted the license and registration from the guy.

James gave himself a mental slap on the forehead. Jeff would never understand what had taken place with the girl. He couldn't believe it happened himself. Was he really dumb enough to try to explain it all to the cynical mind of Jeff? He leaned back against the headrest and closed his eyes. The overheads ticked above him. Her image . . . shimmering in and out, like a piece of sheer silk being moved through light. *No hot, no cold* . . . she said. James wondered what she was going to say when she said, *"There isn't anything to feel like that but . . ."* But what? What did it feel like? Thinking back on it, he should've tried to touch her to see what that essence would be like to him as just a man.

"I can't believe this guy," Jeff huffed as he slammed the door shut. He called in the driver's license.

"What's up?"

"Jerk has already been ticketed for having a four month expired plate and still hasn't gone in to pay for the ticket or get it registered. What a complete . . ." Jeff went off in a string of cussing.

"Do you want me to call a tow truck?" James asked.

"Yeah. He needs to be impounded, plus he's smartin' off to me about how he's got a right to drive whatever he wants on roads he pays taxes to upkeep. He's completely crazy."

"They all are," James agreed.

He got out with Jeff to let Mr. Bornheldt know that he would need to find a ride to wherever he was going. Dan Bornheldt was very unhappy.

"Please step out of the vehicle," James said.

"I most certainly will not!" Bornheldt yelled, spittle flying from his mouth and specking his bottom lip. James rolled his eyes.

"Mr. Bornheldt, we can do this the easy way or the hard way. The easy way is you step out of the car, taking any belongings you need with you, and let us do our job. The hard way is Officer Wicker here gets to get you out of the car." Jeff smiled at the man showing all his teeth. "We arrest you, then sit you in the back of our squad car so we can do our job. Either way, the job will get done, but one is distinctly more pleasant than the other."

"This is police brutality!" the man wailed as he opened the door and stepped a foot out.

"Oh, for cryin' out loud. Brutality would be if we took out our batons and beat you about the head," Jeff muttered, loud enough that only James heard. "Can we call you a ride?" James asked, ignoring Jeff's mutterings as Bornheldt started in again.

"You know my taxes pay your wages," he fumed.

"So now is a bad time to ask for a raise?" Jeff countered.

James laughed at Bornheldt's darkened face. "I think that's a yes, Wicker."

"You enjoy this, don't you? Get a kick out of tormenting citizens, decent taxpayers. Think this is some kind of game?" Bornheldt cursed and shook his fist at them.

"It would be more fun if you keep up your crap there and make us arrest you out of principle," Jeff said.

When the tow truck arrived, Bornheldt wailed even louder. He began swearing every few words for emphasis, but James barely even heard the language. He heard it all the time. Jeff pushed the guy into the car. "Please stop swearing," he asked through gritted teeth. "It is very disrespectful."

Bornheldt shut up instantly. No one could feign courage when faced with the burn of Jeff's gaze. James smirked. It seemed strange that people swearing at him made Jeff so mad when he himself seldom spoke a sentence without adding some of his own color to it.

Back in the car, after Bornheldt had been ticketed and picked up by his ride, Jeff pulled back into traffic. "Okay, so we were talking about this girl."

"Oh, nothing. I'm just glad I was there at the right time."

"Uh huh? Do you expect me to believe that? How many car wrecks have you been to? How many times have you done CPR? How many hospitals have you been to after the fact?" He belted out the questions in quick succession like he would when he was interrogating someone who was about to crack. The first few questions were irrelevant. It was the final one that was expected to be answered. It was the final one that most people did answer.

"And so tell me, James, how many times did you stay all night with the victim?"

"She is just so . . ."

"Incredible, I know. You said that. Why do you say that?"

"I don't know. It's just a feeling I got."

"Well, it was hard to tell with all the bandages and crap all over her, but under all that, she might be pretty. She certainly can't be worse than the psycho."

"Which one?"

"True, there were many, but I mean Pam."

"Yikes, don't remind me."

Pam had believed she was going to die of a dreadful disease and had her funeral planned out to the second. Ali had been a klepto and stole everything from him while he wasn't looking. His parents had liked Tara, but she was too involved with ward choir and didn't care much for the idea of a cop.

That was a huge problem for most women. No one wanted to be married to a guy who could get shot any day and never come home.

"Yeah, she was something else," Jeff continued. "Too bad you didn't get a girl like my Kelli. She's the sort of woman who can tell you where to go and make you like the trip."

"That is exactly what I need."

"My friend, it's what everyone needs."

The conversation continued along that line until they had pulled over seven more cars, interceded on a burglary, and refilled their mugs once. The shift seemed to take forever.

James pulled his car back into the hospital parking lot. His heart beat wildly against his rib cage. The trip to the florist had taken much longer than expected.

The bouquet he pulled out of the back seat of his car was filled with white roses. The bouquet of balloons with a stuffed bear in the center of the largest one had been an afterthought.

He knew his dad would say he was carrying it way too far and that he should take things slow and cautious, but as he looked at the bundle in his arms, they didn't seem nearly enough.

He had showered and changed into his best Old Navy Jeans and T-shirt. He pried a finger free from the tangles of balloon ribbons to punch the elevator button. *Breathe*, he thought. *Just breathe.*

The hallway seemed to stretch into eternity and yet it only took seconds to cross the length of it to the angel's room. *Breathe*, he commanded himself again. The door clicked open and there she was, almost sitting up, eyes open and appearing lost. Those blue eyes widened when she saw him with his arms filled with flowers and balloons. He had agonized on a card and what to write, and finally settled on:

> To the dark haired angel,
> I'm glad I was there
> I'm glad you're okay
> Wear your seatbelt (message from my dad)
> Always,
>
> —James Hartman

James had asked the florist twice what he thought of the message; the answer was a shrug of the shoulders. "How should I know?" the man asked. "I'm sure it's fine."

She blinked at him, her eyes widening more.

"Hi," he said, trying to keep his voice from squeaking.

"Hi?" She couldn't keep the question out of her voice.

He took two quick steps into the room. "You don't . . ." James stopped short. The words "remember me" stuck in his throat.

A nurse came in behind him scooting him to the side. "Honey?" she said to the girl. "Do you know who this man is?" She didn't allow the girl to answer. "This man saved your life. He is the reason you are breathing and talking here today."

The blue eyes surveyed him from under the bandages. She winced as she shifted to get a better look at him. Her arm was casted and he could see her chest was completely wrapped in layers of bandaging. He wanted to hug her. James could only shrug when she finally asked with a tilt of her head, "You saved me?"

"I did," he shrugged nearly dropping the vase of flowers. "Oh, and these are for you." He set the vase down on the stand near her bed and the balloons on the counter across from her.

With his hands empty he felt awkward and folded them across his chest. "Are you okay?'

She smiled softly and said thickly, "I hurt, but I'm glad to be here. I guess I owe that to you . . . er, what's your name?"

James jumped forward. "James. And you are?" Her lips parted to utter the name he had wanted and waited to hear.

"Oh, Darling, I'm sorry it took so long to get here." A man in olive corduroy pants and blue button up dress shirt pushed past James and went straight to the girl's bed. He took her hand and kissed the back of it.

"It's okay, Bradley. I'm not up to any company yet."

"Then who's this? Looks like company to me."

Her blue eyes fixed on James. He hoped she didn't see the heat in his face. "It's James. He saved my life."

"Well then, I guess that's okay!" The man started to stand to greet James, but as an afterthought, handed the girl a box of chocolate.

She smiled faintly. "Oh, Bradley, you shouldn't have . . ." She broke off as she peered into the half empty box. Her smile froze on her lips.

"Oh right, freeway was a mess. I was absolutely starving. You understand, love, don't you?" The man had a clipped, yet lazy, British accent.

The nurse who had been checking the I.V. bag grunted and rolled her eyes at the half-eaten box of candy. "Are you going to need anything else, honey?" she asked the girl.

"No, no thanks. I'm okay right now." She shifted and winced again, a little cry escaping her lips as her eyes clenched tightly closed.

James jumped forward instinctively, not able to stand watching her in pain. "Are you okay?"

She shook her head. "I'm fine."

The nurse patted her blanketed legs kindly and whisked off. The man, Bradley, as she had called him, stared at her. "Well, I suppose we'll need to postpone the wedding won't we? Can't have you kneeling at the altar in a body cast now, can we?"

James felt his legs give way and leaned against the counter to steady himself. Wedding! She was getting married! He looked at her left hand. There was no ring or sparkly gem to indicate this was the case. The guy could buy a BMW but not an engagement ring?

"And darling," Bradley's accent went on lazily, "The car is totaled."

She winced again, but not from the pain. "I'm so sorry."

"What could you have possibly been thinking? Ruddy car cost me a fortune."

"I know. I just . . . they said the roads were wet and . . ." Tears welled up in her eyes.

"It's just a car," James interjected, exasperated by the entire moment. "Be glad she's alive. She almost died."

Bradley looked James over, his eyes half shut like a lazy, fat, uninterested cat. "Yes, she is and all thanks to you, James." He said James' name with an amused smile. Bradley did stand this time. "We owe you a great debt." Bradley put his arm around James and led him the few steps to the door. "Here's a little something for all your trouble." He handed James a crisp carefully folded exactly in half twenty-dollar bill.

James' jaw hung slack, "A twenty?" he asked in disbelief.

Bradley looked puzzled. "Just a bit to help you out. It's a token of gratitude."

James looked from the girl to Bradley. He was certain if his eyes got any wider they would pop right out of his head. Her eyes were wide as well in absolute disbelief. "Bradley," she started, "I don't think . . ." She trailed off with a lack of anything that could be said with dignity.

James furrowed his brow and pressed the twenty into Bradley's blue shirt pocket. "No thanks, pal. I don't need this."

Bradley snorted, "Well, from what I gather cops make, you probably do need it, but all right." Bradley sighed in mock resignation. He pulled the twenty out of his shirt pocket and smoothed out the wrinkles, replacing it again in the pocket of his trousers.

James was too stunned to do more than mutter, "I'd better be going." After a last long look at the nameless angel, he turned without another word and left before he started to cry or before he took a swipe at Bradley. Either was possible.

She was engaged and from the way the guy acted, she was

engaged to the same guy she'd told him about previously. The sound of her laughter filled his head. He felt nauseated. The world's most perfect woman was engaged to someone who deserved to be pounded into the ground.

After reaching his car and getting in, he pounded his fist on the steering wheel and then used that same steering wheel to rest his forehead on and say a desperate prayer.

Chapter 4

"Bradley!" A thousand horrible things to say to him came to her mind, but all she could sputter was his name.

He raised his hands in innocence. "What?"

"How could you do that?" Her tongue felt fat and heavy against her teeth as she spoke, and also on her lips when she tried to moisten them a little. Her lips were fat and the skin under the bandage felt like it was on fire. Her brain felt like it was bouncing against her skull.

"Do what?" he asked, taking another chocolate from the box and popping it into his mouth.

She sighed, the breath exhaling making her ribs feel like they were squeezing her lungs. She leaned her head gingerly back into the pillow. "You demeaned him. Treated him like a busboy or something." As her fat tongue pressed against her teeth, she wondered if her teeth might fall out. They felt loose sitting in gums that felt bruised.

"Right, I certainly don't think he sees it like that, Kitty. I mean, law enforcement always needs financial help. Heaven knows they don't make enough to pay even the electric bill."

"Twenty dollars? You spend more than that on lunch."

"It's all I had on me, isn't it? Really Katherine, I don't see how this is an issue." He hesitated, looking around him for the first time. "Where did all this come from?"

She looked to the flowers and balloons, vibrant and cheery. "James brought them."

"Bit extravagant for a lass you don't even know, don't you think?"

"I think it was very nice." Katherine's head pulsated with every beat of her heart. Everything ached so violently; it was hard to focus on any given part.

"Where are my parents?" she asked thickly through her lips.

"I haven't called yet."

"Bradley," the little she had raised her voice hurt her head. "I really need to see them."

"I just thought we could get a little alone time. Time where I can take care of you." He shot a skeptical glance to the balloons and flowers. "Now we're alone." He leaned down like he might kiss her but grimaced at the site of blood crusted to the uncovered parts of her face and turned away.

Bradley picked up the remote attached to the bed. "Mind if we watch some telly?" Without waiting for an answer, he flipped it on and surfed the seven stations available in the hospital. "Not exactly satellite," he grumbled, settling on a daytime talk show.

Katherine was tired. The images on the screen blurred, became clear, and blurred again. She touched her hands together and felt that her left hand was bare. What did that mean? She wasn't sure. The voices from the hall and television faded in and out as did images she knew, but couldn't remember. James' face. She saw blood on his shirt and hands as he kneeled . . . where? The television meshed finally into white noise as her swollen eyelids closed heavily.

When Katherine awoke, her parents were there along with her brother Gary. Bradley was gone entirely and she was glad. She couldn't explain it, but his presence sometimes made her chest tighten and seem to threaten to cave in on itself. She wasn't up to it, wasn't up to worrying about the tantrum that was sure to come when she was lucid enough for him to really be mad about her wrecking his car.

Gary glanced at her from the windowsill he was sitting on. "Hey, she's awake." He leapt up and crossed over to her, gingerly taking her hand. "Kit, are you okay?" Gary had been her lifeline in every step of her life. Six years younger than she, he allowed her to maintain childhood a little longer. His blue eyes were bloodshot, making the blue appear green. Had he been crying? Why?

Her mother took her other hand. "Kit, honey, we've been so worried." Her mother's eyes were also red, with a film of tears rushing over them and threatening to fall.

"Mom . . ." her voice squeaked and cracked. The energy to say just that one word felt exhausting. Her eyes focused around the room. There were more balloons and flowers from Gary and her parents, she assumed. Her dad put his hands on her mother's shoulders.

"Daddy . . ." She felt the tears fall from her eyes hot and stinging to the still open wounds on her face. She wanted to sit up, but lacked the energy. Her entire body felt heavy and immovable. She stared at her family through tears that fell unhindered by her desire to wipe them away. She wondered if she were paralyzed, but the pain was great enough, she knew that wasn't possible.

At the sound of his daughter's voice, Ryan fell to his knees at her bedside, dropping his head softly to hers and starting to cry silently. "I can't believe you were here all alone all night," he said, his voice filled with apology.

"Oh, she wasn't alone," said a voice in the doorway. It was a woman in her mid forties. She was in street clothes with a white lab coat hanging off her shoulders and a stethoscope around her neck.

She stuck her hand out. Ryan stood and took it, giving a quick handshake. "I'm Dr. Orton. I was the doctor on duty last night."

"What can you tell us?"

"Well, she has three fractured ribs and a fractured collar-bone. Her arm was broken in four places and had to be pinned together. She is pretty bruised but all in all, it could have been much worse. She was lucky there was a policeman on the scene that did CPR on her and revived her to the land of the living." Dr. Orton sat on the bed next to Katherine. She turned on a penlight and flashed it in Katherine's eyes.

"We're glad she wasn't alone then. We're glad you were here," said Marleah, Katherine's mom.

"Oh, I didn't mean me. The young policeman stayed with her. He stayed all night."

"Well, that was very nice of him," Marleah said as she stroked the back of her hand gently over her daughter's hair.

"Yes, he was very nice," the doctor agreed. "I've never seen a policeman so concerned before. In fact . . ." She hesitated. "Are you LDS?"

"Yes, we are," Ryan said. Curiosity lined in his brow. "Why?"

"I think he called in his father to give her a blessing." The doctor said it with admiration, but caution too. She wasn't certain how these people would react to such news.

Ryan contemplated this information, his fingers steepled against his lips. "So . . . he saved her life, gave her a blessing, and stayed with her all night."

"Yes, sir." Doctor Orton hoped she hadn't gotten the young man into trouble.

"I would very much like to meet this young man. I have a lot of respect for policemen and would be honored to shake this one's hand," Ryan said. His wife nodded.

Dr. Orton sighed in relief as she read over Katherine's chart. She herself had been impressed with the officer. He showed compassion that most policemen tried hard to remove themselves from. She respected that.

Gary smoothed his hand over Katherine's fingers. "I'm glad you're okay, Kit. 'Course this means we won't be going rock climbing any time soon, but we can rent movies or something." His face split into a grin. "Hey, you must've hit a nerve with

Bradley. Look at all the stuff he brought!"

Katherine eased herself up as much as her stiff body would let her. She worked her mouth soundlessly a moment before finding her voice. "Wasn't Bradley. James brought it."

"Who is James?" Ryan asked.

"The police officer," Dr. Orton offered.

"Really," Ryan said. It wasn't a question, but Dr. Orton nodded anyway. A smile twitched on his lips and was gone so fast one might have thought it was imagined. "Looks like Bradley has been outdone."

Gary snorted, "Like that would be hard to do."

Katherine closed her eyes; the banter was going to begin: why Bradley was wrong for her, why her life was headed for further disaster if she let him do the driving and why doesn't the guy relax enough to wear jeans? Her dad was her strongest supporter and Bradley's greatest critic.

She couldn't fault her dad for that. He just wanted so much for her happiness. He seemed consumed with it. He always reminded her that she was his little girl and that no one would ever be good enough for her.

"We're just glad you're going to be okay, honey." Her mother looked tired, worn from the experience of the time she had spent at Katherine's side, however long that had been. Katherine was grateful for her mother's ability to gently lead the men of the family away from conversations that tortured her.

Dr. Orton checked her vitals and the I.V. bags. "We'll get you off of this after the bag empties. You were so dehydrated, it was hard to get a vein to take a needle." The doctor nodded to the arm where the needle had been inserted in her hand and wrist and in a vein on her forearm. There were pinpricks surrounded by large purple bruises. These marks were the signs of attempts to get the I.V. in.

There was no pain there, at least none she could discern. The rest of her ached so violently that these small bruises may not have even been there at all. She noticed her ring sparkling against the bruised hand and wondered a moment. Was that there before? She shook her head, the motion swirling pain and sickness through her.

"So how are you really, Baby?" Ryan asked as he scooted Gary aside to take her hand. Gary only scowled a second before taking the chair next to the bed.

"I'm okay, Daddy," she mumbled.

"So is Bradley's car totaled?" Gary asked, grinning madly.

"Yes, it is," Katherine grimaced.

"Aw, don't worry about it! At least you're not totaled and c'mon, Kit, you can't tell me you don't think it's funny."

She stared at him as levelly as her pounding head would allow. "I don't think it's funny, Gary. He's going to kill me as soon as I get better. That was a really expensive car!" She almost started to cry.

"Oh, don't cry. I'm sorry." Gary looked like he meant it which was rare for him.

"It's okay," Marleah cooed at her. "You are all right, that's what's important here. I'm sure Bradley knows that. Don't worry. Everything is going to be fine. Bradley is very responsible and I'm certain he has full coverage insurance."

Gary opened his mouth but snapped it shut at the warning look from his mom. She went back to gently smoothing Kit's hair down and tucking it behind the ear uncovered by bandages. They all settled in to be together, no one rushing to leave or needing to be anywhere at all. Kit was grateful. It was exactly what she wanted.

Chapter 5

James had driven up the canyon. He had paced and circled his car more times than he could count, kicking at rocks as he went. Married! That beautiful angel was getting married! And to that jerk of a guy! James fantasized pulling that guy over and having him resist arrest so he could pound him to the ground. And worse yet, he still didn't know her name!

Married! The word made him want to vomit. How that would be different if it was him she was engaged to and not that little . . . a dozen horrible words went through his mind but none of them captured how he really disliked that guy. He covered his eyes with his arm and sighed deeply.

There was nothing to be done. Nothing he could conceive of that would change the cold facts of what had taken place.

Her blue green eyes were like pools of eternity, the dark around them appearing like ripples in a calm sea. She had stared at him through those eyes for just a moment and it was like receiving a confirmation that he was right in loving her. Then the whole dream came shattering down around him with that stupid British accent.

He felt so tired. He got back in his car and found his way down the mountain to his parents' house in Cottonwood Heights. His mom would have dinner ready and she always made enough in case he stopped by.

When he didn't stop by, she would bundle it all up into various containers and leave it in his fridge when he was away at work. He tried to assure her he could fend for himself, but the plastic containers with notes that said "Love, Mom" continued to appear in his fridge.

He figured showing up saved her a trip to his place. James was the youngest of five children. Everyone else was married with children. He really only ever saw his oldest brother, Brian. The others had moved away. But Brian was enough for James. He had had to sit through enough lectures on settling down, getting married, and adding to the list of grandchildren. In essence, he was as much a family project as he was a ward project when it came to getting him married.

In fact, finding him a wife had become a favorite pastime of everyone he knew, so much that it never occurred to any of them that he may be capable of finding one on his own. Of course he hadn't had much luck on his own, but then he hadn't had much luck with anyone they provided either.

When he arrived at his parents' house, he sighed in resignation at the car in the driveway. The black Lexus gleamed in the lights that bordered the front walkway. Brian was there.

Brian was the oldest brother. There were exactly ten years and one week between them. He had a beautiful wife, Annette, and four kids. He was successful in business, life, love, and everything. As the oldest, he felt an especially strong inclination to marry James off to the right girl.

James loved Brian. Loved him for the example he was and the effortless, unending service Brian gave, but the last thing James wanted was another date set up by his oldest brother. Or worse yet, for his brother to find out he was in love with a girl he didn't know that was engaged to someone else.

James let himself into the house quietly and followed the noise to the kitchen. Annette was there, bouncing the baby on her hip while trying to set the table. His mom was pulling dinner from the oven. She smiled when she saw him.

"I'd hoped you would show up tonight. Your father needs

some help moving one of the bookcases he built out of the shop. Brian's out there now, but it'd be good if your father wasn't involved at all. You know how bad his back is."

James nodded as he kissed his fingertips and tapped them on his mom's forehead, then turned around to go out the side door that led to his dad's wood working shop.

His dad was a chemical engineer by trade. He loved the phrase, "it doesn't take a rocket scientist to figure this out," because, technically, he was just exactly that. He had worked out at Kennecott Copper Company until he retired and took up idling his hours away building things for neighbors and family and anyone else who mentioned they needed something.

It turned out that Gerald Hartman had quite a knack with wood and was making himself busy with all the orders he received from various projects.

Brian was a disembodied voice from behind the bookshelf. Two hands on either side of the shelf were the only visual proof he was there. "Dad," he was saying, "I don't see why we need to move this out. When they come to get it, we can just load it straight into the van from the shop."

"I need it out," Bishop Hartman patiently explained, "to make room for the cupboards I'm building. We can just store it in the hall by the stairs until it's picked up." Bishop Hartman stretched out his arms to embrace the other side of the bookcase when James tapped his shoulder and scooted him aside.

"Let me get that for you, Pop." The two brothers wrestled the case long ways and then each took an end to the house. Caroline scowled softly at it and then shook her head with a smile. Her house had started filling with wooden pieces from chests to bookcases to cupboards to anything else that could be conceived of.

"Dinner's ready," Caroline said as she watched the procession pass by.

"Be there in a minute," James grunted. They settled the bulk of wood against the railing to the staircase going upstairs.

Brian wiped his hands on his jeans and scooped up their toddler on the way to the table. Annette had already started feeding the baby now settled in the high chair. The two older siblings stared at each other in contempt.

James sat down between Brianna, the oldest, and Brett, the second.

"Brett, stop it!" Brianna hissed at him.

"I didn't do anything!" Brett insisted.

"Knock it off, you guys, or James will take you to jail," Brian said.

Bishop Hartman folded his arms cueing the family to do the same. James could feel Brianna glare at Brett over his bent head and twisted his lips into a slight smile.

When the prayer was over, hands fled to the center of the table to snatch up plates of food.

"So, how's your sleeping beauty?" his dad asked as James plopped a helping onto his plate.

James didn't look up. "She's awake."

"And . . ."

"And . . . nothing. She's awake."

"Do you know her name?"

"We didn't make it that far in the conversation." James shoved a forkful of potatoes into his mouth hoping his dad would just go away.

"Who's this we're talking about?" Brian asked.

"Yeah, what's all this?" Annette chimed in.

All eyes were on him. "This is nothing. It's just there was this . . . Look, it isn't anything."

Caroline tilted her head to look at her youngest son better. He could feel her eyes search over him like fingers sifting through sand to search at a small jewel.

"Aw, c'mon, James, tell us," Brian goaded.

Caroline smiled at him and straightened her head. "If he says it's nothing, I'm sure it is just that." She went back to her broccoli without any further look at James. And her words stopped any thought of continuing that conversation. At least until after dinner.

Caroline and Annette were cleaning things up after refusing all help from the men. James suspected it was a nice break from watching the kids.

The kids, Brian, James, and their dad retired to the living room.

Brian was in the rocking chair with a blanket draped over his shoulder and the baby's head resting on the blanket. Her cheek squashed into her mouth making her lips pucker.

The toddler had crawled into Gerald's lap. The older two fought over the idea of TV or Playstation.

"So what happened today?" Gerald asked, shifting the small boy in his lap until he was more comfortable.

"I taught a DARE class, drove around in my car, handled an accident, and gave out a few tickets. You know, the usual."

"I don't think that's what Dad meant, Junior," Brian said.

"Okay fine, she's engaged! Is that what you want to know?" He was pulling at the threads in a pillow on the couch.

Gerald blinked in surprise. "She wasn't wearing a ring," he said.

"I didn't notice," James lied.

"I looked as soon as you told me . . . well, what you told me."

Brian looked confused. "What are we talking about?"

Gerald looked from one boy to the other. "If you want to tell him, then you should be the one to tell him."

"Tell me what?"

James rolled his eyes. "I met someone last night." He told the story quickly, rushing through the details and hitting the highlights that were pertinent. His head spun as the words sank reality home. She was engaged! Heaven help him! She was taken completely. He wanted to slam Bradley into tomorrow.

Brian clicked his tongue in empathy. "So what are you going to do now?" he asked.

"Do?" James blinked. "What can I do? She's getting married."

"Yeah, but you said the guy was a jerk."

"He is."

"So . . . convince her of that."

"Oh please! What, go to the hospital and tell her she should take me, a guy she doesn't even know over the guy she agreed to marry? Whatever!"

"I don't mean storm in there and throw her over your shoulder and take off with her. But it ain't over 'til the girl in white says 'I do.'"

James laughed in spite of himself. "I don't know, Bri. Maybe I'm meant to be a bachelor."

"Nonsense, Junior. No one is meant to be alone. It'll happen for you. Maybe not today, but it will happen . . . someday.

"Someday . . ." James echoed.

He had grown to hate that word. To hate that its meaning meant it *could* happen, but maybe not. And even if it was going to happen, it was going to be something waited for. Waiting required patience and the ever growing gnawing in the stomach that it still *may not* happen. The torture of someday was infinite, a perfect circle of hope and pain.

"Someday . . ." he repeated with an affirmative nod. "Well, Pop, thanks for dinner. I have a long day tomorrow. I better go." James stood. Gerald stood too, scooting the toddler aside gently. He took his son by the shoulder and pulled him into a hug. "Don't worry, boy. Things work out for those who have faith."

"Thanks, Dad. I know they do . . . someday . . . right?"

"Something like that."

James nodded. He knew that meant he'd have to be patient—wait a little longer. Fine. He could do that. Maybe all that waiting would remove the image of the dark haired angel that seemed to have been seared into his mind and the laughter that rippled through his ears continually.

Someday. He laughed at the word as he drove home, and scoffed at himself for thinking any of it mattered. He arrived at his little home in Holladay and sat in the car staring at it. He'd bought it for a great deal when the economy was a buyer's market.

It was probably the smallest house in the neighborhood, but on the largest lot of land. The trees that framed the house in the front yard were towering maples that had been there for nearly a hundred years.

His family had been worried when he bought it. What could it mean that a man of his age should buy a house without being married first?

"It means," he had tried to explain, "that I am tired of paying rent on a building where there are chain smokers below me blowing their smoke into my vents and a deaf woman who for some reason can hear my music no matter how quietly I play it." The deaf woman lived next door and would bang on her wall whenever he turned the radio on.

They still tsked tsked their disapproval and worried to themselves that he was all alone. "I'm only 32," he would say to them. "It is normal for a 32-year-old man to not be married in this world."

That would bring raised eyebrows to which he could only throw up his hands and shake his head and silently wonder if he was abnormal.

He jingled his keys as he wandered up the walk and settled himself on the bench placed on the porch to overlook his yard. With elbows rested on knees, he laid his head into his palms.

He felt uneasy, though this week had been better than last as far as work went. Last week's images floated around his head nearly as often as the face of the dark haired angel.

A young boy of five called 911 because his mom wouldn't wake up. When they got there, they found her in the bathroom. She had bled to death, while trying to have a baby on her own. There were plastic garbage bags set aside.

James knew this woman. He had dealt with her twice before. She had been a drug addict for probably the majority of her life. The first time he'd met her was on a raid on a party that had been tipped off to the police. Drugs and suspected drug dealers were all going to be there. The woman was wasted, spent a few nights in jail, and sent off to rehab to get clean. That was his first meeting.

The second meeting was when they found the body of a newborn in the lake. The baby had been placed in a plastic garbage bag and tossed aside. James had been a detective at that time.

The fingerprints on the child and on the bag matched the prints of the woman he'd arrested the year previously.

They arrested her again for homicide but had to let her go. They couldn't prove the child had been born alive, and she insisted it had been born dead and that she didn't know what else to do.

When the autopsy had been done they couldn't determine if the lungs had filled with air due to the baby taking its first breaths or if it had been because the body had filled with gases over the time it had been in the water.

It had killed James to let the woman go. He knew the baby had been born alive. He wasn't sure how he knew, but he saw the guilt in those glazed over eyes and no one could convince him he was wrong.

They had arrived at the house too late to save this baby, too late to save the woman, and though the scene filled him with horror, it was the hand of the five year old, sticky with blood, slipping into James' hand and asking what was to happen to him now that tore James' heart out.

Child Services had come to get him after James had washed the boy's hands and given him a candy bar. The child never cried, not one tear fell from his frightened brown eyes. James hoped he'd been in time to save the boy. He hoped the boy would go to some family that would love him and teach him about his place in this world and in Heavenly Father's kingdom. He finally had to ask to be transferred from detectives back to a regular patrol officer. Though there were many ugly aspects of both, working with homicides daily was killing a part of him too.

There were some good things about not being married. He didn't have to take the chaos of his day home to a woman whom he loved. He didn't have to lie to her when she asked how his day had been. He didn't have to come up with excuses as to why he couldn't speak without breaking into sobs. He didn't have to hide the calluses that he had developed over his heart to shelter it from the constant beating it took from watching humanity hurt humanity.

He stared over the garden, at the little heads of daisies his mother planted there for him as they bobbed in the wind and then he reached out and touched the scar on his shoulder. What would his life be like without that pink-purple mark? He didn't know, could not even imagine. Sighing, James stood, unlocked the door, and bolted it again behind him.

Chapter 6

Katherine looked up from her plate of untouched food as Bradley entered the room. He looked nice, but then he always did.

"Bought a new car today," he announced as he planted a kiss on her head and he took the seat next to her.

"What kind?"

"Guess."

She didn't feel like guessing. "A Buick?"

He crinkled his nose. "Of course not."

"Ford then."

"No, darling."

"I give up."

"A Jaguar XKR!"

"Oh."

"Red. Four Liter Supercharged Convertible. I got it for under £60,000."

"Pounds? What is that in American?"

Instead of answering her, he scowled. "You really need to learn the conversion rate if you are going to be married to me." He was all smiles again in the next instant. "Right, so . . . it is a very great car! I bet you can't wait to drive it."

"Hmm . . ."

"Aren't you happy? I would've thought you'd like that."

"I don't really know what it is," she confessed.

"Ah, I see. Well, no worries. You'll know in a couple of days when you get out of this forsaken place."

"I've been actually released to go home early."

"Really? Why didn't you tell me?"

"I just found out. My mom's coming to get me in a few hours."

"You had time to call your mother but not me?"

She flushed. "I'll need her help to get dressed."

"Right." A grin spread over his face as he leaned closer to her. His lips brushed lightly over hers.

"Stop it," she said.

"What, darling?" His face was all innocence.

"Whatever it is you're thinking." She smiled in spite of herself, hard as she tried to be angry with him. There was something irresistibly charming about him. Something she couldn't identify, understand, or even see. It was like a light visible from the corner of her eye, but when she looked directly at it, the light was gone.

They had dated almost a year. Known each other for two. Everyone expected them to get married and the couple never gave anyone reason to think otherwise. She found that once she had started dating Bradley, people stopped pestering her about getting married. It wasn't a surprise to any involved when they announced their engagement. Her father was silent at first, but then hugged her and told her how much he wanted her to be happy. Gary had been flat out hostile towards the idea and her mother became instantly consumed with the concept of a wedding.

Bradley took her hand, fingering the ring he'd placed there four months previously. "So why are they letting you out early?"

"Good behavior," she said.

He didn't laugh but smiled patiently. "Seriously, darling."

"I'm doing pretty well. I can sit around at home as well as I can sit around here. My head seems okay, no danger of slipping into a coma or anything, so I get to go home."

Bradley nodded and patted back a yawn. "Well, since your mother is coming, perhaps I shall go home and take a bit of a nap."

"Oh." She tried not to sound disappointed. "You're not staying then?"

"Don't really see a reason to since you won't be needing my help."

"Well, okay then. I'll see you when I get home."

"Sure thing, Kitty." He left without a kiss goodbye. She looked over at the flowers by her bedside and pulled the little card out. She had read its message a million times before, it seemed. At least often enough she now knew it by heart.

Kit had hoped he'd come visit again, but he had stayed away. Probably because Bradley had been so horrible to him. She just couldn't help but think of how he'd leapt to her defense when Bradley started in about the car. Like some knight out of a fairytale, storming in to save his lady's honor no matter how trivial the problem.

Her mother arrived and started bundling things up for her from next to the bed. She pulled out an umbrella. It had a brass handle shaped like a duck head. The name Gerald Hartman had been carved into the wood pole.

"Whose is this, honey?" her mother asked.

"I don't know. I don't know anyone by that . . ." She smiled. "Hartman? The policeman's last name was Hartman. Let's take it home. I can deliver it to him later."

Her mother shrugged and settled it on the top of the rest of things to carry out to the car. Gary showed up a few minutes later to help move things. "Cool umbrella," he said. "Looks like something you'd get from an antique store." He lifted the suitcase while holding the umbrella under his arm.

MarLeah had to call Gary when she realized Bradley wasn't there to help. Kit felt a twinge of embarrassment over his leaving but shook it off. He was what he was. She knew that when she agreed to marry him.

The nurse wheeled her out in a wheelchair while she did her best to balance the bouquet that James had left on her lap. Kit didn't know why she felt more protective of that bouquet over all the others she had received, but it was truly the only one she wanted to be personally in charge of. The white roses had started to open, making the arrangement larger, fuller, and intoxicating with the honey smell.

Going home was more difficult than she had imagined. The painkillers didn't dull the pain as much as they turned her stomach. When Kit stood to hobble to the front door, her head spun like a boat in a whirlpool. The sensation made her curl over with the need to vomit. Probably a reaction to the Lortab. It would be six weeks before she would heal, before she could move and not want to die with the motion.

Die? Kit wondered over that word. Did she want to die? No. Of course not. But the word seemed to brush against a memory. What memory? She saw that policeman, James, kneeling, and his mouth moving. His eyes were downcast. He must have been praying. Why would she have seen him praying? Why did the thought send a tingle of warm electricity through her veins to every part of her body?

Die? No. No matter how much she ached, no matter how she wanted to run from the chaos of her mind and life, she would never want to die. Not with all the things she wanted still to do.

Gary pulled her arm over his shoulder and held her steady. "Just a few more steps, Kit," he said as he led her to the front door and to her bedroom.

Kit sank gratefully to her bed, letting the swirling in her head slow to a ripple. "Can I get you anything?" Gary asked, his head cocked to the side and his face pinched in an atypical expression of concern on his normally mischievous face.

"No, I'm fine. I . . .I'm fine, thanks Gar-bear." His eyes lifted and he flashed his half-grin that seemed to mock everything.

"Yeah, you're okay." He nodded and socked her unhurt shoulder gently. The tiny bump seemed to burrow its way to the shattered shoulder. She winced and his smile vanished. "Did I hurt you?"

"No," she lied. "I'm fine."

His brow furrowed and then smoothed. "Sure you are. You will be anyway. Hey, I gotta go. I'm going rock climbing."

"Jerk!"

"I already had it planned. Can't stay here and stare at you all day. When I come back, I'll set up the TV and VCR in here and rent some movies."

"No action this time."

"No chick flicks."

"Comedy then," they said at the same time.

"When I get back," Gary promised and left. Kit rolled over to her good side to face the nightstand where Gary had helped her set James' bouquet. With a grimace she stretched out to remove a long stemmed rose from the vase.

The thorns had all been removed leaving the stem clean and smooth.

She cupped the bud in her good hand letting the stem rest between her fingers. Had it really been over a year since the last time a man had given her flowers? Her thumb traced over the silky white petals. The way he'd looked at her! In all her life she did not remember anyone looking at her like that.

She blinked and shook her head gently, starting again the whirlpool in her skull. Why was she thinking about him? She was engaged to Bradley! "I am engaged," she hissed softly to herself. She laid the rose on the pillow next to her where she could stare at it. Her eyes blurred, her heavy lids fell, and from behind them her kneeling knight was praying again.

Chapter 7

The three kids from the Jeep that James had pulled over now sat on the curb, hands on their heads, shoes off and set in front of them. Sitting there like that, they looked like the three monkeys; see no evil, hear no evil, speak no evil, except their hands were on their heads. Marijuana was the reason for their predicament. They had four unlit joints in the glove box and one that was being passed around when James happened by. He watched them as they pitched it out the window of the vehicle and started fanning the air around them. The kid in the passenger side had enough frame of mind to try buckling up his seat belt.

James sighed. People who broke the law were always so obvious when they tried to look like they weren't breaking the law. The kid on the right was muttering, "Oh man, oh man," to himself while the one on the left cried softly about his parents killing him when they found out. The middle one glared at James.

He'd been the one driving the vehicle when they got pulled over. He'd been the one to throw out the joint into the bushes. He wore gang clothing, but didn't seem the type. The kid had a mean spirit—the glare was enough to make that evident—but there was more to it than that. He was just so casual about the whole thing. He was casual about being patted down, about the interrogation, and about taking his shoes off.

Were it not for the glare, James would've just figured the kid was high, too doped to know what was going on, but the glare proved the kid was wild. It proved he had reached a level of defiance in his life that, if not properly restrained, would lead him to crime on a much larger scale.

James was doing FTO's this week, which meant he was training a new field officer. The new guy's name was Tony. Tony was eager to learn and do everything that most new guys were, but he had an edge that made him fun to teach. The edge was that he was teachable. That was an uncommon trait for a young guy just out of the academy.

Tony was asking the kids questions and took their ID to call in. James could hear Tony ask what they thought they were going to accomplish by throwing the joint out of the window. He chewed them out for littering. He cuffed them. James held the level glare of the kid in the middle.

"Punk!" James hissed as Tony handed him the IDs. Tony didn't have to turn around to see whom he'd meant.

"Got a serious attitude, doesn't he?"

"Yeah, let's get them out of here." They loaded the three into the back of the patrol car.

"Hey, there's not enough room back here for all of us," the kid with the glare spat.

"Shut up, Rick," said the one that had been crying earlier.

"No! I won't shut up. We got rights."

They'd already been read their rights. James sighed, "Look, I just figured if you guys liked each other enough to puff on the same joint, you must like each other enough to sit real close."

"My knees are in my mouth. There isn't enough room for one person back here."

"Sure there is." To prove the point, James shut the door, leaving the three of them in there.

Tony had checked the shoes for hidden drugs and tossed them into the trunk. They didn't give the shoes back because six out of ten arrestees tried kicking in the divider window.

Without shoes it hurt their feet most of the time enough for them to stop after a couple of kicks.

James wasn't worried with three of them back there; there wasn't enough room for them to move around too much. There wasn't as little room as the punk tried to make it seem like, but it would still be a cozy ride for them. He could feel the glare on the back of his head. The kid was likely headed for serious trouble. The apathy he held towards the law marked him as a society misfit. James wondered when he would be arresting the kid again. They had the Jeep sent to a state impound lot.

After they had released the kids to juvenile custody, they went off to fill out reports. He sat at his desk staring at nothing. The nothing he stared at faded into the image of her face. Her dark hair swirling over her shoulders . . .

"Stop it!" he admonished himself. It had been four and a half weeks since the day at the hospital. It felt like she had somehow crept into his head and curled up there, making herself comfortable as a new resident. Her face was always there. He got her name off of the insurance reports that were filed later. It was Katherine Riley. He had tried to call her once and hung up when a male voice answered, then worried for two days about whether or not they had caller ID.

Sighing, he pushed her image back into the corner she had claimed as her own in his head. Though she was never completely gone, it was easier to work when she was just in the corner instead of the middle of his thoughts.

Once back in the car, James and Tony had just turned onto State Street when an older black Mercedes blew through a stop sign. Tony flipped on the overheads and pulled in behind the car. The driver slowed to a stop on the side of State Street. James got out.

A woman about his age had her window down with elbow propped up on the doorframe and chin cupped lazily in her palm. When she saw him she seemed to brighten and smiled sweetly. “Hello, Officer,” she sang. “Nice day, isn’t it?”

James couldn’t stop his own smile. It was a pretty good day and it was nice to pull someone over without having to put up with the defensive stance most everyone took.

“Yes, ma’am, it is.” He agreed. “Do you know why I pulled you over?”

“You want my phone number?”

James couldn’t stop the laugh. “No, actually . . . no. You went through that stop sign over there without even slowing for the turn.” He pointed behind him with his thumb.

She sighed, the smile never leaving her face, the tease never leaving her voice. “Oh that. Well, I suppose I can’t blame you for my inability to focus.”

“May I see your driver’s license and registration please?”

The smile widened. “So you don’t want my phone number?”

James almost blushed . . . almost. “Please, ma’am.”

“Oh, you’re no fun.” She reached over and pulled the registration out of the glove box and license from her purse. “Here you are.” She made a point of brushing his hand with her fingertips as she handed him the information.

He rolled his eyes as he walked back to the car. It wasn’t the first time a woman had acted like that.

“Got ourselves a flirt,” James announced once back in the car.

“Cool. Is she hot?”

“Not . . . hot exactly; cute though.”

“Right on.” Tony sighed. “Don’t you wish there weren’t rules against taking them up on their offers?”

“Nope. A girl like that is a walking social disease.”

Tony laughed. “Probably.” Tony called in the license. When he was done and the ticket was written, James got out again to give it to the flirt.

She didn't even blink at the ticket. "Thank you," she purred. "I'll be more careful the next time."

He nodded and turned to go. "Officer . . .?" she sang.

"Yes, ma'am?"

"If you promised not to call me ma'am, I'd invite you to my place when you're off. We could have a little . . . one-on-one defensive driving class."

"No thank you, ma'am."

She laughed out loud. "You really are a cop, aren't you?"

James laughed too. "Yes, ma'am. I am."

"Well I think that's great. Such a shame though that you're so cute, but so good." She put her sunglasses on. "Thank you, officer."

"No problem. Drive safe." He tapped the side of the car to let her know she was clear to leave and went back to his own while shaking his head.

"Where were women like that when I was in high school?" Tony asked when James got in the car.

"I'm sure I don't know."

Tony eyed him, his lips pursed. "You probably don't," he grinned. "So tell me, Hartman, how does a guy get as old as you in your religion and avoid marriage?"

"Pain and lack of dignity," James said with a smile. They both laughed as they pulled into traffic.

James got home that night and dropped his keys on the table by the door. The day had gone pretty well—no major problems, or anything that caused stress or grief. He was glad of that. He undid his belt as he walked through the living room to the kitchen where he dropped the belt on the table with a loud clunk.

A smile crept over his tired features when he'd opened the fridge to reveal a meal neatly packaged by his mother. It wasn't a surprise to see it there, just an immense reassurance. A sort of confirmation that the world still worked the way he felt it should.

After reheating the steak and potatoes, he went out to eat his dinner on the patio he'd finished a few months previously.

The cool air from the previous month's rain was gone and left nothing but sweltering heat and cracked earth where the sprinklers didn't hit. Allen and Cindy were supposed to come by later tonight for a video and some chips and salsa.

Allen didn't get off work until 7:30, so James had an hour to kill. He lounged outside after eating under the evening blue sky. A slight breeze rustled the leaves overhead. He sighed and stood abruptly. He felt . . . restless, like something was going to happen, like he was waiting for something to happen. He went back in the house and sat at the piano bench.

He had had quite a temper as a youth and, finally, when his mom got sick of all his tantrums and broken toys, she signed him up for piano lessons and spent time with him practicing every day. She taught him to focus and told him that when he felt angry or sad, he could take it out on the piano keys. She had promised she would hear his pain and needs from there much more loudly than a shouting temper tantrum.

The piano had belonged to his grandmother. He inherited it only because he was the only grandchild that could play the piano. It was a rich cherry wood with only a few nicks in the bottom from where he'd hit it accidentally with the vacuum.

The padded seat was covered with a navy blue cotton. James sat on the bench and looked at the music book resting on the stand. Without opening the book, he lifted the lid and slid his fingers along the keys. The piece was his own—although incomplete. It had come from his heart and then the flow stopped. He couldn't finish it.

He'd carried a fantasy that someday he would meet a woman who would inspire the song's completion. Her heart would mingle with his, and the inspiration would come. He had thought, or hoped rather, that Katherine, his dark haired angel, would be that woman. He had drifted to sleep while waiting in the hospital with a melody in his head, but it was almost as if it had been erased upon the second of leaving her room after meeting Bradley.

He played the beginning again, his eyes closed, and heart pounding with each press of his foot on the pedal.

"Hey man, that is really good!" James jumped and reached for the gun that wasn't there. He spun to find Allen who had just let himself in.

Relief washed over James' face. "Do you have any idea how dumb it is to sneak up on a cop?"

"You're not wearing your gun," Allen observed.

"But you didn't know that." James fell heavily onto the bench.

"I didn't know you still played," Allen nodded to the piano.

"I just mess around mostly. It's relaxing."

"Could someone help me here?" Cindy was outside the screen door, her arms loaded with bags and videos.

Allen smiled as James shook his head at him and got up to open the door for her. "Thanks, James," she said sweetly, shooting daggers from her eyes at her husband.

"No problem."

James and Allen followed her to the kitchen. She unpacked the bags, putting salsa and chips into the bowls; Allen got cups, filled them with ice, and handed one off to James. James topped it off with Dr. Pepper and drank heavily from the glass. He refilled it.

"So what movies did we get?"

Allen rolled his eyes in response. "*Sense and Sensibility*."

"*Sense and Sensibility*?" James was sure he'd heard wrong.

"It's a great movie," Cindy defended.

"Yeah, twenty years ago. C'mon, Cin-ful, tell me you got something else."

"She didn't," Allen interjected before she could answer.

"We could play poker while she watches it," James suggested.

"We won't be able to think once the neighbor's dogs start howling with boredom," Allen said, straight-faced.

"Yeah, even a game of cards would be hard to manage over the wails of dogs."

"Shut up," Cindy scowled. "It's a great movie!"

"It's a chick flick," James observed.

"It's a boring chick flick," Allen added.

"It's moving," she said stubbornly.

Allen laughed outright. "Makes me want to move myself right off the couch and anywhere but in front of that TV."

"You guys are so mean." Cindy sat down at the table and scooped a chip into the salsa.

James and Allen sat too, faced with either that or watching the movie.

They emptied and refilled the bowl twice before James put the bag on the table and chucked the bowl into the sink. Allen then asked, "Do you remember when we dumped all the tar out of barrels they were using to redo the roof at Brighton High?"

James sprayed out his Dr. Pepper in the laugh. Coughing and laughing, he managed to choke out the words, "How could I forget! They closed the parking lot for two weeks while they tried to clean it up!"

Cindy laughed too. She wasn't there, wasn't a part of the childhood her husband and his best friend shared, but she knew the stories by heart and loved to go over them as much as the guys did.

The bag of chips was empty. The laughter quieted into private thoughts.

James had been staring into the empty salsa dish when Cindy put her hand over his. "Still thinking about her?" she asked softly.

James jerked his head up. "No! Of course not. I mean, why think about it. She's engaged."

"You could call her," Allen suggested. James just shook his head not daring to admit he'd done that a few times in the past few weeks. He'd called from pay phones to avoid any caller ID entanglements, but she never answered the phone.

"Maybe you should go visit her," Allen added.

"I can't do that. You know I've got DARE this month, plus I'm doing overtime on graves and I've got to winterize my swamp cooler."

"It's not even September," Allen snorted.

"It'll be cold soon. Hey look, I know you guys mean well, but . . . I mean . . . you have the love of your lives. It's not so easy when the only person I even came close to thinking about is engaged, and, let's face it, she was dead when I decided she was the one. How stupid is that?"

"Oh, would you stop! You had a really cool experience! And let me tell you, pal, I didn't get the love of my life by winterizing my swamp cooler all summer!"

"It's gotta be done!" James rubbed his hand over his velvet fine hair.

"Not for another two months! Jamie, buddy, go see her. You know you want to. You could use the 'hey, I'm just checking to make sure you're okay' excuse and see what happens."

"She's probably married already."

"I doubt it; not with all that's happened to her."

James sighed. "I just can't."

Cindy sighed too, along with frowning. She dropped it; so did Allen. They had been through it before, not only with this

Katherine girl, but with other women, ones they thought would be good for him, ones he thought may be good for him and when he finally decided to give up, there was no turning him back. He was James, the eternally stubborn.

They stayed only a few minutes longer, silent mostly, but not uncomfortable in the silence. When they finally left, James turned off all the lights and sat at the piano in the dark. He didn't need to see. His fingers followed the path the keys took him in their melancholy chords. His eyes closed to the blackness of the house. From behind his eyelids however, there was light. The image of a light everywhere and a dark haired woman standing in the midst of the light, her head haloed, eyes glittering and smiling at him as the chords of the piano filled the room.

Chapter 8

James looked up from his laptop when Tony sauntered over to this desk. Tony dropped a McDonald's bag in front of the laptop. "Got you a ham, egg, and cheese muffin."

"Kissin' up, Poulson?"

"Not to you, Hartman. I'm just a nice guy."

James laughed. "Nice guys finish last in this place."

"Oh, don't you worry, I'm not *that* nice." Tony sat on the corner of James' desk. "Plans for today, O cap'n, my cap'n?"

"You have training with Greg. I'm doing a DARE class with Jeff. I get four hours off to sleep and then I'm pulling a graveyard for some overtime."

"What do you need overtime for?"

"Pay off my house."

Tony smiled. "You are the most responsible single guy alive."

"Not really. I just don't have anything better to do with my time."

"You could come hang out with me; meet some women, get some lovin.' How 'bout it?"

James smiled too as he folded the paper wrapper off the McMuffin. "I doubt I'd like the girls you'd be meeting." He sighed. "And I really doubt they'd like me."

"Yeah, maybe not," Tony stood up. "You are kind of lame, but not a bad lame. A likeable sort of lame. Well, Cap'n, I gotta go. Catch you later."

James finished up his paperwork and met Jeff at the

elementary school. The DARE class went without any major calamities and gratefully all the kids were responsive and well behaved. He had napped, showered, and was back in his patrol car by 10:00 p.m.

The night was dead. The city was shrouded in darkness that was as quiet as its sleeping occupants. He snapped his gum and turned into a neighborhood. The radio was on enough to hear, barely, but low enough that it wasn't a distraction.

James jumped when the dispatch came over the radio "18-J-5?"

"This is 18-J-5, go ahead."

"What's your 20?"

"I am 400 East 5000 South."

"We have reports of a 1091. Backup has been called . . . homeowners are away, no description available on perpetrator . . ." she rattled off the other details of location.

"Ten-four. I'm heading there now." When he entered the street, he flipped his lights off. He parked two houses away from the location of the suspected break-in.

He took out his gun, and with it pointed to the ground, cautiously approached the house. Jeff showed up just moments after him with his field training officer in tow. He and Jeff circled the house to the side door, which stood ajar, leaving the field training officer and the other teams of back up to set up a perimeter of the outside premises.

James inhaled and exhaled and focused on listening as he edged the door open further with the toe of his polished black shoe. The full moon glinted off his shoes and the gun in his hand. James found himself wishing there was no moon. The extra light exposed him to whoever was inside.

His heart pounded the blood past his ears in a rush that made it hard to listen. Without blinking, he entered the house.

The fridge hummed in the kitchen they now stood in. The

moonlight washed the room in a soft glow. Table, chairs and appliances were shadowed against ambient light. He stepped carefully so the wooden floorboards didn't creak. He turned right from the kitchen.

The point of a thorough search in unfamiliar territory was once you started a direction, you needed to stay with it. If you start the search to the right, you could get lost if you made a left turn next, aside from the fact that you would cover ground you'd already covered.

James found himself in a short hallway and side-stepped a dark round object on the floor. It looked like a child's toy. A grandfather clock chimed three times from another room—3:00 A.M. He felt Jeff jump at the sound behind him. Jeff may have startled, but he was quiet and composed in less than a second. They kept their breathing slow and rhythmic. If the adrenaline overtook them, they would be panting loudly. Yet the adrenaline pulsed through his veins, making him grip his gun tighter.

There were stairs to the left of the hallway. He pressed his body against the wall in case someone was watching him from the stairs. He listened . . . nothing. Nothing but the hum of a house running through its late night whirs and clicks.

James peeked around the plaster banister that divided the stairs from the hall and glanced up. The stairs were empty. He stepped tentatively on the first stair. It groaned under his weight. He cursed under his breath, shifting so the weight was more evenly distributed. Jeff sidestepped the stair with the squeak.

At the top he stopped and listened harder. There were shuffling sounds of feet on carpet, of metal clicking softly against metal. It was from the room at the end of the hall. *"Breathe evenly,"* he commanded himself. His body was tucked as close to the wall as he could manage without the items on his belt bumping and scraping against it. Jeff seemed to melt right into it. Hallways were the worst part of a search like this. They called it the fatal tunnel. As James crept forward, Jeff stayed behind to cover him from surprises that could come from the doorways on either side. The noise had been from the end so they were certain someone was there, but someone could still be in any of the three doorways off the side of the hall.

James had just passed the first doorway. Sweat slid between his shoulder blades under the layers of the T-shirt, vest, and the standard button up police shirt. Jeff remained distanced, watching the fatal tunnel as James did a quick glance in each of the side rooms. He made it to the room on the end and stepped in. A shadowy figure stood over the dresser he was emptying.

James' voice caught in his throat, a nano-second of fear enveloping him. And then the adrenaline surged like a tidal wave crashing through the wall of fear.

"Freeze!" he commanded to the shadowy figure. He had raised his flashlight to shine it at the person, but while stepping into the room he tripped on a backpack and dropped the light. He kept his grip firm on his gun and maintained his balance despite the obstacle.

The face looked up sharply. At the same instant the hand raised to aim the familiar outline of a gun at James.

"Drop it!" James barked. The moonlight from the window in the hallway that James stood in front of along with the light of the flashlight now pointing his direction made him a perfect target, unlike the figure over the dresser shrouded in shadow.

To James' surprise, not only did the figure not drop the gun, but he moved forward, casually, and unconcerned. Sweat dripped down James' shoulder blades now in a steady stream. It was an itch he could not scratch.

The low growl from James' throat was calm, yet forceful.

"Don't come any closer! Put your weapon down!"

The figure snorted in derision and stepped enough to the light that James could see him clearly. James' jaw went slack, all moisture evaporating instantly from his mouth.

It was the kid he'd arrested a month previously. The one that for all purposes should still have been in detention in Provo.

The level glare of defiance was still there and a glint of something more . . . triumph maybe? A long dark strand of hair hung over his left eye, touching his cheek when the kid moved.

"Well, well . . ." the kid said. "I figured they'd send a cop, but I never dreamed they'd send you." The kid's face was smooth, the face of a boy who had yet to grow into a beard of manhood. James felt the sweat, cold against his back. The roar past his ears was so loud every other sound was drowned by it, yet he could hear the boy's every word with clarity.

"Drop it, kid. The house is surrounded and I just have to squeak and my partner will be in here shooting."

"You think I'm just some punk . . . some gang banger, but you're just like me. Cops are nothin' but a gang with guns. I shoot you and your boys shoot me out of revenge. What makes little boys grow up to be gang bangers? Everyone asks it, but I ask another question. What makes little boys grow up to be cops, bullies with uniforms and guns? So how about it? What makes you a member of the blue and badge gang?" James could only stare. The kid snorted, "See. You think you're some good guy, but you . . . are . . . just . . . like . . . me . . . ." James saw the kid's hand twitch to pull up the weapon and in the millisecond before the kid's gun fired, James had shot his own weapon off and rolled to the side to miss the bullet aimed for him. He was out of the roll and on his feet before the kid hit the ground. James kicked the boy's weapon from reach and knelt down by his side. Jeff came crashing into the room weapon up and scanning everything.

James only allowed a glance and a nod at Jeff before looking back to the boy.

The boy gasped and stared at James wildly. He gripped his fingers into James' arm. "See, man, you're just like m—" He wheezed and went still. The blood bubbled from the hole in his chest and James pulled the kid's hand from his own shirtsleeve and settled it next to the still body.

Jeff spat out a curse, lowering his gun. James cursed too and stumbled off to find a bathroom, leaving Jeff alone with the boy's body.

James lurched forward to the toilet just in time before his stomach released everything. He retched again and then spit. Standing up, he leaned over the sink and ran the water using his left hand. His hand smeared blood on the faucet handle. He didn't notice. He splashed water over his face, into his mouth. He spit some more, closed his eyes and leaned his forehead against the cool metal tap.

The boy was dead. He had killed a kid, just a kid. Dead, oh no, the boy was dead. What if he'd made a mistake? What if the gun was just a toy gun? What did that mean? Was he in trouble? Would he lose his job? Would there be a trial? If arrested, would he go to jail? He almost retched again. The things that happened to cops in jail were unspeakable. The thought of such torture was enough to keep cops from straying to illegal activities.

And then another thought struck James. His eyes clenched shut along with teeth that bit the scream into a sob.

He killed someone! Did he have to go to the bishop? Would there be a court held there? Would he be disfellowshipped, lose his temple recommend, be excommunicated? The ache that filled him tightened every muscle in his body. Was he, in just a moment's action, in danger of losing his soul?

There was noise in the hallway; the sounds of heavy boots

thumping as other cops rushed the room where Jeff waited with the dead boy.

James sat heavily onto the floor, his legs sprawled in front of him, his hands hanging limply in his lap with his gun resting on top of them. He stared at the gun, but wasn't really seeing it. He was not really seeing anything. The sounds from the other room floated to him and around him, but were not able to penetrate his conscious mind. There were calls on radios, boots scuffing, and snaps from the cameras. People were talking, but the only words he heard were the echoes of that kid's voice saying, *"You're just like me . . ."* James touched the purple-pink scar on his shoulder. *"What is it that makes little boys grow up to be cops?"*

A tear hovered on his eyelid, finally gathering enough weight to fall. He watched the splash on his gun and wondered numbly at it until finally the dam broke and he could only cradle his weapon in the crook of his arm and sob as he rubbed his hands furiously together to get rid of the blood.

He wept silently, tears mingling with flakes of dark red that had fallen to the floor. *I'm not like you!* James growled to the voice in his head. But he wondered . . . .

What did make a boy grow up to be a cop? He knew for himself it was that moment the wild eyed man stood in front of him with a gun. The bullet that ripped into the muscles of his shoulder also re-patterned his future. *But that doesn't make me like you!*

Or did it? Cops were a society of people sworn to protect other people. He wanted to protect others, to serve them. What was a gang? A society of punks sworn to protect each other.

This is crazy, he thought. *I'm the good guy. I am* not *just like you.* He touched a finger to the red puddle his tears had created with the blood and smeared a line through it. James bowed his head and prayed. He prayed for the boy; the man the boy would never grow to be. He prayed for himself; the soul he feared he lost. "Forgive me," he repeated over and over. But there was no feeling in the words, just desperation.

James had no idea how long he'd sat there. Was it minutes, an hour, two hours? Someone knocked at the door. He didn't answer. They knocked again and Jeff's voice floated to him in the void he'd surrounded himself with.

"James? C'mon, James, open up. You okay?" Jeff tried the knob and, finding it unlocked, let himself in. He cursed instantly upon seeing James.

"Are you hurt? Did you get shot?"

James looked up, bewildered by Jeff's reaction and then looked around himself. There was blood on the handle of the toilet, blood on the faucet handle and blood in small puddles in front of him. His hand was smeared with red and was placed subconsciously on his shoulder, clinging protectively to the place his scar was, making it appear as though he'd been wounded there.

Instantly, James removed his hand and dropped his gun into the holster at his belt.

Jeff looked him over. "Are you okay?"

James shrugged and looked away so Jeff wouldn't see the tears that had newly filmed over his vision.

"You're not hurt then, are you?"

"No, I'm not hurt," his voice squeaked. He cleared his throat. "I'm . . . fine." As he said it, he wondered at the dull, barely perceptible throb in his shoulder. It felt almost as though if he were to look at it, it would be glowing bright red. He knew he was only imagining it and that truly if he were to look, it would merely be the same dull pinkish purple that it has always been. "Really, I'm fine."

Jeff didn't look convinced. He reached out to James' shoulder to inspect for himself, but James shifted so Jeff couldn't touch him. "I'm fine," he said again firmly. The quiver in his voice was gone, but he still felt it in his heart.

Jeff nodded. "Sure thing, man." He looked doubtful, but James didn't care. He'd just killed someone, not just any someone, but a kid. A boy barely old enough to shave and drive.

He led Jeff out into the hallway and back to the room with the body. The desire to run screaming from the house was consuming but no one would ever call him a coward. This was something he had to face.

When James entered the room, everyone went still. They stared at him, the remorse and compassion evident in their eyes. Nodding to each person as he passed them, James felt something tear his heart. *I am just like you*, he thought. I am a member of a gang of members who all pack heat and shoot to keep from being shot.

The body was in front of him. Instead of looking at it, James turned to Jeff who had followed him into the crime scene. "If anyone needs me, I'll be out in my car." He pushed past Jeff and out of the room, taking the stairs three at a time. He jumped the last four.

You're just like me . . . the voice followed. The cocky over-confident gaze levelly searched into James' mind. He threw himself out the door and to his car, falling into the front seat and leaning his head against the steering wheel. James' breath sounded ragged, like bread that had been ripped through with a dull knife. It nearly felt like he wasn't getting any oxygen with each breath in. He was suffocating. He glanced up. There were more patrol cars there now than there was when he'd gone in. The newest arrivals had their overheads on; the blue, red, and white flashing shadows all around him.

A tap came at his passenger side window. It was Jeff. Jeff got in the car and turned in his seat to look at James.

"We'll need your weapon."

James nodded, watching the lights dance wickedly over the trees and bushes.

"Detectives are in there now. They just got here."

Again, he could only nod. His head hurt. Of course they were there. Where else would they be when a cop shoots a kid? Internal Affairs would be showing up, too. He pulled the gun from the holster and handed it to Jeff. Jeff seemed relieved to take it away from James. He handled it carefully so as not to mix fingerprints. "Will you be able to come to the station?" Jeff asked.

"Will you drive?" James heard his voice say. It sounded hollow. "I don't think I can."

Jeff looked relieved. It was what he'd come to do. He had hoped James would allow him. "Yeah, sure I'll drive. Let me tell everyone what's up and I'll be right back."

James got out of the car when Jeff did. Numb fingers pulled the handle to the passenger side and opened the door. His body felt heavy as he settled into his seat. He concentrated on the lights from his overheads. Blue, red, white, blue, red, white single lights, yet mixing like a kaleidoscope. Nausea from the swirling lights caused him to shut his eyes.

It seemed natural that he would pray then and there at this time in his life while his eyes were closed. It would seem right to pray were he able to summon the words. He tried to focus, brow furrowed. *What could he possibly say?* Nothing. There were not words to give back the life he had taken. A kid, a child that with the right care, the right help, may have become a useful member of society.

Did he believe that? He didn't know. He hadn't ever before. He had seen so many times that kids were arrested for small things that progressively got larger; the penalties more severe. Not to say they all grew up to become drug pushers and car thieves, but a great many did.

Which group did the life he took fit into? Was he one that could have been reformed and made useful in society, or would he have always been a misfit skirting the edges of decent living to prey upon those innocents that wandered there? Numbness flowed from his fingers, through his arms, and straight to his heart. No prayer ever coming to mind, no words ever finding a voice to utter them.

Jeff returned. He adjusted the seat forward to accommodate his shorter legs, and swiveled in the seat to look at James.

"Hartman, I am going to say this, because it needs saying. The kid pulled a gun and fired at you. You are a lucky wretch to still be sitting here and if you think it should've gone any other way, then you are a bigger fool than I could imagine and don't deserve the badge you are wearing. Don't ever forget this fact. He fired first! You defended yourself. Case closed."

James ground his teeth together and nodded. What could he say? Jeff couldn't possibly understand. The blood wasn't on his hands. He hadn't fired the gun, and yet, James knew what he was saying was true. The logic could reason it out and separate the facts. It was the heart that screamed in denial against any innocence. His heart was chanting the word "murderer" at his mind as it desperately clung to the logic of the situation.

Chapter 9

"James, please come on in." It had been a few days since the shooting. He had been given leave with pay until he could come back. The sergeant was now bringing him in to discuss just that. James sat on the chair in front of the desk. His stomach growled. He hadn't eaten much in the last few days and it seemed everything he did eat came back up.

Sergeant Steve Allred sat in the chair on the other side of the desk. "How are you doing?"

James shrugged. "I'm fine," he said stiffly.

Steve grimaced. "I thought so. Listen, Hartman, you know you have garrity here, but more important than that, I am not just your sergeant . . . I'm your friend. I am really worried about you."

James frowned and looked away. "I know, Sarge. His mother filed a civil suit today."

"I know. I heard. Don't let that bother you. It won't come to anything. You did everything by the book and the fact remains that he fired first. We have the bullet holes in the wall to show where he fired at you, plus the powder on his hands. Nothing will come of it, Hartman. You need to believe that. You know I am not going to candy-coat all this for you."

"I know you won't. That isn't the problem."

"What is the problem?"

James wondered if he should share the questions he had about his role as a cop. He had always imagined his reasons to be altruistic, but now he simply didn't know. He believed in the job. He believed in the badge, but he wondered if he truly belonged there. "He was only a kid . . . he was just a child."

"He was a child with a gun," Steve said, his brows beetled together sternly.

"I know that. It's just that he was somebody's son, Sarge. Some woman, the same one that is now filing charges against me, had to hear that her child got gunned down. Imagine that! She gets news that a man in blue took her kid out and he won't be coming home. Sorry, ma'am, thank you for your time." James shook his head against the image he created.

"It was his fault!" Steve countered.

"He was somebody's son!" James shot back.

"So are you!" Steve stood up, pushing his chair back gruffly. He stomped over to James, poking a thick finger hard into James' chest. "Do you think it should have gone the other way? Is that it, Hartman? Are you willing to go back and change things so that your friends in the uniform have to go to your mother's house? Should it have been your mother that got that news? Should we all be planning your funeral right now so we can fold a flag and give it to your mom while she cries? If you think it should have been like that, then you should just turn in your badge now, because you have no idea what you are doing here."

James blinked at Steve's face, near enough to his own that James could feel his sergeant's hot breath. He wanted to break down and sob like a baby, but couldn't do it. Not in front of this man that he respected so greatly. "I . . . don't want that," James admitted. It was true he didn't want that and had honestly not thought too much about it being like that. He had only pictured the boy's mother.

"You're not ready to come back yet. I can tell that by looking at you," Steve said, straightening up. "We have a counselor we would like you to see. I have already made the appointment for you. You meet him Monday at 2:00 pm. Here is the address." Steve pulled a paper off his desk and handed it to James. He stepped back behind his desk. "Don't you forget, Hartman, you did what you had to do. You did your job and there is no shame and no sin in that. Think how many times a week you have to pull your weapon. Did you really think you would never have to use it?"

"Have you ever had to?"

Steve frowned. "No. I've been lucky. But if I did have to, I would know that I did the right thing. It is better he dies than . . ."

"Than me?" James finished.

"Yeah."

James blew out a long breath. "Sure." He stood up to leave. Steve watched him go, clinging to his paper, and wondered if James would bounce back. He was a great member of the force and a good man besides. Steve wanted to cry for the kid. He understood where James was coming from. He was LDS, too. He had held a special fast for James the day before and asked his wife to fast with him. He knew that James would need all the help he could get right now and there was nothing Steve was not prepared to do to give him that help.

Chapter 10

"You had to go see a shrink?" Brian asked after dinner was over at their mom's. It had become a sort of tradition to gather together at regular intervals.

"Yeah. They think I'm crazy."

"Well, I think you are, too," Annette chimed in. "But maybe not certifiable yet." She smiled warmly at him. He grinned back.

"I have been three times this last week. It isn't so bad as I thought it might be."

"Do you lay down on a sofa?" Brian asked.

"I could if I wanted to. There is one there. I just sit in the chair, though."

Brett poked at Anthony who had toddled over in front of the television. Brett was seven and had little tolerance for his small counterpart. Anthony cried and scowled at Brett. "Hey guys, knock it off or James will take you to jail," Brian warned.

"Cool!" Brett said jumping up. He grabbed James by the shirt. "C'mon, James! Let's play cops and robbers! I'm the cop!"

James rolled his eyes but got down on the floor to play with Brett. He pretended to take money out of Annette's purse. Annette laughed, "You can try that all you want. There isn't anything there to take but some lipstick, and I might get a kick out of you wearing that!" James pulled out the lipstick and started to run away with it.

Brett chased him around the living room a minute,

knocking into Brianna who was reading a book and looked up long enough to stick her tongue out at Brett. Brett finally yelled out, "Freeze!"

James kept going around the couch. "Bang! Bang! You're dead!" Brett shouted, his finger pointed out at James like a gun. James turned and stared at Brett in horror. The room seemed deafeningly quiet.

James fell to his knees in front of his nephew. "Why did you do that?" he demanded.

Brett shrugged. "You're the bad guy. If I let you get away, you will hurt somebody else. I have to catch you so you don't."

James stared, tears pricking at his eyes, and took his nephew by the shoulders into a hug. "That's right," he said finally.

Annette stepped in and took Brett by the hand. "I don't think we should play this game right now," she said softly.

Brian looked worried. "You okay, Junior?"

James stood up. "I will be. I think I will be."

James awoke that Sunday morning with dread. Too much, too soon. Although he felt better, he didn't want to go to church and no one would fault him for staying home. It had only been two and a half weeks since the incident and he wasn't ready.

Brian's words from the previous night replayed in his head. "You need to have faith in God's plan for you. You need to believe that He is aware of everything you go through and isn't going to give you too much to bear." He spit the toothpaste into the washbasin and gargled a cup of water. The mint floss was next, gliding easily between his teeth. He knew he had to go to church. If he stayed home, he would lose the right to any help God might want to give him.

James had to admit he did feel better. His small nephew had been able to explain what the psychiatrist and everyone else at the department could not. The child had explained their purpose. If cops don't catch the bad guys then lots of good people would get hurt.

The logic was simple. He knew it in his mind, but it took the voice of a small child to explain it to his heart. After knotting the tie at his neck, he grabbed his scriptures and left.

There was a homecoming during Sacrament Meeting. The young man looked fresh . . . eager. His shoulders set straight in confidence.

James smiled. That was a kid who'd served a valiant mission. His eyes blazed with the conviction of an unshakable testimony. Tears pricked James' eyes as the youth shared the stories of serving in Lithuania, and then finally bore a humble testimony.

The spirit had been so strong. It was exactly the salve James' heart needed. He stood up and wandered to the front where the newly returned elder shook hands and gave hugs. The kid's face was vibrant in animation as he spoke to a woman with dark hair. James fell into place behind her, not knowing why he felt such a need to welcome a complete stranger home.

Perhaps it was the calm of the young man's voice or the strength in his testimony . . . perhaps it was simply that James had needed to feel the spirit so desperately that he felt the need to embrace the man that brought it to him.

The woman laughed, hugged the elder again, and turned right into James, nearly knocking him over. "I am so sor . . ." she broke off.

Her eyes blinked and widened. Her burgundy lips fell open in a gasp. "It's . . . it's you," she whispered.

"It's me." He shrugged, feeling all moisture from his mouth evaporate as his jaw hung slack. He felt tears behind his eyelids at the sight of her in perfect health. "Katherine . . ." he hesitated, fearing she heard the caress over her name when he spoke it aloud. "I . . . I can't tell you how glad I am to see you again. I mean, it's just nice . . . good, really, to know you're okay."

He wondered if there was a film of tears in her own eyes as she nodded and held her arms open then stepped into his personal space to embrace him. "I can't tell you how many times I have thought about calling you."

"You have?" Bewilderment flashed over his face. "Why?"

"To thank you for saving my life, giving me a blessing . . . the flowers." They both paused, uncomfortable in the brief silence.

"So, hey . . . you're LDS," he said with a grin. "I am too . . . LDS, I mean."

Her smile seemed to consume her face. "I figured . . . your name embossed in gold on your scriptures kind of gave it away."

James smiled back. Beautiful, spiritual, and funny! "This isn't your home ward. What brings us the honor of your visit to my ward?"

"Oh, my best friend's little brother came off his mission. It was his homecoming."

"Right, of course." He had only lived in his home for a year and was not very familiar with many of the families in the ward. He wondered which family her best friend belonged to.

As he was about to ask that very question, Katherine's fiancé sauntered up with a short blonde girl talking a million miles a minute to him. He looked bored. James wondered if that was just his natural facial expression.

Either way, it didn't matter. James felt sick just looking at him. He scowled when Bradley slipped an arm over Katherine's shoulder. The gesture of ownership seemed clear to James and it annoyed him.

The blonde whispered something to the missionary and they hurried off.

"Hey, darling?" Bradley said, bending down close to her ear. He looked up and saw James standing there. Bradley straightened. "Bit of a small world isn't it?" Bradley said to James, extending a hand. James took it.

"Yes, very small world."

"I am sorry, but I don't recall your name."

"It's James. James Hartman." Bradley nodded, not really interested, and turned back to Katherine.

"I've got to clear out of here. Something's come up."

Katherine's countenance fell. "But we were going to go to Ashton's homecoming party at Whitney's house and then you said we would go visit my grandfather."

"You got to see Ashton here, didn't you? And sincerely, love, we'll see your grandfather next week. I promise."

"But, I already told him I'd be by today."

Bradley sighed in exasperation. "Really, Kitty, he is an old, old man. It isn't as though he's bloody planning on you. He probably doesn't remember speaking with you."

Katherine's face flushed as though Bradley had slapped her. He saw the reaction and instantly took her hands in his. "Kitty, darling. I'm sorry. I didn't mean that. Really. I know you need to go; I just can't be the one to take you. Couldn't Whitney take you?"

"Her brother just got home. She couldn't do that today!"

"Right, 'course not." Bradley searched around him quickly, his eyes picking through the crowds leaving the chapel. His eyes passed over James and then darted back and settled there, making James shift uncomfortably.

"I'll bet James could take you."

Both James and Katherine blinked in surprise at Bradley and then looked at each other.

"Bradley, no, we don't really know each other and James doesn't want to drive me all over the valley," Kit stammered.

"What's to know; he's obviously trustworthy. After all, the man did save your life once. You'll do it, won't you, James?"

James' ears were ringing as he stared from Bradley's pleas to Katherine's discomfort. Through the ringing he heard himself say, "I'd be happy to take Katherine anywhere she needs to go. I didn't have any plans today."

"Right," said Bradley, grinning with satisfaction. "See, Kitty, all taken care of. You go have a great time. Tell your granddad hello for me, won't you?" He brushed a kiss over her lips and was gone, leaving James and Katherine to stare after him with wonder.

"You don't have to take me," she said finally. "I can get my brother to come pick me up."

"No, really, I want to take you."

"I don't want to be a bother." She looked down.

"Are you kidding?" James said, ducking his head to peer into her face. "Katherine, you could never be a bother to me."

"You only say that because you don't know me very well." She tilted her head. "You know, the only people who call me Katherine are my grandfather and my mom when she's upset."

"Do you prefer 'Kitty'?" James doubted she really preferred that nickname, but he would call her whatever she wanted.

She grimaced at the sound of Kitty. "No, actually, I really don't like that one very much. Most people call me Kit. My brother calls me Katy-did, but that's another thing entirely."

"Kit?" James smiled. "I like it. It seems to fit you. But then, I thought Katherine fit nicely, too."

They started walking. James had forgotten he had wanted to shake Ashton's hand and congratulate him on a well-served mission. He couldn't be certain Ashton was even still there. The only thing James saw was Kit.

She had eyes so deep, James was afraid he would get lost in them, and more afraid that he wanted to get lost in them.

"So why 'Kit'?"

"My mom loved the book, *Witch of Blackbird Pond.* The main character's name was Katherine and her nickname was Kit. My mom just always liked it."

He unlocked the passenger door to his car and waited for her to get in before closing it. He loved the simple process of opening her door and sighed as he walked back around to his door. *Don't set yourself up for the biggest fall of your life,* he thought to himself.

Kit gave him directions to Whitney's house only two streets down from his own. She then swiveled in her seat to look at him, her seatbelt pulling tight over her shoulder.

"I never had a chance to thank you properly," she said.

"You thanked me just after Sacrament Meeting."

"Yes, well . . . that wasn't a proper thank you."

James grinned. "So what constitutes a 'proper' thank you?"

She focused her blue green eyes on him seriously. "For what you did, there isn't enough I could do to thank you." She leaned closer to him as though about to whisper a secret and then pulled abruptly back. "Oh, turn here on the right!"

James pulled the car over in front of a house where a dozen other cars had piled into the driveway. He got out quickly to try to beat Kit to opening her door but hadn't even rounded the corner when she was out and locking her side up.

"You know, I could have gotten that for you." He motioned towards the door.

"Why?" she winked. "I'm a big girl. I open doors, jars, and my own mail."

She reached past him to open the front door without bothering to knock or ring the bell. He followed her down a short hall to where all the noise was.

The gathering wasn't too large. Mostly family and people who may as well have been family. James felt uncomfortable at first but the blonde girl who had been with Bradley earlier at the church grabbed his arm.

"Who is this?" she demanded of Kit.

"This is my friend, James."

"He's adorable!" the blonde exclaimed, as though he wasn't there.

"What's your name?" James interjected before she could start pinching his cheeks.

"I'm Whitney Brunatti. I'm Kit's best friend."

"Brunatti? You don't look Italian."

She grinned. "I'm not actually. Brunatti is my married name."

As if cued for that moment, a dark haired man stepped into the kitchen with a small baby. He passed the baby off to Whitney. "I think she's hungry," he explained.

"I'll take care of her." Whitney cooed into the tiny face as she snuggled the baby into her arms. "James, I hope you'll excuse me. It was nice meeting you. You really are adorable."

She giggled softly as she walked away. James flushed furiously. Kit grinned. "Don't mind her. She thinks everyone is adorable."

"Does she think Bradley is adorable?"

Kit stopped. "I don't really know. She hasn't said." She furrowed her brow slightly then turned to lead him into the living room. Whitney's brother, Ashton, was there, now in jeans and a sweatshirt with a BYU logo on it. Smaller cousins, all adoring at the feet of their newly returned family member, surrounded him. He was trying to talk to Whitney's husband as a ten-year-old tried to tackle his back.

They all noticed James. Whitney's parents recognized him from church and welcomed him to their home. "Isn't it strange how people can live so close to each other and never really get acquainted?" her father asked. James nodded.

"So what do you do?" her mother asked.

"I'm a policeman."

The cousins' worshipful eyes turned from Ashton to James. "Do you have a gun?" one asked.

"Yes, I do."

"Can we see it?" another chimed in.

James smiled patiently. "Not right now."

"C'mon, please." The child put up his hands clasped together in pleading.

"I don't have it on me," James said truthfully.

"So you must be Kit's new boyfriend," Whitney's mother said trying to steer the conversation away from the small boys.

Kit smiled. James' eyes nearly popped out of his head. "No . . . I . . . I'm not," he stammered. "I'm just a friend. She's engaged you know."

Whitney's mom looked disappointed. "That's too bad. You looked like such a nice boy."

James cleared his throat then said with a smile, "I am nice."

"Have you ever shot anyone?" the ten-year-old said from Ashton's back.

James' smile froze on his lips as his blood ran cold in his body as though someone had put in an IV of liquid ice straight into his veins. "I . . ." He had no response. The question had taken him completely off guard and he found he could only blink at the child in the now still room.

"Oh really, Steven! What kind of question is that?" Kit had her arms folded across her chest.

"Yes," Whitney's mom agreed. "That's a terrible thing to be asking. People have to do all sorts of things at their jobs, but you don't need to bother them about it."

Steven slid off Ashton's back looking adequately penitent.

"I was just asking," he grumbled and stalked off. Ashton looked relieved to see him go and stretched himself to straighten his back out again.

"Are you in our ward?" Ashton asked James.

"Yes, I am," James said softly. He was still a little shocked by the boy's question and it was hard to quell the image of the body lying on the floor of that bedroom that seemed to rise into his mind unbidden.

Kit leaned over to James. "I need to get going soon."

"Oh sure, take him away just as we start to get acquainted," Ashton whined.

"You'll see him in church next Sunday." She smiled and knuckled the top of Ashton's head. "Bye, little boy. Be good."

"I'm always good," Ashton declared with a wink.

James shook Ashton's hand. "It was good to meet you. I really enjoyed hearing you speak. It was what I needed to hear."

Back in the car, James scowled at Kit. "You need to put on your seatbelt," he said. He'd almost made it to the end of the street before he realized she wasn't wearing one.

"You gonna arrest me?"

"Nope." He pulled over to the curb. "But I'll wait for you to put it on."

She grinned, pulled the belt over, and snapped it into place. James moved back onto the road.

"So did you grow up in the neighborhood?" he asked.

"No. Whitney used to live by me in Sandy, but her parents moved here after she got married about three years ago."

"So where did you go to high school?"

"Hillcrest."

"Hmm. We were rivals then."

"Why, where did you go?"

"Brighton."

"Too bad. You seemed like such a nice guy too."

"Hey, don't hold it against me. I hated high school and would've done anything to get to go to a different school."

"I liked high school. It was fun. Not that I'm one of those groupies that want to go back, but it was okay while I was there."

"So what year did you graduate?" he asked.

She told him and directed him to turn left.

James turned. He already knew when she had graduated, had figured it out when he was able to pull her birth date from the report files on the accident. She was two years younger than him. He berated himself for memorizing such details as her birth date, height, weight and everything else listed on her driver's license. He almost felt like some crazy stalker.

"So where do you work?" he asked after making another left turn into a neighborhood.

"I work as the director of communications for the March of Dimes."

"Wow. Sounds technical. What does that mean exactly?"

"It means I handle the media relations for them. I design the pamphlets and handle all the big public fundraisers like Walk America. I help bring people an awareness of who we are and what we do."

James nodded thoughtfully. "So who are you and what do you do?"

"March of Dimes was started originally to stop polio. We are the first and only non-profit organization to achieve our goal, which we did when we found a vaccination for the polio disease. I truly believe that every person who is born and lives without the fear of having polio owes March of Dimes a debt."

"That's cool. I didn't know that. I mean, I did Walk America when I was a kid, but that was because my older brothers and sister did. We read 'Choose Your Own Adventures' while we walked."

"Our big push now is to educate people on the importance of nutrition and—oh, it's this house, here." She pointed to her right to a little white house with a navy blue tin awning over the front bay window. James pulled over to the side in front of the house. He got out and hurried to her side of the car to let her out. He was glad she waited for him. She thanked him and bounded up the steps to the front door, which was red. There was a doorknocker in the shape of a Scotsman in a kilt holding up a large brass handle that made up the knocker. It was set in the center of the door.

The doorbell also was made up of a brass Scotsman with the buzzer centered in his belly.

"Is your grandpa Irish?" James asked as she used the knocker on the door.

"Scottish. He's very proud of his heritage. Our family, the Buchanans, immigrated from the lowlands of Scotland." She furrowed her brow and knocked again.

"Why not use the doorbell?"

"It doesn't work. Grandpa disconnected the wires last year to keep from being bothered by solicitors. He does a lot of reading and hates to be bothered by nonsense."

She almost knocked again, when, in a moment of decision, she opened the door and just walked in. "Grandpa?" she called out. There wasn't any answer. She walked further into the house. James followed in behind her.

"Grandpa?" She looked nervous as she hurried through the front room. James wandered the room, uncertain if he should follow her or just wait. The house smelled like an old person mingled with a musty scent as though the house had been shut up for a while.

Despite the smell, the place was incredibly clean. He ran a finger over a shelf on the oak bookcase. No dust. The walls were lined with bookcases. James figured that was where the musty smell came from. The books looked ancient, the pages yellowed and brittle. The leather covering the spines of the books sagged with wrinkles of time and gravity.

There was a huge rug on the wall above the fireplace that had strange symbols on them. A triangle over another triangle which was upside down.

Bagpipes were placed next to the fireplace and a plaque with a coat of arms sat on the mantle. A clown figurine was to the right of the plaque.

Something about the room, the books, and the Scottish memorabilia commanded respect. And as Kit called for her grandfather from the back rooms and James circled the room, he felt an encompassing amount of respect.

Kit came out from the back rooms, wild with panic. "I don't know where he is," she said running a hand through her dark hair.

Just then, the back screen door in the kitchen slammed shut. Kit leapt to the kitchen. "Grandpa!" She hugged him furiously. "Where have you been?"

"You said you were coming to visit, so I went out of here and cut some zinnias for you." He held out a small bouquet of multi-colored flowers. "They're outta here for you."

She smiled softly, taking the flowers from his hand, and burying her nose into them. "I knew you'd remember I was coming by," she whispered.

He pointed outside as if to explain again. "You said you were going to be outta here and I went outta here . . ." He paused and furrowed his brow. He looked as though he might cry and then he shrugged and pointed at her ". . . flowers," he finished, shrugging again.

"I love them." She planted a kiss on his cheek and hugged him again. "And I love you."

He pulled away and put a hand on either side of her face and peered into her eyes as though searching for something in them. "I see you, Katherine." He nodded and released her, turning away and walking carefully to the chair by the bookcases in the living room. "I see you," he said again as if puzzling the words out in his own head.

They followed him, taking their places on the couch opposite his chair. He seemed to blend into the books on the shelves. His skin, yellowed and parched like the paper, wrinkled and sagging like the leather covers. He fit into the scene behind him as perfectly as if an artist had set him there in a painting.

He smiled fondly at Kit. "I have a new book outta here, Katherine."

"Really? What book?" she asked.

He thought a moment and then shrugged with an embarrassed smile. "Can't get it . . . outta here . . ." He stood and pulled a book from the shelf and handed it to her.

The book certainly didn't look new or smell new for that matter. Kit turned it over in her hands reverently. "*Toilers of the Sea* by Victor Hugo . . ." she said. "It's perfect, Grandpa." She handed it back to him. He took it and placed it on the gilded stand next to his chair. Though the stand, with its ornate workings, did not match a single item in the room, it belonged there as perfectly as the old man did.

He gazed at James a moment, noticing him for the first time. "New boyfriend, Katherine?" He poked a bony finger in James' direction.

"New friend. He's my guardian angel." She smiled. "His name is James."

"James is a good name . . . outta here."

"What's your name?" James asked, finding his voice.

"Gene Madison." The eyes were clear when he said it, bright with memory, but they seemed to haze into ambiguity when he started to turn away.

That happened frequently while they talked. When he mentioned his books, his eyes were clear. When speaking of the day or a party or the weather, they hazed over. He threw in the words 'outta here' frequently, randomly into most sentences. Many times when he could not pull up the words he'd intended to say, he would simply shrug and smile.

Although the situation seemed odd, being in a strange old man's house with a girl he'd met only once before and fell in love with, James was very much at home. Even the musty smell of aged leather seemed inoffensive and actually inviting.

Kit went and fixed her grandfather a Coke with ice and the old man seemed to ponder James when she had left.

"You love her," he said finally and leaned forward, his pale blue eyes crisp with clarity.

James felt the hairs on his arms raise. Hesitantly he nodded. "I do."

"There is a part of her, a part that loves you too, but she doesn't know why, so she hides it. Hides it even from herself."

It was the longest sentence the old man had uttered without the phrase 'outta here' in it.

James leaned forward as well. "How do you know?"

The eyes clouded over like neglected cataracts. He whistled a raspy whistle through his teeth a tune that sounded like a military march cadence. When Kit came back and before she could hand him the drink, his shoulders sagged. "They're shooting again," the thick voice wailed. "Get down! Get down!"

Kit put her arms around him. "Ssshh. It's over. That was a long time ago. You're safe now. Tell me about Gaston LeRoux and the Phantom." The wails stopped as his eyes closed. His thick voice took them through France to the Paris opera house. The memory of the book, prompted by Kit in places, seemed to ease the furrowing of the old man's brow.

Once they were back in the car, Kit gently held her bouquet in one hand while fingering the petals of each flower with the other.

"I think he likes you," she said after a minute.

"Why?"

"He remembered your name when he said goodbye to you."

James supressed a grin. The old man had said, "James . . . outta here." It sounded like a genuine kick out, but James knew it hadn't been. It just sounded funny to him.

"Why did he say, 'I see you, Katherine'?"

A half smile lazily drifted over her face. "That's how he says I love you. He had a stroke seven months ago. No one can believe it didn't kill him or at least turn him into a vegetable. He has had a hard time speaking ever since. He understands what is being said to him and knows how to reply, but sometimes the words get lost on the way to his mouth. It's frustrating to him and to everyone else. They want to stick him in a home."

"Who does?"

"My mom's stepbrother."

"Why? He looks like he's doing okay."

"I guess because he's forgetful. Sometimes he gets lost in a memory. Sometimes he's still fighting World War II, like today." She sighed. "The sooner you get him out of the memory, the easier it is to get him out. I'm afraid sometimes when he's alone and has a long time to think that he'll get trapped somewhere in his past."

"You two have a good relationship."

"Yes, we do."

"He has lots of cool stuff."

"Yeah, he has. He has a bunch of World War II things and Scottish things and then there are the books . . ."

"Do you like to read?" James asked.

"I love to read." She grinned. "My friends were books when I was little. I guess I was socially deficient that way, but I chose it. One time I had a friend over and I still hadn't finished the book I was reading. It was Rudyard Kipling's *Jungle Book*. She got mad because I wasn't entertaining her so she picked it up and ripped out the last pages I hadn't read and threw them away."

"Oh, no way! She ripped up your book?"

Kit giggled. "It was just a cheap paperback. No harm done."

"Still, that's one friend you'd think twice about crossing."

"Oh, I don't know. Whitney grew up to be pretty nice."

"That was Whitney? Wow. Who would've known that girl had a temper?"

"All girls have tempers. All guys do too."

James pursed his lips. "Yeah, I guess they all do." He flipped on the car radio. "What kind of music do you like?"

"Everything. Not too fond of Heavy Metal or the hard alternative stuff, but even some of that isn't too bad."

James swallowed hard. Everything she said wound her tighter into his heart. He pulled into her driveway with regret. He wanted to think of an excuse to drive forever and learn everything there was to know about her.

"I guess this is it," he said simply.

"I guess so . . ." She paused, letting the air out between her teeth like her grandfather's whistle. "Walk me to the door."

"Sure." He'd walk her to Saturn if she asked him to, but was surprised she wanted him to take her to the door. At the doorstep she leaned forward and kissed his cheek.

"Thank you," she said.

The place her lips had touched him seemed to burn. His breath felt shallow as he searched the inner pools of her eyes.

"For what?"

"For saving my life." She gave him a hug too. "That may not be enough to thank you truly, but at least it is a proper thank you."

"Oh . . . of course."

"And thank you so much for dragging me around today. Probably bored you to tears, but I'm glad I had the chance to spend some time with you."

"I'm glad too. I had a great time. It wasn't boring at all." He wanted to reach up and touch her dark hair, but stepped back instead. "Anytime you want to visit people who keep such good company, let me know," he grinned. "I'd better be going." James hesitated, shook himself, and then commanded his feet to carry him back to his car.

She stood there a moment after he'd reached the car and then smiled, waved, and disappeared with her zinnias behind the screen door.

Gary was there, waiting for her with a grin that split his face into two separate pieces. "Bradley's here," he whispered to her. "He's been here waiting for over an hour. He called six times the hour before that."

"Why?" Kit hissed.

"I think it had something to do with the guy that just walked you to the door and the flowers in your hand."

"Oh my word! Did he see me walk up?"

"Yep."

"But . . . but . . . Is he–" The word she wanted to use was jealous, but she knew it wasn't that. Bradley *expected* her to be his. There was never any question about the fact that she would belong to him. She had tried before to make him jealous by flirting with another guy or whatever, but it never fazed him. His confidence in her loyalty was almost admirable . . . almost.

It hurt too. It sometimes felt that his apathy was because he really didn't think her attractive enough or fabulous enough to catch the eye of anyone else.

In her mind she knew it wasn't true. She dated half the world in college, and had been proposed to seven times before Bradley. She knew she looked okay, but somewhere the feelings of inadequacy inside her kept growing.

It didn't help that Bradley scrutinized everything she wore and sometimes went as far as to ask her to change her clothes if he didn't think she looked good enough. She had come to learn that sweats or T-shirts were a definite no. Her hair was another item of scrutiny. He liked it long and down. She preferred it swept up off her face, or kept shorter. For some reason she could not explain, she let it grow and wore it down.

Gary smiled wider. "He looks pretty annoyed."

Kit grinned with him. "And you love that, don't you?"

"Absolutely. I do say it was delightful to bother the ol' chap." The accent was lazy, in perfect imitation of Bradley.

"You know, young Riley," the voice behind them said with an edge, "it's bad manners to mock behind a man's back."

"You're right, Bradley," Gary said. "It's ever so much more fun to do it to their face, don't you agree, Old Bean?"

Bradley didn't bother to answer, but continued to glare until Gary was tired of glaring back. Gary winked at Kit and went up to his room.

"Nice of you to come home."

"I've only been gone three hours."

"I thought you were only going to Whitney's and your grandfather's."

"I did."

"What took so long?"

"We stayed at Grandpa's for a couple of hours." She hated that he was drilling her as if she'd done something wrong.

"You don't stay that long when we go."

"That's because you are always in a hurry to leave."

He scowled but didn't respond. She stepped toward him.

"What's the matter, dear darling Bradley . . . Jealous?"

"Of what? Him? Oh please be serious, Kitty. He's the last person I would be jealous of. Bear in mind, I sent you off with him. Would I do that if the man were capable of making me nervous?"

"Then why were you 'nervous,' darling?"

"Simply worried about you."

She raised her eyebrows. "Worried about me?"

"Certainly. We just got you put back together, didn't we? Certainly would hate to have anything else happen to you."

She sighed. She knew he hadn't been jealous. In some ways it made her angry he wasn't; in other ways she was relieved. Did he have a reason to be jealous? No, of course not.

James was handsome, smart, sensitive and every other thing that might attract a woman to a man, but he was . . . was . . . what?

Anyway, it didn't matter. She was engaged. She had made a promise and Katherine didn't break promises. Besides, she really did love Bradley. She told herself that while she made dinner and he droned about his new car. She told herself that when Gary and Bradley fought about trivial details of gospel doctrine that only ended when Kit's father silenced them with a growled "enough!"

"I'm sorry, Ryan," Bradley said. "I didn't mean to bring contention to your table."

Gary rolled his eyes and belted out a snort of derision. Ryan turned an icy glare Gary's direction. "Sorry, Dad."

Kit pushed the brussel sprouts around on her plate. She hated it when Bradley chose to argue with people. It wasn't just that he did it with Gary, but with everyone. To Bradley, the entire world was open for debate; one in which his argument was the right one. Marleah was flushed. She hated the debate arena too. She was the type that moved mountains with gentle suggestions, and as the Young Women's president, she excelled with that attitude.

"How's the stucco business going, Ryan?" Bradley asked

conversationally. Ryan Riley owned RMR Stucco and had owned it his entire life. He loved to talk about it, to thrash over details of deadlines and employees. Changing the subject to business was a tool Bradley used with precision.

"Things are going well, but I'm having issues with my new haudie—you know, the guy that hauls the mud for the stucco."

"What's wrong with him?"

"Oh, he calls in sick a lot, always late, and takes too long of lunches."

Bradley tsked in sympathy. It was Kit's turn to roll her eyes. Bradley didn't care about her father's problems in his business. All of his empathy, sympathy, and helpful suggestions were an act. "You should fire him," Bradley said.

"Well, that's the hard part. He works hard when he's there, and right now we're short of hands with the explosion of new building. I'm backed up for months to come. I need every hand I can get."

"I understand completely, Ryan," Bradley said, taking a second helping of corn bread.

Ryan sighed. Marleah quickly hid a frown in her glass of milk. She felt her husband's frustration. Employees were truly hard to come by and the business seemed to keep growing. Ryan's back had gone out five years previously, so he was little more than a foreman now. He hated not getting down into the thick of work and pulling his own weight, and the paperwork end of the business bored him senseless.

"I wish I could help," Bradley said. "But even on my day off, I'm supposed to fly to California and meet up with my father. He's having some difficulty with his business as well. His are from an administrative point, of course. The shareholders are in the throes of mutiny. I need to go put things back together." He chuckled lightly. "Light knows what they'd do without me in the little enterprise Dad started up."

The "little enterprise" was what brought the large amounts of money to Bradley's checking account every month and made it so he would never sweat for a dollar again. Bradley's father, Max, started a computer graphics firm in the early '80s creating and designing games for Atari and Commodore. When those companies dwindled and the computer industry changed, Max's company adapted to the changes and boomed.

Bradley went to college, but quickly became bored with it and went home to his dad to get a job. Max was getting older and wanted to retire. He was glad to turn the business over to his son.

Bradley stared lazily over the table at Kit. "Kitty, I almost forgot to tell you, you'll need to take next weekend off."

"Why?" she asked.

"Since I'll be going home for the week, Mother thought it would be nice if you came down for the weekend for dinner and maybe brunch on Sunday. She's been worried about you since your little mishap and needs to see for herself that you're fine."

"Bradley, I . . ." She didn't want to start this conversation in front of her family. "I'll have to check with my schedule. We'll talk about it later."

The rest of the meal was taken in silence. Everyone knew what Kit meant when she said "later" and Gary grinned malevolently. Maybe this would be the fight that would finally break them up so he didn't end up with British arrogance for a brother-in-law.

James drove to Allen's house instead of driving home. He replayed the day in his mind over and over again. He had spent those hours with his angel and had come away loving her more than ever. He badly needed advice.

"Hey Cin-ful," he said as she opened the door wider to let him in. He kissed his fingers and tapped her forehead. "Is your lazy, good-for-nothing husband around?"

"He'll be back in just a minute. He went to borrow some CDR discs to burn an image from his hard drive. What's wrong?"

He went with her to the living room. "I don't know that anything is wrong exactly. I just needed someone to talk to."

"What happened?"

"I saw her again." He let out a long breath. She waited. "Cin-ful . . . I don't know how to describe it. She is beautiful, funny, and smart—did you know she works for the March of Dimes?" He stood up to pace. "She loves to read, she wants to save babies and stop childhood diseases. She makes intelligent observations about life and the whole world. She—"

"How do you know all this from just seeing her again?"

"I met up with her and that rotten fiancé of hers. I really don't like that guy and it isn't just because she is engaged to him."

"Why don't you like him then?" Cindy folded her legs underneath her on the sofa.

James scrubbed a hand over his head. "I don't know, I mean he says the right things, but they just seem wrong." Cindy wrinkled her nose and arched a brow. "I know what you're thinking, but you're wrong. I am not being judgmental. He acts like she is something he owns; as if he could snap his fingers and she will be there to feed him grapes and fan him with palm fronds."

"Maybe she likes him that way."

"No, Cin-ful. I don't think so."

"How did you guys meet up again? I'm lost."

"I went to sacrament meeting and there was this returned missionary speaking and he really helped me to feel the spirit so I went up to thank him. You know things have been rough for me lately with all that's happened." She nodded. "Anyway, he was talking to this girl and when she turned around, it was her!"

"Wow, small world."

"Yeah, her fiancé was there too, and I tell you, the guy is a creep."

"What did he do?"

"He left her stranded when they already had plans to go see her grandfather. He asked me to take her instead."

"And you did it?!"

"I had to. I mean, it was a chance to get to know her."

"But you already said you were over it."

Allen came in and put his backpack down. "Over what?"

"Over Katherine."

"The dead girl?"

"Yeah, that's the one. James just spent the day with her."

"I thought you said you were over her," Allen echoed.

"I thought so too." James hung his head in his hands.

Allen looked at Cindy who smirked and shook her head.

"But you're not," Allen observed.

"She's just so . . . everything!"

"So what are you going to do now?" Allen asked, scooting next to Cindy.

"I have no idea."

"I could drive over, pick this guy up, and ship him back to England for you," Cindy said.

"Or we could call him and give him an anonymous tip to leave town before the green card office finds out about him," Allen said with a grin.

James smiled at both of them. "Or we could just spend some more time with her so she has something to compare him to."

"So you're going to see her again?"

"Yep."

"You never struck me as the type of guy to date another guy's girl."

James stared levelly at Allen and then hung his head back into his hands. “I’m not.”

Cindy smoothed a hand over James’ head. “It stinks to always be the nice guy, doesn’t it?” She rubbed his head quickly. “Your hair feels like velvet.”

“Oooohhh, let me feel!” Allen laughed, climbing over Cindy to rub James’ head. He gave James a noogie, to which James retaliated with Allen in a headlock. They began wrestling, landing on top of Cindy and rolling onto the floor.

It ended with Allen crying out for mercy. James looked to Cindy. “Should I let him go?” he panted. She pursed her lips thoughtfully.

“Hmmm. Well, maybe. I might need him later and he’ll be useless to me if you break him.”

James let him go with a small push. “Aw, he’s useless anyway, Cin-ful. He got the better end of marrying you.”

Allen looked up; his hair tousled, his grin lopsided. “That’s for certain,” he agreed. Allen growled at her and then leapt to attack her. He had her pinned before she had time to blink.

“Let me go!” she laughed.

“Say the magic word.”

“Now!”

“Aw, c’mon, honey. There’s no magic in that.”

“Please.” She tried to move her arm from under his grip. He pulled it back. She laughed harder.

“I’m gonna tickle if I don’t hear it soon.”

“No!” She gasped between fits of laughter. “No tickling.”

“And I’ll help,” James chimed in.

“Say it, Cin-ful.”

“Never!” she declared.

Allen tucked her hand under his leg and started tickling. She squirmed and squealed with laughter.

“Say it,” he asked again. James moved closer in case Allen needed any help.

"You're the best looking guy I know," she squealed.

Allen let her up and hugged her. She pounded his arm playfully. He grinned at James. "It's so sad I have to torture her to get her to say it." He winked.

"I just can't believe you make her lie to you," James smirked.

"Ooohh, honey, don't listen to him . . . it isn't lying," Cindy cooed and kissed Allen on the forehead. James couldn't help but grin at the two of them. He sighed, too. What was he going to do about Kit?

Chapter 11

Marleah made Gary do the dishes after dinner. He grumbled as he cleared the table and took everything to the kitchen. She went with Ryan to plan out the work schedules for the next week, leaving Kit alone with Bradley.

"It's later," he observed.

"I know." She stood up. "Let's go downstairs."

When they had finally settled on a couch in the rec room, he said again. "It's still later. Tell me why you don't want to go to California for the weekend."

"I never said I didn't want to go." She picked at the loose threads on the sofa. After a moment he took her hand in his to stop her from fidgeting.

"Tell me what's wrong, love."

"Bradley, your mom hates me," she said in a rush.

"My mom does not hate you, Kitty! Why would you say such a thing? Where would you get such an idea?"

"She argues and lectures every time I see her. 'Kitty, you're too thin; Kitty, you should wear more makeup, you look so pale; Kitty, please fold the napkins horizontally, not vertically when setting my table!' I'm serious, Bradley, she hates me."

"Oh, I hardly think that being thin, pale, or in need of napkin folding lessons are reasons to hate the woman I love."

Kit smiled, tired but grateful. "Do you love me?"

"Of course I do. If anything changes, I'll let you know." He chuckled at his own joke. "Seriously, Kitty, my mother does not hate you. Come to California. It's only a few days that I'm asking for. Come Thursday night after work and you can go home Sunday night."

She bit the inside of her cheek. "She may not hate me but she is still mad that I am having the wedding in the Salt Lake Temple and not the San Diego one like she wanted. And I'm not going to brunch on Sunday. I won't break the Sabbath. I'm tired of the way she tweaks gospel principles and justifies her actions."

"I understand. I really don't see how that's a problem at all." He smoothed her hair and kissed her.

Slipping into the covers later that night, she was surprised to find James as the last thought she had before drifting to sleep. He was also the first thought when she woke up. He seemed to occupy every thought throughout the day.

What surprised her most was the way her mind created scenarios for her to see him again. Was that wrong? She didn't know, but she wanted to see him again.

As she got ready, she wondered if she could find a reason to go to church with Whitney's brother Ashton again. No. She couldn't do that. Maybe she could just start speeding whenever she saw a police car and he would pull her over and . . . And what?

Kit grinned in the mirror at herself. *You are insane,* she berated herself. Look at yourself. You're thirty years old, educated with a phenomenal career doing what you love to do. People respect you and here you are acting like some sixteen-year-old with a crush!

A respectable person would be sensible enough to simply walk up to the front door and say, "Hello, I enjoyed your company. Would you like to go to lunch?" But she couldn't do that! Frustrated, Kit pulled her hair up into a sloppy twist and latched it there with a big black clip, letting the ends topple loosely over the side.

Bradley hated this hairstyle. It looked juvenile to him. But he was in California or at least he would be in less than an hour.

She looked at the clock and then back in the mirror. She frowned and looked back to the clock. Next to the stand the clock sat upon, resting quietly and quite forgotten in the corner, was an umbrella with a brass duck head handle and the name Gerald Hartman engraved on it.

Kit thought about the umbrella all day. She had a meeting with Channel 2 to help them write up a story on March of Dimes with all the proper statistics. They were on a campaign to help bring out an awareness of folic acids and how important it was to take folic acids during pregnancy to prevent diseases like spina bifida. She gave them a list of people to interview and had to work hard to focus on the task at hand.

James and the umbrella were at the front of her thoughts. Everything else was secondary. When she got home, Gary was in the kitchen. He was still in his work clothes. He worked with their father in the stucco business. Little chunks of cement and smears of color stained his clothes. He was reading a magazine on four-wheelers and eating Oreos with milk.

"You could use a shower," Kit said, sitting next to him and pulling an Oreo out for herself and dunking it in his milk.

"You could use one, too, but I didn't want to hurt your feelings by telling you you stink."

"You are not capable enough to hurt my feelings."

"If you say so, stinky."

"I should go get packed," she mused, taking another bite of cookie.

"So, you are going to California?"

"I guess so."

"I swear Kit, you've got 'spineless wimp' engraved on your forehead."

"Don't start, Gary."

"I'm not starting; I just don't get why when British boy snaps his fingers, you snap to attention."

"I don't!" she protested. "I don't at all! There is nothing wrong with me wanting to please him."

"There is when you sprout strings from your shoulders and hands, and he's the puppeteer working them."

"It isn't like that at all."

"Look at you. Be honest with yourself. When was the last time you wore your hair up?"

"I don't remember. What difference does it make?"

"The last time . . ." Gary said above her protests, "was the last time British boy left town."

She thought about that a moment and then looked away. "It wasn't that long ago," she muttered, but by Kit's voice, it was obvious Gary was right and he'd struck a nerve in showing her the truth.

She got up absentmindedly, taking his glass of milk to the sink and dumping it. "Hey!" Gary leapt up, but not in time to salvage the contents of the glass. He frowned into the sink.

She shrugged. "Sorry, I wasn't paying attention."

"Obviously," he growled.

"Oh well. You needed to go shower anyway."

He stalked off. "Yeah, I'll save some hot water for you, stinky."

She glared at this back. "I don't snap to attention," she grumbled.

She pursed her lips and stared at the phone. She could call . . . she *should* call James. After all, she had his dad's umbrella.

She pulled out the phonebook to look him up. She found Gerald Hartman, his dad, but no James or Jim or anyone with a number from the Holladay area. She frowned. Maybe he just moved there. She called information but they showed his number as not listed.

Frustrated, Kit hung up the phone. *This is crazy,* she thought as she picked it up and called the number to Gerald

Hartman.

A woman answered. "Hello?"

Kit took a shot in the dark. "Is this Mrs. Hartman?"

"Yes, it is."

"Hi, my name it Kit, er, Katherine. I'm a friend of James and I have something for him."

"Oh, well, he doesn't live here."

"Yeah, I know, but I don't have his phone number."

"Well, I can't give out his number. He has asked me not to, but I will give him the message you called and have him call you back."

"Oh, sure. I understand . . ." Kit gave the number and repeated her name. She frowned and picked at the phone. Why could he not have his home number listed? He didn't seem like the paranoid type.

The next day she spent designing pamphlets to hand out at parenting classes in the high schools. They were meant to educate young girls to start healthy habits now in order to have healthy babies later.

After work, she went to a meeting with "The Road Home." She was co-chair for the Great Annual Chili Affair fundraiser that year.

Kit was involved in lots of committees for causes. Her parents praised her, Gary criticized her, but ultimately she still felt like she wasn't doing enough. The cries of humanity had reached her heart and she couldn't *not* listen.

She came home tired with a list of things that still needed doing. Gary was just heading out on a date. They passed in the front entry hall. "Hey, you got a message to call that guy at his mother's house."

"He called?" All the tired left her bones.

"Yeah, why wouldn't he call?"

"I don't know. I'm just glad that he did."

Gary snorted. "I'll bet. Who wouldn't want to talk to British arrogance long distance?"

"Oh." Her elation plummeted. "You mean Bradley."

"Uh yeah! Hello? Who else?"

"Right, there isn't anyone else. Thank Gar-Bear." He shrugged into a leather jacket and left her alone in the entry hall. The uneasiness from before settled deeper into her bones than ever before.

Kit went to the kitchen to use the cordless phone so she could fix herself something to eat while she talked to Bradley. She pulled out fixings for a sandwich and dialed Bradley's parents' number.

Bradley's mom Dianna answered. Kit shuddered involuntarily. "Hello, Dianna. Is Bradley there?"

"Yes, he is, who's asking?"

Kit felt your teeth grind. "It's me, Kit."

"Oh, Kitty. Didn't recognize your voice."

Kit stabbed the knife into the Miracle Whip. "Not a problem, so may I speak with Bradley?" She tried to coat her voice with honey, but the pepper of hearing Dianna still burned in her ears.

"Certainly, Kitty. I'll let him know you're on the phone."

Kit sighed. She spread Miracle Whip over her bread, piled on tomatoes, lettuce, and bacon she'd cooked in the microwave. She took a bite before she realized she was still on hold. She was wondering if Dianna had really gone to get Bradley at all when he finally picked up.

"Hello?"

"Hi, Bradley."

"Kitty! I'm so glad you called back. I was starting to think you weren't going to."

"Yeah well. I was thinking you weren't going to come to the phone."

She took another bite and held the phone away from her

mouth so he wouldn't hear her chewing.

"Oh, sorry, Dad has some people over and one was telling a fabulous joke and I wanted to hear the punch line. Darling, it was truly so funny."

"Why did you call?" Kit asked. She took another bite.

"Oh, right. I need to tell you that you'll need to come tomorrow after work."

"What?" She managed astonishment with bread stuck to the roof of her mouth.

"The ticket's already paid for. It'll be waiting for you at the airport. You'll need to get there by 5:30 to get luggage cared for and all that."

Kit swallowed painfully. "But what if I have meetings?" She blurted thickly. She swallowed again.

"Just reschedule them. It isn't a big deal, Love. You always make such a deal over everything."

"But why?" The thought of two extra days with Dianna were enough to make her want to throw up her sandwich.

"Mom has a little pre-wedding party planned. Kind of like a shower. You can't not come. She's invited all the guests already and you're the guest of honor."

Kit wanted to scream, but to what end? He would tell her she was being irrational and childish and he'd be right. He usually was and Kit could admit that, but she didn't have to like it.

She ran a mental inventory of her schedule and found she didn't have anything that couldn't be done with a laptop and a fax modem. She conceded and hung up. Instantly, Kit was glad Gary was out on a date. His teasing was intolerable. She threw out the rest of the sandwich she had made and stomped to her room to pack and call her supervisor to let her know what was up.

Chapter 12

James met with his therapist the next morning. He was a nice man with salt and pepper hair cut short and feathered back. He had a tidy little beard and moustache and warm wrinkles in the corners of his eyes. His name was Dr. Meyer.

James found himself humming the Oscar Meyer Weiner song while he was in the waiting room. He stopped mid-tune when the receptionist cast a glance his way. James cleared his throat and sat deeper in the stiff chair, raising the magazine so it covered his face from the receptionist's view until the doctor came out to get him.

"Hello, James. How are you this morning?"

"Good, you know . . ." James shrugged. "Pretty good." James hated how even the simplest of questions felt like the Spanish Inquisition as though the therapist may take an answer wrong and call the guys in white coats to come take him away in a strait jacket.

"Been sleeping well?"

"Off and on."

"What do you mean by off and on?"

"Some nights are better than others."

"Tell me about the sleepless nights. What do you think about while you're awake?"

"A lot of things." James scrubbed a hand over his head. "I wonder when I can go back to work again. I wonder about the officer I was in charge of."

"Do you want to go back to work?"

"Sometimes. I'm a doer. Sitting around all day is not good

for people like me and I can only mow my lawn so many times in a week."

"So do you want to go back?"

"I guess."

"What do you think would happen if you were to go back today?"

"Today?" James started wringing his hands. Dr. Meyer tilted his head. James forced his hands still. "I don't know. I don't think I want to go back today."

"Why not?"

"I just think everyone will look at me differently."

"Why?"

"Because I am different now. I mean, we pull our guns four or five times a week, but actually shooting and killing are totally different." James started wringing his hands again. "The kid's mom has written letters that are so accusing. I just feel so bad for her. He was her son. He was somebody's son."

"James, you're somebody's son too."

"I know that," James frowned. "My Sergeant keeps telling me that."

"Do you believe him?" Dr. Meyer leaned forward.

"Yes, I do. I just . . . There are a lot of conflicts with my religion and my job. Things that maybe I should have thought about before now."

"Like what?"

"Like killing people. That is wrong."

"The Nephites went to war to protect themselves and had to kill others. Do you think Captain Moroni was any less of a righteous man because of it?"

"Well, no, but . . ."

"What other things are there?"

"I don't know. I'm around drugs and violence and cussing all day long. I swear sometimes it is eating at my soul. I just wonder what I'm doing it all for."

"Well, James, I can give you my take on it, which is this: my house was broken into last year and a policeman came and took care of things. My wife was terrified to have our home invaded like that. The policeman found the crook, threw him in jail, and my wife feels safe now. Your job is important. It makes it so that regular people like me feel safe. I don't think you will lose any part of your soul for that, but I tell you, you may get praises sung to you for your valor."

"I understand that . . . I really do."

The soft crinkles creased further with a smile. James relaxed. The smile was always there, but it definitely had to mean something. It had to mean the guys with the strait jackets weren't really coming.

James felt better after the session. He laughed at the idea that he had gone to see his therapist and actually felt better. He shook his head and drove to his parents' house.

He kissed his fingers and tapped his mom's forehead. "Hey, Ma, where's Dad? His car is gone."

"I sent him to the store. He was driving me nuts and I needed him out from under my feet." She put down the book she was reading while he sat down. "What have you been up to?"

"I saw my therapist this morning."

Her brows furrowed. "What did he say?"

"He said to pack my bags; they got a padded room all set up for me at the Provo hospital."

"Oh, Jamie! That isn't funny."

He grinned. "Sorry. No really, I'm fine, Ma. I'm good." He stared at her, picturing her being told he'd died on that confrontation and not the boy. He shook himself out of it before he started to cry. That was not an option. Things had to turn out the way they did. "I'm good," he repeated, clearing his throat.

She creased her brow further. "Oh, honey . . ." Caroline

perked up. "There's a message for you."

"From who?"

"Kathryn or Kit or something. She kind of mumbled through her name. She left a phone number. Said she had something for you . . ." Caroline trailed off. "I'm not sure what I did with the message though. Your dad had dropped a cabinet down the stairs and was in the middle of catastrophe. You know how your father gets."

"Kit called?" Just saying her name sent shivers through him. She called! What did that mean? He didn't know. "Maybe, I'll go over there, since she has something for me."

"Is this the . . ."

"Yes, Mom, this is the dead girl." Everyone called her that. He rolled his eyes and stood up. "Bye, Mom." He kissed his fingertips and tapped her forehead again. "I'm out of here. Tell Dad I said hey and I'll call later."

James' mind whirled as he drove to her house. "Hey, Kit, I heard you called. I was in the neighborhood . . . so . . ." He frowned at his reflection in the rearview mirror. This was crazy; big tough cop can't find the courage to face a girl?

It seemed time had raced to drop him off on Kit's doorstep. He scrubbed a hand over his head. *Here goes nothing,* he thought as his finger reached out to punch the doorbell.

A young man opened the door. He looked like he'd just got out of bed. "Can I help you?" the kid asked.

"Yeah, is Kit here?"

"Naw, she's gone to California for a few days. Want me to leave a message for her?"

James hesitated. "Yeah, my name is James and I—"

"Gary!" A voice thundered from the driveway.

Gary looked white as a man stomped over from a car he'd left running. "I cannot believe you slept in; as short of hand as we are right now and all those contractors yelling at me to get these houses done and you're standing out here in sweats."

"Dad, I'm sorry." Gary looked as penitent as James had seen a man. "I must have slept in. I'll get my clothes on and be right down. It'll only take me a minute. I swear." With that, Gary vanished into the house.

Ryan sighed and leaned against the doorframe to catch his breath. "No such thing as reliable work any more." He mumbled and then looked up. "Sorry about that. We're just so short of hands right now, I don't know where to turn."

"What are you doing?"

"I own a stucco company. We have five houses due to be finished with our part by the beginning of next week."

"Need some help?"

"Don't tease an old man."

"Seriously, I'm off for a few days. If there's anything I could do . . ."

"What's your name?"

"James Hartman."

"What do you do normally?"

"I'm a cop."

Ryan cocked his head. "A cop?"

"Yep."

"Are you the guy that was there that night of Kit's wreck?"

"Yeah, that was me."

Ryan stuck his hand out. James took it hesitantly. From the handshake, Ryan pulled James and clapped his other hand around James' neck. "I have been wanting to meet you for a long time now."

James' eyes widened. "What for?"

"I've just heard rumors." Ryan inspected him. James could almost feel Ryan's eyes picking him apart looking for faults or something else. "So you want to work for me?"

"Sure. I'm not doing anything for a while."

"Do you know anything about cement?"

"I helped my dad put in a patio last year."

"That'll do. Lets get you some clothes."

James followed Ryan into the house and down the hall. Ryan thumped a fist on Gary's door. "I'm coming!" Gary called out. He flung the door open while tucking a T-shirt into jeans. The clothes looked like they were badly in need of washing.

"Hey Gary, James here is coming with us. Get him some clothes to wear."

"Cool, no problem." Gary led James into his room. James followed with a degree of hesitance. There were posters of Star Wars up and CDs stacked haphazardly with action figures on top of them. Clothes were piled on the floor like land mines that had to be skirted around. There was a huge audio system set up against a wall with an enormous music library. Jewel cases were scattered on the top of the cabinet.

Gary opened a drawer and pulled out clothes that were just as grimy looking as the ones he was wearing. Gary handed them to James. "I know they look bad, but they've been washed. Stucco color doesn't come out."

"Thanks." James followed the hallway to the bathroom and changed quickly. When he came out, Ryan had left.

"So what do you want with Kit?" Gary asked conversationally after getting in the car.

"I was there when she got in her accident."

"Oh, you must be that cop!"

James smiled. He wondered if he was merely referred to as "that cop" the way Kit was referred to as "that dead girl." If they were referring to him at all, what would they be saying? "I guess I must be."

"That was a gorgeous bouquet you sent her and the balloons . . . . So, do you like her?"

Startled, James shifted in his seat. "Why would you ask that?" He gave a short uncomfortable laugh.

"You brought her home on Sunday and I haven't seen her that giddy since college. 'Course she flipped out into psychosis when she found out Bradley was there."

To that James could only cough nervously and shift again in his seat.

They arrived at the work site. Ryan was there, already pouring buckets of water into a large cement mixer. "Dad!" It seemed it was Gary's turn to shout. "Put that down! You know you can't be lifting stuff like that!" Gary pulled free the bucket labeled DryVit from his father's white knuckled grasp. The water sloshed around stirring little chunks of grit at the bottom of the bucket. Gary finished emptying the water into the mixer.

James watched everything with interest. It felt good to get out and work hard on something for the benefit of someone else. They started him shoveling from the wheelbarrow to the hock with mud. They then took the mud and smoothed it onto the wall that looked like it had been covered with tarpaper, chicken wire and blue foam. Gary later informed him that that was exactly what went underneath a layer of stucco.

After a while, Ryan let him try his hand at putting the mud on the wall. James found it wasn't too hard and did that for most the rest of the day.

Gary worked hard for his father and was very watchful that Ryan didn't lift or strain too much on his back. The other guys, Mark and Glen, worked methodically. From the work they did, they showed they respected their employer and cared about doing a good job. They got along well with James, even though they had the radio cranked with country music.

James and Gary teamed up to harass them about the music.

Gary at one point climbed up the ladder to the roof and tiptoed to the other side where Glen was working. He had a small bucket of the cold water from the garden hose. When Glen squealed, cursed, and swore vengeance, they had all guessed what Gary had done with the water. Ryan turned his head and bent down to mix colors to hide his smile.

Once the house was mudded all the way around, they started the house next door with color. It was getting later in the day and Ryan was slowing down. He got chattier with the falling sun too.

"Tell me about my Kit's accident," he said.

"What do you want to know?"

"I want to know what happened, from your perspective."

Ryan ran the trowel over the wall to spread the color evenly. James came along behind floating it into smooth, barely perceptible swirls. James thought about what he could say. "Well . . . we were getting off the freeway. I was in the car behind her and she was going way too fast to take the curve and rolled it. It happened so quick and at that time, I just wanted to avoid getting involved in the mess with my car."

"And then what?"

"Well, then I called 911 and went to check everything out."

"And . . .?"

"She was, um . . . on the side of the road. She'd been thrown from the car." James allowed himself a little laugh. "Not wearing a seat belt."

"Isn't that odd? Kit always wears a seat belt."

"Well she didn't when it counted."

"Then what happened?"

James slowed the swirling "wax on, wax off" motions. "She was dead." He swallowed hard seeing the scene in his mind.

"Dead?"

"Yeah." The image of her shining all around him filled his senses like he was drinking her in and drowning but not caring.

"Then what?"

"What?" James looked startled.

"Then what happened?"

James shrugged. "I did CPR and she was okay."

"Hmmm." Ryan smeared another coat of color into the

army green mud of the wall. “What about the hospital?”

“Excuse me, sir?”

“I heard your father came in.”

“Oh that. I just, um . . . wanted to give her a blessing and needed some help.”

“I appreciate that.”

“Oh well . . . It wasn’t like I did anything special. She needed it.”

“You’re a good man, James Hartman. You are exactly what a man should be.”

“We all have problems, imperfections that no one ever sees. I’m not all you think I am, sir.”

Ryan grinned, stretching out a smear of color across his cheek. “I’m too old to be told what to think, son. I say you are all right.”

“Thanks.” James hesitated. “You’re all right, too.”

Ryan laughed and plopped more color onto the wall. It had been a good day. James had worked hard and felt great about it. He had been useful and hadn’t had to pick up a gun, hadn’t had to put on a badge, hadn’t had to face the silent stares of sympathy from his friends at the station.

“Mind if I come back tomorrow?”

Ryan and Gary looked at him like he was nuts. “You’re crazy to want to, but sure . . . if you have the time off, you are welcome back.”

“Thanks, I’ll see you in the morning then.” James smiled the whole way home. He could feel the sweat and grit in his pores and the lime from the cement had opened a cut up wide and stung terribly in his finger. With all that, he felt great and the smile seemed permanent on his face.

Chapter 13

"Kitty girl, put this on." They were in a boutique of gowns. Kit bit back the scream. If she was called 'Kitty girl' one more time, she was going to lose her cool and punch Dianna in the face.

Dianna had been imported straight from Britain. Max was American through and through, but he loved Dianna and so conceded when she wanted to go back to her homeland. It was twelve years before he was able to convince her to leave again . . . but the bitterness at leaving never really disappeared from her.

She hated America, hated the culture, the grammar (or lack thereof), and hated that no one could make a decent Earl Gray tea. She had to import her tea along with other must-haves once a month. It seemed odd to Kit that Dianna displayed such pious attitudes of religion when she drank her tea nearly every morning. Every time Dianna thought of anything she hated in this forsaken country, she needled her husband. Max took it silently, but Kit wondered how long it would be before he broke, bumped Dianna off, and dumped her in the trash behind the house.

Not soon enough, Kit pouted sourly as she jerked her head through the neck of the gown Dianna insisted she put on for her little wedding party.

With all the caterers and the humbly sized orchestra that were on order for the next evening, the party didn't seem so little and the gown made Kit almost as furious was being called 'Kitty girl.'

She looked at herself in the full-length mirror and

suppressed the desire to throw up. It was lavender. Kit hated lavender and this horrible gown had matching heels.

"Now that is absolutely lovely!" Dianna exclaimed. Her Cheshire cat grin made Kit clench her fists. Dianna had a growth of some sort just under her left nostril. It had a pale yellow coloration that made it look as though Dianna hadn't wiped her nose properly. Kit had tried to train herself not to gawk at the growth, but it was difficult.

"Dianna, I really don't think this dress is necessary. I have three dresses that I packed from home that will be fine. This dress is a waste of money."

"It is precisely that attitude, Kitty, that keeps me assured you are not marrying my son for his money."

"What attitude?" Kit asked indignantly.

"Your peasant attitude of waste. Honestly, Kitty, one would imagine you were raised in a ghetto. Now, here, put on the shoes so the gown doesn't drag the floor."

Kit obeyed. She fumed over being called Kitty and for being told she was a ghetto peasant. Who would ever take a woman named Kitty seriously? "Can't we get a black gown instead?" She'd seen one on the rack just outside the dressing room that had a long scarf that came with it. It was breathtaking and probably cheaper than the purple number that she was in.

"Black is fine, I suppose, but it wouldn't do with your dark hair and pale features. You'd be like some vampire. Be sensible, child. So what do you think, girl? Isn't it lovely?"

"It's kind of purple . . . but you know it's nice . . . I guess."

"The floral arrangements are also being done in lavender. It will be perfect."

"Perfect . . ." Kit echoed with a sigh. It made no difference, she supposed, that the cost of the dress would have been a "perfect" donation to March of Dimes or that it could feed all those people in the homeless shelter for a month. Dianna had decided.

Kit wondered how she had become so push-aroundable. In her life she had always been independent from what others thought. But here she was like a young girl watching sullenly as they wrapped the dress in paper and carefully placed it in a box big enough to be a coffin.

She stared out into the streets of San Diego. Her fingers tapped furiously on the leather seat of the red Jaguar Dianna had chosen for the day. They entered the freeway. Palm trees wooshed by along with ivy clad overpasses.

“Child! Stop that infernal drumming!”

Kit’s fingers froze. “Sorry,” she said through gritted teeth.

“Don’t be sorry, girl, just don’t do it. Can’t be helped I suppose . . .” Dianna stole a glance from the freeway to Kit. She sighed dramatically and looked back to the freeway. “With your upbringing, I’m stunned you don’t slouch or chew with your mouth open.”

“What is that supposed to mean?”

“Oh please, Kitty, I’m not picking a fight with you! Light, you’re sensitive. I just meant that it seems improper to raise a girl on a construction site.”

“Why?”

“Ladies don’t work like that. Ours is a work of the mind.” Kit had had enough.

“My mind is worked daily, Dianna. I have been through eight years of college to get my master’s and read every piece of literature known to intelligent man. In case you haven’t noticed, I’m very smart.” Dianna sucked in to respond, but Kit cut her off. “I think working at my father’s sites helped me gain a work ethic, too. It means that not only am I vastly intelligent, but I am a hard worker. That may not sound like much to you, but it rates pretty high on my list, so cut out the peasant talk, okay?”

Dianna’s eyes narrowed on the road. She pulled off the

freeway in jerky motions. They were almost to the house. If Dianna would've slowed enough, Kit would have jumped out and walked. Dianna said nothing, but the wall of ice she had surrounded herself with caused enough of a chill that Kit shuddered.

As soon as the car had pulled into the driveway, before it had even stopped, Kit was out. She stormed into the house. "Bradley!" she called out. He didn't answer.

Max came out of his office and smiled at Kit. "I'm glad you guys are back." His smile melted into concern when he saw the fresh tears on Kit's face. "What's wrong, Kit?"

"The dress is purple!" she sobbed as she fell into him.

"Oh honey, you should have told her to forget it," Max said.

"I couldn't! She's just . . . Oh just . . . I'm sorry . . . never mind." Kit turned and fled to her room.

Dianna entered as Kit shut her door. "What did you do to her?" Max asked.

"Absolutely nothing! The girl is so sensitive. Honestly, imagine her as a teenager." Dianna put her purse and keys on the credenza by the door.

"What's wrong?" Bradley asked from the staircase.

"Oh, Kitty's in a fret." Dianna waved her hand dismissively.

"Your mother has been working her magic."

"What happened?" Bradley asked.

"I just asked her to stop drumming her fingers; honestly, that girl is so fidgety she makes my nerves stand right on end."

"I'll talk to her." Bradley went down the hall to Kit's room. He didn't knock, but went right in and closed the door behind him.

Kit was sitting on her bed, legs folded underneath her, a book opened on her lap. There were no evidences of tears, no remnants of sobbing, but there was a tightness around her eyes and her mouth was shut tight in a firm straight line.

"What are you reading?" He sat on the other side of the bed, brushing away the key lime truffle that the maid had left on the pillows after tidying the room and making the bed.

"I'm not reading. I just barely opened the book."

He was ready for a response of banter. "So, should you set forth in your actions of opening this book and put your eyes to the page and the words therein, what would you be reading?"

She allowed herself a smile. *"The Finest Story In the World."*

"And what story might that be, love?"

"No, Bradley, that is the story. 'The Finest Story in the World' is a story written by Rudyard Kipling."

"Bloody arrogant title, don't you think?"

Kit grinned. "Well, he is English, after all; arrogance is their forte."

"Is that a personal attack?"

"Of course not." She set the book aside. "It's actually about a young man named George who fancies himself a poet of astounding genius. He comes up with a plot for the finest story in the world which he promptly sells for five pounds to a man who understands how ingenious and perfect the story is."

"So he sells off a fortune for a fiver?"

"Mmm-hmmm."

"Poor devil has no business sense at all. No wonder he's a poet." Bradley sighed. "What am I to do with you and your books?"

"Buy me a library?"

Bradley laughed. "A library is not nearly so full as the shelves in your bedroom." He paused. "Heard you had a rough morning with Mom."

She blew out a long breath and chewed the inside of her cheek thoughtfully. "It really wasn't anything. She just seems to always be picking at me like a hem she wants to take down. I feel myself unravel every time I'm near her."

"Stand up to her. She'll respect you for it."

"Why can't she just leave me alone?"

"Darling, she's just like that. It isn't anything personal. She does it to everyone that matters to her; I mean look at me. She's picking at me all day."

"Bradley, you're her golden child. She hasn't ever picked at you."

"Well, maybe not like all that, but . . . you're just being sensitive. Don't let her badger you like that."

"You're probably right. I'm just so frazzled lately. You know with work and the homeless shelter and this wedding."

He put an arm around her. "Oh, I know the wedding is a lot to deal with."

She laughed with an edge. "She bought me a purple dress." He snorted and leaned his head on hers. "I look like a bruise in it."

"Dad said you might need a true break today. He cancelled the meetings I had and rescheduled them for tomorrow. Why don't we take a little day trip south of the border today?"

"What, like Mexico?"

"That would be south, now wouldn't it?"

"You're mocking me."

"Only a little."

She smiled. "I think getting away is a good idea."

He jumped up suddenly. "Great, let's go!" He pulled her up by the hand, the quick movement bouncing the truffle off the pillow altogether.

In her haste to get out the door without another confrontation with Dianna, she left her bag in her room. It felt strange not to have it. The wallet, laptop, notepad, everything she may need was in it. But there was freedom in the bag's absence.

On I-5, heading south, Bradley took her hand in his while

lazily draping the other over the steering wheel. "So the dress is purple?"

Kit blew out a long sigh. "Purple."

"Could be worse, couldn't it? Could be pink."

Kit grinned. *That* is the *only* thing that would be worse.

"So tell me about the wedding plans. Is everything set? Are the invitations ready to go out?"

"The invitations are still at the printer's, but it's okay, we don't want to mail them for another week and a half."

"What about the reception hall? Everything reserved?"

"Bradley, I told you already we couldn't get the hall for the rescheduled date. We're having it at a church."

"Oh Kitty." His voice went tight. "I thought you were joking. We can't do this at a church!"

"Why not?"

"Mother would die. The idea of basketball hoops looming over us is simply . . . well . . . simply not doable."

"Bradley, I told you this a month ago! We aren't having it in the gym. There's a beautiful church called the Garden Park Ward over on Yale Avenue. It has a beautiful garden and a pond and it was inexpensive. Remember, my parents are footing this bill, not yours."

"My mother offered assistance—"

"And then what? She has my bridesmaids in purple with pink dots? Everything is fine. Don't worry about it."

"Sorry. You're right. This is your wedding. I just want to be relaxed for it. Whatever you want is fine."

She blinked that he had cut off the beginning of an argument so quickly and easily and then settled deeper into her seat. Today wasn't going to be as bad as it had started.

Bradley eased his dad's Lincoln into a parking space just north of the border. "Why don't we just drive in?" Kit asked.

"You don't just drive expensive American cars into Mexico.

That would be begging for trouble, aside from the fact that you can get right in, but the line getting out is hours."

He got out and hurried over to pay the parking lot attendant. Kit let herself out and made certain the doors were locked. He came back and took her hand to lead her over the cement hedge between countries.

"It's hard to imagine . . ." his breathing was rapid with the exercise, "that you've never been to Mexico."

"I've never had a reason to," she said, her breathing even and her voice chatty in tone.

"I used to come here a lot." He paused and bent slightly, propping his hand on his knees.

Kit leaned against a graffiti covered wall and stared out over a place where it appeared water ran through. It was very wide and seemed to be where they ran sewage from the smell. "I remember, back in your days of debauchery and sin."

"Yep, those were the good old days; a shot of tequila and dancing 'til morning regardless of the fact we weren't old enough to drink." His breathing evened out as they stood there.

"I'm surprised Dianna didn't ship you to a boys school in England where you'd be raised like a gentleman."

"Oh, she wanted to; Dad wouldn't allow it. He told her 13 years was enough for a child to be in a cold damp country. He told her I needed some sun and sand to make me a respectable man."

"I don't think he meant Mexico in your coming to manhood."

"No, he didn't. He was pretty well buggered when he found out about our little ventures and shut us down completely."

"I don't blame him. I can't believe you ever did that."

Bradley straightened himself. "Oh c'mon, love. I was a teenager sowing my wild oats or whatever. You can't tell me you never did anything wrong in your past."

They started walking again. "It isn't the doing something wrong in your past that bugs me. It is the fact that you take pride and joy in the memory of it."

A great iron fence stood in front of them with a rotating gate that had large bars jutting out from it like a turnstile. The bars had an inch of black grime that was sticky and unidentifiable. Kit pushed through it. A line furrowed deep in her brow. Old papers, browned with the muck of the street, twirled away in the slight breeze the movement of the gate created. The California humidity seemed to adhere her shirt to her body and her hair hung limp and lifeless in the moist motionless air. Bradley passed through the turnstile behind her. It felt they walked a million miles before finally reaching anything; small children with layers of dirt and odd clothing jutted out tiny hands her direction. Others held up small candies and jewelry for her to buy.

Kit's head twisted back and forth as she took in all the people selling their wares on the crumbling curbside. "I'm sorry, no money," she heard her voice say over and over. "I'm sorry."

Bradley's head never swiveled except to peek at her every now and again.

"See anything you want?" He nodded to the street now loaded with shops, vendors, and people.

"Want?" The word tasted foul on her tongue. "Want?" She stared in disbelief at the poverty around her and wondered if it was a sin to want at all in such a place. She knew she should be used to it. She worked in the shelter and soup kitchens, but this wasn't like that. Kit couldn't discern why it felt different, but it did.

Up on the bridge, there were people staring over the way to the buildings cropping up like gold and silver on the American side of the border. How that view of America so near to them must taunt one who wanted more from life.

A small band played their instruments in the square, kicking up a lively tune. A young boy danced under his mother's watchful gaze as she organized the bracelets on the blanket she used to display them.

There was painted stonework, chimes, jewelry, and puppets dangling from hooks lining the roads. Bradley bought churros from a street vendor and held one out to Kit. She hesitated a moment before accepting the strip and taking a bite. To her surprise, it tasted wonderful.

They wandered in and out of little shops and eased their way between the blankets and booths along the sidewalks. Bradley bought a blanket from one shop and a rose from a woman peddling flowers. He handed the flower to Kit and pressed a fistful of coins into her hand.

"What is this for?"

"Are you joking? I've watched you all day. Your expression changes from worry to concern, but is never happy. So go on, darling. Feed your starving huddled masses. Your heart is bleeding so violently, I can almost feel the droplets splashing me. I'll be needing to get my shirt laundered."

Kit stared at him, gasping openly. She then reached up and kissed his cheek. "Thank you." She whispered, unable to hide the wonder.

"For what? It's just pocket change, love."

"For understanding." She turned and doled out the coins to every child she saw until her hands were empty.

She came back to Bradley with a grin.

"Now that is the Kitty I like to see," Bradley said.

They stayed in Mexico for another few hours. Kit relaxed and enjoyed the country much more after Bradley had given her the change for the children. As they pulled out of the parking lot on the northern side of the border, she stared at him, a faint smile on her face.

"What?" he asked under her scrutiny.

"Thank you."

"For?"

"For taking me around today and being so great."

"Ah, but the day has yet to be completed." His glance melted lazily over her. Bradley drove on, sticking to the coastline. The ocean seemed to stretch right into the horizon of clouds. Bradley turned down a narrow winding road through what appeared to be a seaside village and then parked.

"Where are we?"

"La Jolla."

"What's here?"

Bradley snorted softly. "What isn't here isn't worth worrying about."

He got out and went to the back of the car to rummage through the trunk. Kit got out and followed him around and grinned. "A cooler? What's all this?"

He took the blanket he'd bought in Mexico and pushed it off to Kit. "It's dinner, love."

He unplugged the cooler from the outlet in the trunk and set it on the wheels to pull it.

"This way." He directed her down a stone path that led down some stone stairs that wound around a cliff. He carefully thumped the cooler over the stairs. Kit followed in awe.

Bradley took the blanket from her hands and spread it over the stone ledge that hung low over the incoming waves. Every now and again, a large wave would break, sending up a cool spray to sprinkle over them.

She sat on the blanket and turned her face to the warmth of the setting sun. Bradley flipped up the cooler top and pulled out a bottle of cold grape juice, a large bowl of sliced fruit and sub sandwiches.

"You had all this set up before I got home this morning?"

"Actually, my dad had it all set up. He said you didn't look happy. He packed the dinner and suggested I take you somewhere peaceful. I thought you might like La Jolla."

"It's beautiful," Kit agreed, picking up a sandwich and taking a bite.

"I've been thinking . . ." Bradley started after a moment. "Dad is looking to expand business to Europe."

"Oh yeah. He told me. He looked really excited about it."

"He is. I think it will be a huge development for the company to go international."

"Well, that's great." Kit agreed, leaning back against Bradley's chest. She closed her eyes and listened to the water.

Bradley blinked and sighed. "Yes, it's great. It will be a very successful move for everyone. You know I served my mission there, grew up there . . . I know a lot about England." She wasn't paying attention anymore. He was certain of that. He sighed again. "We'll talk about it later, love."

"About what?"

He snorted softly. "Exactly."

"Is something wrong?"

"No, Kitty. Nothing to worry about at all." He wrapped an arm around her, pursed his lips thoughtfully and watched the sun melt into the sea.

They drove the coastline as far back to Bradley's as possible. Kit kissed Bradley lightly on the lips and hugged him. "Thanks again. And thank your dad for me. It was a break I really needed." She went to her room and shut the door softly behind her, taking care to lock it. Bradley had a habit of just walking in whenever he wanted to and she didn't want him to catch her dressing.

Kit yawned and changed quickly. She tiredly swiped her bag and some odds and ends off the bed onto the floor, not noticing the bag was opened. When she woke the next morning, her eyes popped open. "My bag . . ." she murmured softly. Kit rolled to her side to peer over the bed onto the floor. The things that had been placed there from the bed the previous night were all spread out.

She dressed quickly and hurried to the kitchen. Bradley was gone; so was Dianna. Max was putting his briefcase together. "Kit, I'm glad you're up. Would you be willing to drive me to the airport?"

"Umm, yeah, sure." She looked around. "Everyone's gone then?"

"Everyone but you and me. Bradley went to work and Dianna is getting the dog fluffed up."

"Where are you going?"

"London. I have some papers to sign to close this deal."

"Wow, this is going to be really big for you then."

"No, this is going to be big for all of us. I'm sure Bradley has told you about it."

"Yeah, he has. We've talked about it."

"Good. I'm glad you're excited for it."

"I better get some shoes on if we're going to the airport." She went back to her room, took some socks out of her suitcase and pulled them on. Kit frowned while tying her shoes and staring at the contents of her bag spilled out like they were. Had someone been going through her stuff?

She knelt to pick it all up and put it back into her bag.

Bradley's dad drove to the airport. "What's on your mind?" he asked.

"Nothing; not really. Did your maid come back after Bradley and I left yesterday?"

"No. She didn't. Why?"

Kit smiled and shrugged. "Oh, it's nothing. I'm just getting absentminded, I guess." She paused. "So, if you're going to London, you won't be here for the engagement party."

Max slapped the steering wheel with glee. "I'm off the hook!" He took a sideways glance at her. "Too bad I can't get you off the hook and take you with me."

"That would be wonderful. Unfortunately, I'm stuck in the purple dress."

"You know, I don't understand it; you are smart, charismatic, educated, well opinioned, and self-assured and yet you cower like a puppy when Dianna comes around. Why do you let her scare you like that?"

Kit shrugged. "I honestly don't know."

"Well, it's nothing to be ashamed of. She scares me, too," he laughed softly. "Business trips are absolute bliss. There is nothing worse than having to ask that woman's permission to put my foot down on a subject."

"Well, this trip might be bliss for you, but you should feel bad for leaving me."

"I feel just terrible." He smiled and turned into the airport short-term parking. "The car is yours for the day. There's money in the glove compartment if you need it. Do whatever you want and don't worry about the party. You'll look like a million dollars no matter what color the gown is."

Kit smiled gratefully and gave him a hug. "You are the only sane member of your family."

"What about Bradley?"

She laughed. "Well, even he is a little crazy sometimes."

Max kissed her cheek. "Be happy and don't let her walk on you."

"I won't."

"Good girl." He turned and disappeared into the crowd. Kit watched after him longingly, wishing she were getting on one of those planes and heading home.

She sighed and put the car in drive. She drove to Buena Park. It was a distance and Dianna would be mad she was disappearing for such a long time the day of the party but she didn't care. She could sit in the gardens and work on the wording for the new brochure March of Dimes was putting out.

She wandered the park before settling down, stopping to watch a guy who looked to be her age juggling and telling jokes. He flipped a half a dozen brightly colored balls into the air in a swirling rainbow and catching them neatly into a tall stovepipe hat. He had on a multi-colored patched-together cape that he flourished when he bowed at the end. He was very talented. He held the hat out to the crowd for donations to his talent and grinned mischievously when Kit dropped in a few dollars. "Your phone number, ma'am? Why, thank you!"

Kit grinned back at him and laughed while shaking her head and walking away. Sometimes it felt good to be flirted with . . . even just a little.

Sitting down in the sun with her laptop and notes, she was able to complete the brochure as well as lay out the schedule for the spot Channel 5 was planning on running. She actually accomplished more than she would have had she been in the office.

Shutting the lid to the laptop, Kit turned her face to the sun. It had been a few hours and she know from the way shadows seemed to be creeping up behind her that by now Dianna was in a panic as to where Kit had wandered off to.

With a scowl that she cared at all that Dianna was in a panic, Kit gathered her things and drove back to Bradley's parents' house.

She had been right. Dianna was furious when Kit entered the front door. "Kitty! Where on this earth have you been?"

"Doing some finishing work on a project."

"Girl, I have scoured the entire city for you! I had Bradley calling everywhere! Why isn't your cell on?"

"Because I was working." Kit tried hard to not sound like

she was biting back anger at the questioning.

"Well, it was irresponsible not to contact us!" She tsked and tapped her toe before saying, "Well, girl, don't just stand there! Go get ready!"

Kit turned like a sullen child getting punished for breaking a fine china plate and went to her room. She set her bag on the bed and stared at it. There was no doubt the bag had been left closed on her bed the day before. Kit was certain it had not been opened when she had left it; and she had certainly not left anything out of it, which could only mean that someone had been rummaging.

The only person home was Dianna. Would she have done it? If she did, what reason would she have for doing it? Kit's ears burned to the tips with animosity. She pulled the gown over her head and yanked it past her hips.

The zipper had been tricky to get all the way done up, but she wasn't about to ask Dianna for help. She fastened the little silk buttons at her wrists and pulled the shoes on over bare feet. Dianna would likely balk at her bare feet and legs, but there was no way she was putting on tights that no one would see. Besides, Kit was tanned from helping her father on his sites during the summer; and her toenails had been painted recently. Granted, the burgundy polish didn't really match the purple gown, but Kit was far from caring.

Why would Dianna be rooting though her bag? What gave her any right to be so darn nosy? Kit twisted her French twist a little too tight in her anger and put in a pair of gem-studded combs to hold it there. After a mental inventory of the contents of the bag, Kit gasped at the image in the mirror. She had left the card James had written and left with her flowers in the bag. It was something she had read and reread, so the card looked worn and faded. What if Dianna had seen it? Would it matter if she did? There was nothing in it that was incriminating, and by reading it, Dianna would have no idea how Kit's heart beat faster when she read it. Chewing the inside of her lip, Kit pulled the bag onto her lap. She unzipped the side pocket and pulled out the little Book of Mormon she kept there. She opened it to Jacob 6:12. The card James had given her marked that scripture. It was still there, appearing untouched.

Dianna must not have seen it and there was nothing else in her bag worth worrying about. Kit frowned and stood abruptly. She went out to face the criticism of Bradley's mother.

Dianna smiled sweetly at her as she entered the patio where the party was to be. The tables were decorated with real china and silverware and the small band was already playing. Kit rolled her eyes. She was certain Dianna wrote the book on pretension.

"You look stunning, Kitty!" Dianna exclaimed. "You could've used a bit of rouge, child, but altogether you look stunning."

"Thank you," Kit said uncertainly. Compliments had not been expected at all.

"Bradley is off with his friend from high school. Why don't you come meet some of the guests?" Kit was surprised people were already there.

Kit followed Dianna through the tables and gatherings of people to a table by the pool. A girl Kit's age was sitting talking to an older woman and man. The girl was wearing the black dress from the gown shop where Dianna had ordered the purple thing Kit was wearing.

"Leann . . ." Dianna simpered. "I'm so glad you and your parents could come."

"We were thrilled to be invited, Dianna," Leann cooed back, sweetly flashing impossibly straight white teeth.

"I wanted you to meet Bradley's fianceé, Kitty."

Dianna stepped back so that Kit and Leann had a full view

of each other. Leann smiled as her eyes trailed over the purple folds of gauze that made up Kit's gown. She made no move to stand to be properly introduced. Kit put on her very best hostess smile and stepped forward to shake Leann's hand.

"I'm pleased to meet you," Kit said.

"Kitty? What kind of name is that?" Leann asked. She smiled casually and it never faded completely.

"It's actually Katherine. Most people call me Kit and for reasons unknown to me, Bradley and Dianna have persisted in calling me Kitty."

Leann's hair was swept up into a half twist with the ends curled in ringlets that seemed to tumble and spill from the top of her head. Her makeup looked so blended it was as though she had none on at all and accented every feature that needed noticing about her face. The black dress was perfect on her slim body and Kit disliked her completely.

"So you snagged our Bradley?" Leann's mother commented. "Truly, I imagined the boy was not snaggable. We had so hoped . . ."

From the mourning look that passed over Dianna's face and the tsk of empathy between the two women, it was obvious what they had so "hoped."

Kit maintained the smile on her face and held Leann's gaze. Her cheek muscles were starting to numb from holding the smile while grinding teeth at the same time.

"Well, Kitty, what is it you do?" Leann purred.

"I work for the March of Dimes."

"The March of Dimes?" Leann's eyes lazily flicked from Dianna and back to Kit. "How interesting." Kit smoothed her hands over the gauzy folds of her dress. She was certain Leann was not interested at all.

"I think I'll go find Bradley now. It was nice meeting you." Kit turned on a purple heel and stalked off flexing her fingers like the claws of a cat. She had never hated rich people until meeting Dianna and slowly she learned to loathe them by Dianna's example. There was nothing worse than dealing with a woman who sniffed at everything decent and noble. How nice it must be for Dianna to have found a little drone exactly like her.

The band was playing. In the setting sun the patio lights and twinkle lights in the trees came on. Kit wandered through the guests, picking up a tiny sandwich from a tray and swallowing it nearly whole. She went back and grabbed two more.

She finally found Bradley as she swallowed the last of the third sandwich. He was outside talking to his friends from high school. "Oh, Kitty darling, there you are!" He pulled her over by the arm so she was standing in the middle of their circle. "I want you to meet some old friends."

"This is Phil." Bradley pointed to a guy with flaming red hair. The guy was quick with a smile and shook Kit's hand enthusiastically before kissing it.

"Pleasure to finally meet you, Kit."

Kit grinned. He hadn't called her Kitty. "Nice to meet you too, Phil."

"Oh, I'll be right back!" Bradley exclaimed. "There's someone I need to speak with!" He dashed off, leaving her alone, encircled by strangers.

"So how did a nice girl like you get caught up with this family?" Phil asked. The others listened with half interest. They had started looking around for something else to do besides talk to her.

"They're a nice family," she said.

"So are the Munsters, but you wouldn't want to spend a weekend with them," Phil declared.

"They really aren't so bad," she insisted.

Phil shrugged. "Yeah, they aren't so bad. I get along with them alright."

Phil's eyebrows matched his hair, back set by a smooth pale face. Kit imagined if he was cut in half and put in green, he'd look like a leprechaun.

They talked about work, his and hers and the schooling they had. The others slowly sifted off to various groups that littered the gardens, bored with Kit and Phil.

"Bradley sure is smitten by you," Phil remarked.

"Why would you say that?" Kit asked, genuinely curious.

"He asked you to marry him for one thing. No one ever imagined Bradley to be the marrying kind; believe me, lots of girls tried."

"Girls like Leann?" It was out before she could stop it.

"Leann?" Phil laughed, his cheeks flushing shades of red and white. "Yeah, girls like her, I guess. But she isn't like you. You are smart and it isn't like she isn't smart, but she's more calculating, like a spider spinning a web. You don't have to worry about her."

Kit smiled. "I'm not worried."

"Yeah, you shouldn't be. She hasn't got anything on you."

The music stopped. Dianna was on the bandstand with a microphone an inch away from her bright red lips. "I'd like your attention, everyone!" People quieted down and gazed in her direction.

"We are all here tonight to celebrate the engagement of my son Bradley to Katherine Riley." Kit let out a breath she hadn't realized she was holding. That was the first time ever Dianna hadn't called her Kitty.

People applauded and whistled as Dianna beckoned both Bradley and Kit to the bandstand where she was. Phil tapped Kit on the back to prod her forward. She hadn't realized this was part of the party.

She was comfortable getting in front of people. She did it all day with her job and she was beyond being nervous about such things. Dianna smiled at her as though she was waiting for Kit to show signs of fear. Kit flashed a smile back, and opened her arms to give Dianna a small hug. Dianna fumbled in surprise at the hug. Kit felt a twinge of elation at taking the woman off guard. She took Bradley's hand in hers and with the other gave a gracious thanks-for-coming wave.

Bradley took the microphone. "I'd like to thank you all for coming and wishing us well. I'd like to also make an announcement about some new developments in our company." His accented voice was lazy and confident. "We are expanding to Europe and will be headquartered in England. Dad is there now closing the deal and we'd like to excuse him for his absence tonight. I'm sure he would have wanted to be here. As you all know, that is where I am from. After much deliberation, we the board, Dad and I decided . . ."

Dianna cut in taking the microphone from him. "Oh, Bradley, no one wants to hear about business." Kit wanted to hear.

Decided what? What had they decided? She scowled at Dianna for interrupting. Dianna was now giving a sappy speech on marriage and true love. Kit's feet were killing her in the purple heels. She slid a foot out of the shoe under the cover of the gown to give it some relief.

What had they decided? Bradley nodded and grinned at some memory his mother had recited to the crowd. They all had a courtesy laugh. Kit's mind reeled. What? What? What? Bradley pulled her closer and rested an arm over her shoulder nearly knocking her off balance with the shoe that wasn't on. Dianna thanked everyone again and apologized once more that Max couldn't be present. More applause and then Bradley led Kit off the stage. Music kicked up again.

Leann was waiting at the bottom of the stairs to the bandstand. "Oh, Bradley," she cooed, "I just so wanted to congratulate you." She slipped her skinny arms around his neck and kissed his cheek leaving a pink shadow from her lipstick. Kit flexed fingers as she blinked and felt the smile freeze to her face. She wasn't jealous, not like that. There was no fear of losing Bradley, no concern of infidelity so to speak. But there was the urgency of competition, showmanship, and a need to prove she was worth her salt. Her cheeks started to hurt again as she watch Leann smooth Bradley's tux lapels and straighten his black bow tie.

He puffed his chest out and straightened under her attention then snapped his fingers in a jolt of memory. "Oh, Leann! Have you met my fiancé, Kitty?"

"Yes, I've met Miss Kitty," Leann murmured demurely. She turned away from Kit and back to Bradley. "Why don't you come sit at my table? I'm certain Mom and Dad would love to speak to you and then . . ." She flicked a glance at Kit. "Then I could hear more about your Kitty." If she had poured syrup over the word Kitty, it would have sounded less sugary.

"We'd love that, wouldn't we, darling?"

"Oh yes, love it." Kit wondered if she was going to need to ice down her cheeks by the end of the night as she followed them to Leann's table.

To her delight, Phil was there. He arched a red eyebrow at Leann and grinned, taking her arm and leading her to the side of the table opposite Bradley and Kit.

After they were all seated, Phil started asking more questions about the March of Dimes.

"What kind of education did you need for a job like that?" Phil asked.

"Well I have my bachelor's and my master's and . . ."

"To work for a non-profit organization?" Leann sniffed.

"It is what I want to do," Kit said simply.

"With an education like that, working for less than a

common policeman seems a little unorthodox."

"Why?"

"It just seems a waste of a decent education," Leann shrugged.

"I don't see it like that," Phil said before Kit could respond. "Kit was telling me about the importance of the work the March of Dimes does. I'd be honored to work where I was enriching the lives of millions of people and saving the lives of babies."

"Oh really, Phil," Leann purred. "Be sensible. People on wages like that couldn't afford philanthropy. Noble deeds are for people who can afford it."

Phil didn't look convinced. "Kit was telling me their big push right now was for women to understand the . . . what was it, Kit?"

"We want to educate women that if they just take 400 daily micrograms of the folic acid B vitamin, they can reduce the incidence of neural tube defects such as spina bifida by up to 70 percent . . . that is, if they take it prior to conception. And I think that's a very ignorant blanket statement for you to make, Leann. Anyone can afford noble deeds," Kit countered, looking as uninterested as the blonde feline across from her. "Because I am well educated, I can educate the entire world on the importance of nutrition and immunizations and help with the research in prevention of birth defects and infant mortality by curing diseases that have plagued our world since the world began. I, with my education, can bring enlightenment to people who can't afford that education and by so doing, I will leave this world a great place to be born into. Nobility belongs to anyone who wants it."

"Well said, Kit," Phil nodded and then looked to Leann to dare to defy it.

"If you say so, Kitty," Leann shrugged.

"What do you do?" Kit asked genuinely curious as to what

the high and mighty simpering female did to support herself.

"I own La Galerie Vogue, a day spa for women."

Kit nearly choked on the peal of laughter that tried to escape her.

"Really? A day spa? How . . . fulfilling."

"It's a really excellent program they have, Kitty, love. You should go tomorrow," Bradley interjected excitedly.

"Yes, you should," Leann agreed. "We could fix you up quite well. Get your eyebrows waxed and a facial. Your nails could stand a manicure."

"My nails are fine, thanks. I won't have time tomorrow."

The two women stared at each other, neither blinking.

"Congratulations, Bradley!" An older man beamed at him and clapped him on the shoulder. "We're very glad to see you settling down." It was the man who had been sitting in the seat Bradley now occupied when Dianna had dragged her over here earlier. It was Leann's dad.

Bradley stood and shook his hand enthusiastically. "Brent! Perfect to see you!"

"Yeah, good to see you too. Your dad sure says some wonderful things about you and the work you're doing with the business."

"He's lying to you." They both laughed quite agreeably.

Bradley put a hand on Kit's shoulder. "Have you met my bride-to-be?"

"Yes. Your mother introduced us briefly a while ago. Hello again, Kitty."

"Hello."

"So what does your father do?" Brent asked.

Kit felt Bradley's fingers tighten on her shoulder. "He owns RMR Construction."

"Well, very nice, very nice. He does buildings then. Has he built anything I'd have heard about?"

Kit cleared her throat slightly. "Ummm . . . No. I really doubt it. It's a stucco company. He owned a brick masonry business too, but when work got too hectic, he sold that off."

Brent's face went blank. Bradley's hand felt like a death grip on her shoulder. Leann's laughter tinkled sweetly as the breeze. "Stucco, brick, construction . . . Goodness, those words have a cacophonous sound to the ear. They're almost painful to hear." Leann hid a smile in her crystal goblet as she took a long drink.

Kit's face went hot. She stood abruptly despite Bradley's hand trying to force her back down. "Well, Leann, not everything can be as euphonious as the words 'day spa' . . ." Kit purred the words out like silk being rustled to the side by sarcasm.

"I rather like that, Kitty. It would be a nice ad for the spa: A day of euphonism. You're brilliant. You really are as bright as they say."

"Yes, I really am. The correct usage of the word you are trying to implement in that sentence would be 'a day of euphoniousness.' Now, if you'll excuse me."

"Leann," she heard Phil hiss behind her.

"What did I say?" Leann asked defensively.

"Excuse me, Brent. I'd better . . ." Bradley scooted past the people and chairs and followed Kit.

She had moved quickly despite the shoes and had made it to her room before he had caught up with her. She already had one pulled off and tossed to the bed when he came in.

"Just what exactly do you think you're doing?"

"Changing."

"You're in the middle of a party where you are the guest of honor."

"I have been insulted, mocked, and tormented pretty much since getting off the plane, and I'm going home."

"You have got to be joking. You have just embarrassed me

in front of Leann's father. There was no excuse for you to act like that!"

"Embarrassed? Are you insane?"

"I think you owe him and Leann an apology."

"What's going on here?" Dianna stepped in.

"Nothing, Mother. Everything is fine, isn't it, Kitty?"

"No. It isn't." Kit folded her arms across her chest. "Dianna, what were you doing in my bag yesterday?"

Dianna's face registered the shock as she took a step back. "I don't think now is a good time for . . ."

"Now is a perfect time," Kit said, yanking off the other shoe. "Because I am leaving now, so we don't have later."

"Be reasonable, love. You can't just leave."

"I need to just leave, okay? So I am going to. Now why were you going through my bag?"

Dianna's eyes narrowed into slivers. "I'll show you." She disappeared and reappeared within moments with a card in her hand. Kit blinked at it.

"So you recognize it?" Dianna scowled. The card was black with a red heart on it and a white rose resting on the heart. Dianna opened it and began to read. "Roses are Red, Violets are blue. I can see that you're blushing when I say I love you. Know always, I adore and worship you. Love, the greatest guy you'll ever know." Dianna's smile was triumphant as she held the card to Kit.

Kit took it and rolled her eyes. "What's going on? What is this?" Bradley asked.

Dianna's cheeks huffed out. "The handwriting isn't yours, Bradley. She got that from someone else. Trite and tacky as it is. It certainly says quite a bit."

"Oh please! Give me a break. You are so right. It isn't from Bradley. It's from my baby brother, Gary. He sent it to me as a joke because I hate Valentines Day. I keep it in my bag because it makes me laugh. Now please leave so I can change. I need to go home."

"Mother, you need to go so we can talk." Bradley started to push his mom to the door.

"No, Bradley. You both need to get out. There isn't anything to talk about and I am getting out of this Easter egg nightmare of a dress now!"

"What will we tell everyone?" Bradley asked, dazed.

"Whatever you want," she said simply, not looking up at him.

Mother and son looked identical in their shock. Neither had ever seen Kit lose her temper and neither had ever seen her not easily placated. In their surprise, there was nothing left for them to do but obey her, meekly shutting the door behind them.

Once Kit had on her own clothes, she felt better. It was as though she had been suffocating before and now she could breathe. Her clothes were thrown into her bag along with her personal items and she was ready to go.

She nearly asked Bradley to take her to the airport, but didn't want to deal with the argument. She tossed Max's car keys in the air and caught them neatly. Max would understand why his car was in long-term parking at the airport and he would never hold it against her.

No one was awake when she finally crept into her house, down the hall, and into her room. Her door skimmed over the carpet and made a quiet click as she closed it behind her. Kit was suddenly tired; tired in a way that she felt she could sleep forever. She didn't bother to undress as she slipped under her covers.

When Kit awoke, the sun was higher than it should have been. She stretched lazily. No one would have known she was home. She had parked behind the house where the RV used to go. She was glad. It meant she got to sleep in for the first time since she could remember and it meant there were no questions as to why she was home early.

Kit had already scheduled time off work and had finished anything that needed doing urgently the day before at Buena Park.

She dropped down to her knees and pulled a box out from under her bed. Inside were old stucco clothes. Her dad had complained about needing help and since she had a few days off, she might as well help him. She pulled her tennis shoes on and went to the message board in the kitchen.

The board was there so that anyone could find their father in a matter of minutes. She skimmed the board, repeated the address a few times to herself and left.

Chapter 14

Glen handed James a can of Coke as they leaned against the scaffolding. They had been at it since 7:00 a.m. It was now 11:30 a.m. and the sun climbed up onto its pedestal of midday glory to bake them completely. "I got an idea for getting Gary back for the water thing."

"Oh yeah, what?"

"Just wait."

James grinned. The guys on this crew were great. The endless practical jokes and the physical labor were better than anything his therapist could do for him. Today was his last day helping Ryan. He had felt like it was time to go back to his job.

James grabbed an iron pole above him and hoisted himself up onto the scaffolding. He pulled a hammer out of the tool belt that hung over his stucco stained jeans and started stretching wire over the tarpaper.

Ryan was on the other side of the house with Gary.

Kit pulled up next to the curb and looked at the new building with chicken wire over half of it. She got out of the car and pulled her hair back into a sloppy ponytail while looking for her dad. She smiled widely when she saw him.

"Hey, Daddy!" she said, bouncing over to him and shading her eyes with her hands from the midday sun.

"Hey there, Princess. What are you doing here?"

"You said you needed help."

"Well I know that, but why are you home? I thought you were in California."

Kit grimaced. "I had some problems and needed to get away."

"Overrun by British babbling, Katy-did?" Gary cut in. "Arrogance thick enough to walk on?"

"Leave your sister alone," Ryan admonished. "Do you want to talk about it?"

"No. Just came to help."

"Well, you can go help Glen on the other side. We're pretty well covered here."

"Okay. Sure." She climbed up to give her dad a peck on the cheek, climbed down and disappeared around to the other side of the house.

"We could too use her help," Gary whined.

"Yeah, but so could they."

"Glen said they were fine."

"It isn't Glen she needs to help."

"Ho," Gary grinned. "Nice move, dad. Seems very much like a checkmate."

"We'll see."

"Hear you guys need some help." The high clear voice called up.

James felt as though a breeze swept through his soul. He could hear her laughter like chimes in that breeze fill his senses as though he were in that moment again.

"Sure, Katy-did," Glen called down. "Come on up and bring a hammer."

"I'm wearing the belt, Glen," she said as she swung onto the scaffolding. "My belt has everything stocked."

"Yeah. It's 'cause you're so lazy, you never use any of it!" he chuckled.

She socked his arm. "Whatever!" James' heart raced. He hadn't looked up yet. He wasn't sure what to say without it seeming like he was stalking her.

"Who's the new guy?" she asked.

"Oh, this is James. He's not really our new guy. He's just helping out."

Her breath caught when he finally faced her. "James."

"Hey, Kit."

"Oh, you guys know each other then? Well good. Hey, Katy-did, you forgot to bring up the foam for the pop-out on this window."

"You didn't mention foam, just the hammer." She smiled at James. "You are the last person I expected to see here."

"It's a long story of how I got here."

"It would have to be."

"Your dad said he needed help. I had some time off so I figured . . . you know . . . that I could help."

"You just go work for a guy you don't even know just because he said he needed help?"

"Yeah, wouldn't you?"

She twitched. "Well, yeah, I would, but . . ."

"But Bradley wouldn't." James said it too fast to think about what he was saying. Glen snickered and ducked his head pretending he was coughing.

Kit scowled at him. "He's busy," she defended.

"Everyone's busy, Katherine. You make time for what you need to even if it doesn't fit."

Glen hopped down to get foam for the window trim. When he got back up, Kit swiped a stray strand of her hair out of her eyes and pulled out her Estwing hammer. James watched her when she wasn't looking. The tool belt hung loosely at her hips. Her muscles flexed with the swing of the hammer as she tacked the foam to the wall and then the wire to the foam. James continued working next to her, pulling out nails from the front pouch of the tool belt he wore and swinging the hammer. The stray strand of hair was finally left in her eyes, as it seemed a futile effort to swipe it away.

"I thought you were a cop," she said after Glen had left for more nails. The two of them were sitting on a plank, legs dangling down in the air. Kit's eyes were closed and her face lifted up to catch the sun entirely. James tried not to stare, but couldn't stop himself.

"I am a cop."

"So why are you doing cement work?"

He let out a slow breath. "I had time off," he said finally, not sure if he wanted to get into what that meant.

She opened an eye to look at him. "Why?"

"Why?"

"Yeah, usually when people take time off, they go on vacation, not go get another job."

"Hmmm, good point. This was unplanned time off. I had some problems at work."

"What kind of problems?" She had closed her eyes again.

"It's a long story."

"Meaning you don't want to tell me, or you don't feel like taking the time to tell me?"

"I'll tell you sometime, but I don't really want to right now."

"Fair enough. So how did you end up with my dad?"

"I umm . . . got a message you called and thought I'd stop by to see what you needed. You weren't there, but your dad mentioned he could use some help."

"And so you helped him?"

James shrugged "Well . . . yeah . . ."

"Impressive."

"Why?"

"Most people wouldn't do that for a stranger."

James only shrugged again. Kit tilted her head to study him. "You don't eat a lot of doughnuts, do you?"

He laughed outright. "What?"

"You don't have the stereotypical body of a cop. No spare tire or anything."

"Thanks. I think."

She reddened "I didn't mean it . . . well, you know, like that. Sorry."

"No, it's okay."

Glen's face popped up over the plank. "You ready?"

James smiled and got up on the balls of his feet.

"You doing it now?"

"I have to," Glen chortled.

James started climbing down.

"Do what?" Kit asked, genuinely intrigued.

"Gary is getting some comeuppance."

"What are you doing?"

"Nothing big. Just going to embarrass him."

Glen went to the cooler and pulled out a Dr. Pepper and sort of meandered by the truck. Gary was behind the door to the truck. Kit grinned. He was answering nature's call. On the construction site, bathrooms were unheard of and it became the standard protocol to open the door of the truck for the guys to offer a shield of privacy.

Glen cleared his throat. "Yes, ma'am, I know that it seems wrong to do that in public, but there's nowhere else to go," he exclaimed loudly in his sincerest voice possible.

Gary's head shot up and the *zzzzip* of a zipper was heard being frantically pulled up.

He came bailing from around the truck. "I'm sorry. I thought the coast was clear. I didn't . . ." He trailed off as he looked around and saw only Kit, Glen and James.

"There's nobody else here," Gary sputtered.

"Nope." James started laughing. Kit was choking it down without success.

"You guys bite!" he grumbled, stalking off.

Glen burst into laughter, slapping his knee and doubling over.

"Ok, break it up. Fun's over," Ryan said. He wasn't smiling but it was obvious he was amused by the moment. "We need to get the north wall mudded before tonight."

"Sure thing, boss," Glen said, wiping an eye.

Kit didn't move as she watched James and Glen go to the north side of the house clapping each other on the back and laughing.

"He sure is a nice guy, isn't he?" Ryan asked dropping an arm over her shoulder.

"He is. He gets along so well with everyone." She couldn't hide the wonder from her voice.

"He's been great. Last night we had him over for dinner, and he stayed half the night playing Monopoly with Gary and me. He taught Gary how to gang up on me though so I won't be playing with them ever again," Ryan chuckled.

"Wow, he gets along with Gary," she snorted lightly. "That's a miracle."

"Miracles happen every day." Ryan looked to where the guys had disappeared around the corner. "Miracles seem to follow James everywhere he walks."

She nodded awkwardly. "Well, I better go help."

"Everywhere he walks," Ryan mused aloud, walking back to the side of the house.

When Kit got to the north wall she found Gary and James spreading mud. Glen had left to get another trowel. James lightly backhanded Gary's shoulder to which he got a playful slug. They were talking too low for Kit to hear, but she couldn't help but smile while watching them.

It had been a long time since Gary had liked a guy she was dating. A long time since she'd felt like her father approved. She shook herself violently. What was she thinking?! She wasn't DATING James. She barely knew him and she was engaged to Bradley. She shook herself again for good measure.

"Will you be our haudie?" Gary called over to her.

"I'm everybody's hottie!" she replied playfully.

"You're delusional. Get over here and get me some mud on my hawk."

She complied, supplying them the cement mud that made the base coat of the stucco. They had done most of the wall when Glen finally came back.

"Sorry I was gone so long. I was helping Ryan to finish the pop-out on the other side and I—" He stopped walking and blinked at the wall they had almost finished. Scratched into the mud on the side of the wall was written: "Glen has a fat head." He read it aloud. "You guys are so childish!" he spat.

He folded his arms and glared at them. "And fat head? That's the best you could come up with?" They all laughed as they kept working.

"Man, I am hungry," Kit said once the sun started falling lower in the sky.

"Yeah, you weren't here for lunch." James trowled the mud upward, smoothing it over the wire. "You know, you could come to my parents for dinner tonight. They're having a little get-together and my mom is a great cook."

"I don't want to be a bother," she said hesitantly.

"Wouldn't be a bother. It'd be fun."

Gary rolled his eyes at Kit. "You have nothing else to do, Katy-did. You should go."

"I . . ." Kit looked to be searching for excuses.

"You don't have to go if you don't want to. There's no arm-twisting involved here."

"No. I would love to go," she said promptly after catching a scowl from Gary. "Thank you for inviting me."

James winked at her. "Thank you for saying yes."

They finished the wall and James stretched. "I'll pick you up after I get showered."

"Great, I'll be ready." She grabbed Gary's collar after James had gone and pulled him up close. "You've got to come with me!" she insisted.

"Why?"

"Because Bradley would be furious, it's like a date."

"It isn't a date. It's a guy asking you to his mom's place for an informal dinner. Geez, Katy-did! Lighten up!"

"Are you sure I should be doing this?"

"Definitely. He's a fun guy. You will have a blast."

"But Bradley . . ."

". . . Is in another state and I honestly don't think he'll mind anyway."

"Why wouldn't he?"

"He's a flaming Brit! He's so arrogant he would never imagine you with anyone else when you've got HIM!" Gary smirked and wiped the edge of his trowel on his jeans.

"Let it go, Gary. Not all British are snobs."

"Oh, I know, but that one definitely is."

"I'm engaged though!" she hissed in a last ditch effort.

"Oh for Pete's sake! No one said you needed to marry James! You're just going for dinner. Besides you owe him."

"Owe him for what?"

"He saved your life. Spent a half a million dollars on flowers and helped Dad catch up with the business . . . not saying we're caught up exactly, but we're scads closer than we were three days ago."

"Fine. I'll go."

"Sure you will. And you'll be glad you did."

She looked down at her clothes. "I better at least clean up a little."

"Yeah, you should." He pinched his nose. "You stink!" He started fanning the air with his other hand.

She went home to change and clean up. After showering

and changing clothes twice, she braided her long dark hair back, and frowned at the image in the mirror. There was a thin scar along her jaw-line from the wreck that was still pink. Nothing covered it. Makeup attempts seemed only to make it worse.

It seemed accented somehow when her hair was pulled back. Her frown deepened and she pulled out the braid, letting her hair hang loose over her shoulders. Leaning into the mirror to inspect the scar, Kit jumped when the doorbell rang. "I cannot believe I'm doing this," she thought.

His jeans fit him nicely along with a T-shirt that showed off the fact he was not the stereotypical donut-eating cop. The day's sun bronzed his face, which nicely accentuated his brown hair.

I'm not on a date! she reminded herself.

"Your dad sure is a great guy. And Gary! What a clown!" James commented once they were on the road.

"I don't know how he'd feel being called a 'clown.'"

"It's not the worst thing I've called him these past few days."

"Are you always the good Samaritan?"

"Nope. I'm the good American—never been to Samaria." He grinned.

"I'm serious. You help the damsel in distress. You help some old construction worker merely because he mentions he needs help. You drive me to my grandfather's and hang out just because I wanted to. I swear there isn't one selfish bone in your body."

"Now don't go making me out to be noble. Everything I do is selfish. All that stuff I did, I did because it made me feel good. Hang what it does for someone else." He paused and flicked his gaze from the road to her. "How is your grandfather?"

"He's good. He's having a lot more memory loss. It seems

every day he struggles harder to stay in today. He seems to live in his books and in his memories. They're talking about putting him in a home." Her voice cracked. She hadn't meant to tell him that. She hadn't even told Bradley yet. She paused, not knowing what to say.

"Your mom told me," James said softly.

"My mom told you?" The widening of her eyes showed the surprise she felt by that.

"Yes. Is that not okay?"

"Well, it's fine. It's just . . . she's usually so introverted. It's not really like her to share things that are personal like that."

James gave a quiet chuckle. "She said the same thing about you."

"She did?" Kit's face felt warm.

"I think she's worried you do too much."

"I don't really do all that much," Kit said, shaking her head.

James clicked his tongue. "Your job is enough to keep four people busy from what I hear. You volunteer at the Chili Affair for Travelers Aid and the homeless shelter every year. You are planning a wedding, dealing with a relationship, helping your dad, and still find time to amuse a sorry old cop by going to dinner with him." He grinned at her. "It's a wonder you speak clearly around all that you've bit off and are chewing."

Kit smiled. "When you put it that way, I feel tired just thinking about it."

"So do I." He pulled into the quiet Sandy neighborhood and into a driveway of a large, but cozy home.

Another vehicle, a burgundy minivan, pulled in behind them. Young children streamed out of it and across the lawn to the front door. They didn't knock but went right in.

A woman got out and opened the side door to take an infant out of its seat. The man that was driving met her to help with a diaper bag and a casserole dish of some sort.

"Should we have brought something?" Kit asked.

"We did." James reached into the back of his car and pulled out a grocery sack with a vegetable tray in it.

She almost waited for him to get her door when she realized once again this is not a date. Hurriedly, Kit opened the door and hopped out.

The other couple met them at the door. "Hey, Kit, I'd like you to meet my brother Brian and his wife Annette. The baby is Elisa." He tickled under the infant's chin. "Hey guys, this is Kit. She's the one from the car accident a while back."

"Nice to meet you, Kit," Annette said and gave her a hug.

"Yeah, it's real nice to meet you," Brian echoed.

They all went in and set the things they brought on a buffet stand. "Hey, Ma," James said kissing his fingers and tapping her forehead, "Where's Dad?"

"Take a guess . . ." She looked out the back to the shop.

"Figures," James said.

"Are you going to introduce us or are you going to just let this poor girl stand around ignored?"

James smiled patiently. "Kit, this is Mom. You could call her Caroline, but nobody does. She's just Ma."

Kit smiled. "Nice to meet you." She carefully left out a title at all to be on the safe side.

"Nice to meet you too. Isn't this the de—"

"Yes, Ma, it is," Brian interjected before she could say 'dead girl.' "Let's get dinner on the table."

When dinner was set, kids settled, Gerald returned from the shop and prayer had been said, conversation floated pleasantly. Kit marveled at the family unity. It felt like her house. Like . . . home.

"So have you been wearing a seat belt lately, young lady?" Gerald Hartman asked.

Kit ducked her head in embarrassment. "I have been.

Thanks for asking."

"It's a miracle you're alive after a wreck like that," Annette said, passing peas to Brianna who scowled and continued passing to Brett without taking any. Brett scowled too and passed it off faster then Brianna had.

"Hey, James, will you do career day at my school?" Brett asked.

"Sure."

"Cool! Will you tell everyone what it was like to shoot that kid?"

The undertow of chatter was silenced instantly. James held his fork in mid air and stared at his nephew in disbelief. "Mister!" Brian sent Brett a warning look.

"What? I didn't say anything wrong," Brett defended himself.

Brianna rolled her eyes. "You are such an insensitive creep."

James cleared his throat and managed to set his fork back on his plate without dropping it. "If I go to your school, I will not talk to them about that," he said quietly.

"Why?" Brett asked. Brianna rolled her eyes again.

"If I did talk to them about that, I would tell them about some kid's mother who is crying every night because her son isn't coming home again. I will tell them that gangs are Satan's tool to give us something that makes us feel a part of something, makes us feel like we belong. I will tell them that a kid died for a group that didn't have the guts to support him in his final moment! I will tell them about . . ." he stopped abruptly, noticing the wide eyes and hung jaws of everyone at the table. Kit's eyes were the widest of all. He felt his cheeks and ear tips burn.

"I'm sorry," he said after a moment. "Maybe you should get someone else for your career day, Brett."

"I think you should do it, James," Brian commented softly. "I think that is exactly what they need to hear about gangs. I think if they knew that truth now, they'd be less likely to get involved later."

James nodded numbly, feeling the motion of his head moving and wondering why it was doing that.

"You okay?" Brian asked.

"Yeah." James allowed a self-depreciative laugh. "I'm great. No, I mean I really am. Working these last few days with Kit's dad has been better than therapy. I'm going back to work on Monday."

Gerald nodded his approval. "Good to get back in the saddle, son. I'm sure you'll find there's nothing to it."

"I'm sure you're right, Dad." He smiled thinly. "And stop looking worried, Ma, I'm fine."

He turned to Kit; she blinked at him. He shrugged, "Told you I'd tell you later."

She furrowed her brow in confusion but nodded and went back to passing food. The rest of the conversation circled Gerald's wood building hobby-turned-business and carefully skirted around James and police work.

"I really like your family," Kit said once they were in the car.

"They seem to like you, too."

Before James could pull out of the driveway a tap came on the window. Kit jumped, her bag slipping from her lap to the floor. She looked up to see Gerald's face in her window, and pushed the button to make it roll down.

Bishop Hartman leaned his elbows on the window frame and handed Kit a small sack. "Your Mom is sending this with you. She doesn't think you take good enough care of yourself."

James snorted in derision and shook his head. "She sends home more food than a small army could eat. Tell her thanks for me."

"Oh I will . . . I will." He started chewing his lip and stared at Kit a moment. She shifted expectantly wondering what he was going to say.

"You're not wearing your seatbelt, Sweetheart." He pulled it forward so she could take it. "I'd hate to have to know James spent another night bringing you back from the dead."

"I'm sorry. I was going to put it on. I just, well, thanks for worrying." She smiled warmly at him.

"You two be good." He tapped the car and stepped back so they could drive away while Kit fussed with the seat belt, buckling it into place.

"So like I was saying. They seem to like you, too."

She giggled. "It is nice to be liked by someone's family."

"Doesn't Bradley's family get along with you?"

"I really like his dad . . . but his mom is like a Steven King novel on mothers-in-law."

"Wow. That bad, huh?"

"Worse that that. Oh well . . ." Kit sighed and then blinked and turned to him. "So tell me more about what happened."

"What?"

"Why you had time off work. Something about shooting someone . . . ?"

"Oh yeah. That." He laughed uncertainly. *Well,* he thought, *why not tell her?* "I went into this burglary in progress. The kid was still in there when I arrived. He had a gun, pulled it on me, and I ducked faster than he did."

"Oh my gosh!" she exclaimed. "That had to be horrible for you!"

"Yeah, well, it was, actually. He said something before he died that I've had a hard time dealing with."

"What did he say?"

"He was a gang member and just before he died, he told me I was just like him. Part of a gang who protected each other with guns."

"But you don't believe that?"

"No." He felt relief that he could say that word and mean it. "I don't believe it."

"Good; you shouldn't. The police keep the rest of us safe. I have always respected law enforcement . . . except when I get speeding tickets. Those just tick me off."

James cast her a sideways glance. "You shouldn't speed." After a moment he added, "Especially when it's raining on an S curve and you're not wearing a seatbelt."

"You guys are never going to let me live that down."

"You're lucky you got the chance to try and live it down."

"How old was the guy you shot?"

James paused. "Sixteen," he said finally.

"Wow, so young."

"So young," he repeated.

"So, what happens after something like that?"

"They take my gun, give me a few days off to cool down; give me a therapist and wait for me to be ready to go back."

"You said you were going back on Monday."

"Yeah. I am."

"So you're better then?" She looked at him curiously.

"Not over it. I can't imagine ever being over it, but, yeah, I'm better." He closed his eyes for a second to stop tears from leaking out. He let out a deep breath and laughed self depreciatively. "It's been an exciting month."

She smiled, "That's one way of putting it."

"So how are wedding plans coming?"

"Oh yeah, that. Not bad. I have the dress, the bridesmaids picked out along with their dresses, the menu, and guest list."

"It's a lot of work to just get married."

"Thinking back on it . . . had it not been for that night . . . had it not been for that wreck, I would already be married." She frowned. "Funny, huh?"

"Hysterical," James said dryly.

"Postponing it and re-planning it was one more plate thrown in the air."

"Plate?" James glanced away from the road to her with an eyebrow arched in question.

"P L A T E." She sounded out each letter of the word like they do on Sesame Street when learning to read, making it sound long. "It's like there are a dozen porcelain plates spinning over my head and sometimes . . . sometimes it feels like if I look away or breathe, they will all come crashing down on top of me."

"What kind of plates?"

"Well, there's the usual. My job, church calling, Daddy's business, which I try hard to help with. And the wedding, Bradley's family, my grandfather being so sick."

"That is a lot of plates," James agreed. "Why don't you quit some of them?"

"Oh, okay, which should I pick?"

"Hmmm, good point. Put a stop on the wedding. That would free up ten plates all by itself." He winked at her.

"Or just get it over with and in the past."

"You know, if you ever need help, I'd be happy to spin a plate or two for you." He pulled into her driveway and put the car in park.

She turned to consider him a moment. "You really are the good Samaritan," she said finally. "Thanks for dinner. You have a great family." Kit put her hand on the door to leave when a rap came at James' window. Both James and Kit jumped.

James rolled it down to reveal Gary standing there. "What is it with people knocking on windows tonight?" Kit asked.

Gary ignored her. "Hey, Hartman, I'm going rock climbing tomorrow. Want to come?"

James shrugged. "Sounds fun. Sure."

"Cool." Gary pursed his lips and looked at Kit. "Yeah, I guess you can come too if you want." He shrugged and disappeared into the house.

James smiled. "Weren't you supposed to be in California?"

"I came home early."

"Why?"

"Needed to . . . I guess."

"Did Bradley come back with you?"

"No. He had to get some work done on their business expansion. He won't be back until Tuesday."

"So are you going rock climbing with Gary and I?"

Her smile was slow crawling over her face. "Sure, you'll need a *good* teacher, not a Gary teacher."

"Then I'll see you tomorrow."

"Yeah. Okay, thanks again." She wondered if she should hug him, decided against it, and opened the door to let herself out.

He let out a huge sigh watching her walk to the door. He wondered if he should've walked her to the porch, but finally decided he was right in staying put. A porch scene with an engaged girl was the last thing he needed. It was bad enough that every word she said sealed his heart more tightly to hers. James didn't dare even think of her in terms of a date, someone to kiss goodnight, someone to hold tightly, and wish the night were beginning, not ending.

But even as he reminded himself he was not allowed to think of her like that . . . he was thinking of her exactly like that.

He started to whistle softly the beginning to his song and then blinked in surprise. He could hear how it needed to end.

He dropped his keys on the stand by the front door and moved his hand over his midsection where his gun belt would be. It wasn't there to remove. He felt silly, even though he was alone and there was no one to notice his mistake.

James took off his shoes, then sat at the piano, placing bare feet upon the cold brass pedals. His fingers pressed the keys, his eyes closed and he pictured her dark hair framed by a halo of light. Then her kneeling beside her grandfather's chair and then with a tool belt buckled over her hips and her arm flexing with the swing of the hammer. Flying down and then up. Fast, slow, soft . . . perfect. It was finished. He opened his eyes and blinked at his hands on the piano, unable to determine how he felt about that.

The song was finished, each note fitting perfectly to the one before it, like pieces nesting against each other in a bridge that spanned from the beginning to the end, seeming to cross eternity.

He rested his elbows on the keys making a loud clunking sound of notes and hung his head in his hands. Confusion clouded through his mind like a rising storm. How could the song be finished? How is that possible?

It was supposed to be finished with the inspirations of the girl he would marry, not a girl that was marrying someone else.

In some ways he was angry he felt the way he did. Angry for allowing himself to fall for a shimmering essence and teasing laughter. And even more angry to know that a woman of her intelligence, charm, and beauty was going to marry a sloth of a guy like Bradley.

James played the song again. It seemed to end with a crescendo of human emotion. Love, anger, pain . . . hope. But hope in what? He dropped the cover over the keys and went to bed. For the first time in two weeks since the shooting, he didn't see the boy's face. He could only see hers.

Chapter 15

"The harness tightens here and here so it feels snug."

Gary pulled straps as he talked, completely invading James' personal space. Kit watched the two of them while unrolling the rope. She had on a mountain appropriate outfit; a tee shirt over khaki shorts and rock climbing shoes. She looked like she belonged there, as did Gary. James didn't.

James had on Levi's with a tee shirt, his typical staple outfit of any non-cop working day. He wondered if his tennis shoes would be instrumental in his falling since it seemed everyone else had on shoes made for rock climbing. Once he'd arrived and stared up the sheer face they were planning on scaling, James realized how much he really disliked heights.

"Don't worry about it," Gary said, noticing James getting paler by the second.

"Oh, I'm not worried," James tried to sound nonchalant, but his voice cracked.

Gary grinned. "I'll be belaying you."

"Belaying?"

"That means I decide whether to let you fall or not," Gary responded with a smile on his face. "The rope attached to you goes through the ring at the top of the wall and back to me. I'll take up the slack as you go up so if you do fall, I've got you locked so you can't go anywhere. It's perfectly safe."

"What about everyone else?" There were two other girls and a guy that had shown up just after James had. One of the girls James recognized from church. It was Kit's best friend

Whitney and the guy was Whitney's younger brother, Ashton. The other girl was Dawn, a girl that Gary was obviously trying to woo.

"They will be taking turns at belaying each other."

"Since you're the new guy, we'll need to watch you a little closer to make sure you're comfortable," Gary assured James.

Kit tapped Gary on the shoulder. "I think Dawn is getting lonely. I'll take care of James."

"You trust her to do that, Hartman?" Gary asked.

"I don't see why not. I really think we'll be fine."

"Okay, Katy-did, he's all yours. Try not to kill him."

Kit stuck her tongue out at Gary in reply. "He's just jealous because he knows I'm a better climber than he'll ever be." She laughed. "Actually, that's not true. Gary is the last of the mountain men. He is the ultimate in creating outdoor experiences."

James motioned towards her perfectly fitted climbing gear. "But it does look like you can hold your own."

She smiled. "I get by. It's been tough getting my muscles to work right since the accident. I was afraid they would never work again."

"Do you remember the accident at all?"

She looked down, fidgeting with rope and then stuffing her hands into tiny thin gloves that left her fingertips exposed. "Oh, look, they're going up now. We should get you up there."

The change of topic evident, James shrugged. He felt dumb spilling his guts the night before about the shooting when she didn't feel their friendship was strong enough to share personal things with him.

He started working his way up the cliff face. His fingers felt for any kind of hold. He wasn't thinking about the climb though. He was giving himself a mental chew-out for being annoyed with her. She was engaged. She had someone to pour her personal life out to. Just because he didn't, didn't give him the right to feel put out by her.

He put his left knee into a divot in the wall to hoist himself up to the next outcrop of rock. He could feel the tension on the rope that would leave him suspended in midair if he were to fall. Kit was keeping up with him without a problem. He stopped and looked down, feeling suddenly dizzy with the height and a little nervous. Kit wasn't looking up. She was looking over at Gary who was belaying Dawn. They were chatting together and it felt like maybe she wasn't paying enough attention to what she was doing. What if he fell and she couldn't steady herself in time to catch him? The whole concept of her catching him at all when she was half his weight seemed doubtful at best.

Gary looked up from his conversation with Kit. She looked up, squinting, to shield her eyes from the glare of the sun. "Hey, Hartman!" Gary called. "C'mon, man, fifteen feet of vertical and you're already resting?"

"I'm just looking around," James said defensively, worrying still that Kit may not be paying enough attention. He started climbing again, hefting himself up on a little ledge with his left knee and then pulling himself up with his hands, which had found a crevice to grip.

After a few minutes of upward movement, he looked up and realized he was at the top. James looked over to where Dawn had also reached the top. Instead of climbing up and over she tapped the bolt at the top, and leaned back, letting the rope hold her weight. It now appeared she was walking backwards down the cliff face as though she were on a sidewalk taking a stroll and not defying gravity. Dawn ran across to one side and then the other letting out a shout of exhilaration with the freedom.

"Try it, James. Touch the bolts and then try what Dawn is doing," he heard Gary call up to him.

He tapped the shiny metal bolt. "Try what?" he called back, not looking down.

"Walk down the wall!" Kit answered.

"Ummmm . . . no. I don't think so."

"It's easy," Gary yelled. "If Katy-did can do it, anybody can."

"Oh great," he muttered. "Peer pressure." James let out a deep breath. "So what do I do?"

"Lean back until you are straight. You know . . . perpendicular to the wall, and then walk," Kit said.

James started leaning back. He cursed under his breath. The tension in the rope was now tight. Kit was holding him. "Oh wait, you mean she's going to hold me up while I do this?"

"Got a problem with that, Hartman?" Kit called. He flinched at her calling him Hartman. Even though her voice had that same lilt of teasing, it felt like he'd offended her.

"I just . . . I just weigh three times the amount you do."

"Physics, Jamie," she sang up to him.

"Physics? What's physics got to do with—"

She cut him off. "Leverage. The rope allows me the leverage to hold you even if you did go visit Dunkin' Donuts before getting here."

He rolled his eyes, "You've reduced me to cop jokes?"

Everyone was laughing now. Dawn had stopped running the wall so she could laugh at him openly. She was bent back, the way they wanted him to do. She appeared to be just standing there, defying the physics of gravity that all present seemed to believe him ignorant of. He glared at Dawn. She had started jumping and running again.

"Show off." It was said loud enough, he was certain she'd heard him. She laughed even harder.

"Baby," she replied. The word echoed off the cliff face.

That did it. He closed his eyes, said a quick prayer for mercy and life, and leaned back. He must've caught Kit off guard because he felt himself actually beginning to fall. When the rope was taut again she had control.

"Blast!" He exclaimed staring straight into a sea of blue sky. It was as though he could walk straight into it.

"Try going to the side with little jumps and use your feet to keep from slamming into the wall," Gary said.

James looked down and did a little jump to the side. "Okay," he thought. "That wasn't so bad." He went to the other side and then started hopping all over the place and running along with Dawn. "Wahoo!" he yelled. He heard Kit's laugh echo and bounce up the wall toward him and he seemed to breathe it in. It filled his senses. He looked down at her and could hear his song in his head.

"I'm coming down," he yelled.

"I got you!" she replied.

"Yes, you do," he said to the wall and started hopping backwards. His knees bent to absorb the shock of each hop and quickly, much quicker than climbing up, his feet were planted on the soil next to Kit.

She impulsively reached up and hugged him. "You did great!" He slowly moved his arms up to hug her back, but before he could she had already stepped back and was readjusting the harness on her. "It's my turn. Unclip yourself."

He looked down at all the straps around his midsection and between his legs then back up to her doubtfully. She hesitated and moved forward when Gary stepped up. "Here let me help you out of that," he said. Gary unstrapped the ties around his thighs. "So did you like it?"

"Are you kidding? I absolutely loved that. I could do that all day long!"

"Well, anytime you want to go, just let me know. I'm always willing." Gary handed the harness to Kit. She stepped into it and had herself strapped up snugly in just a moment.

"Want to belay me?" she said to James.

"Uh . . . What if you fall?"

"That's why you'd be holding me," she said. "All you do is pull the rope through your belt to keep a bit of tension. When I come down you feed it back slowly. Keep it in your right hand tightly and let it slide through your left. You can put your foot against the wall to balance if you need to."

James nodded and adjusted the rope on his hands. Kit started climbing. She seemed like Spider Man scaling the wall, finding holds that didn't seem to be there to the naked eye. Gary watched as she put a knee into the wall for leverage.

"No knees, Katy-did," Gary yelled up to her.

"Why no knees?" James asked, pulling the rope tighter.

"No rock climber worth their salt uses their knees."

"Oh," James said, feeling dumb, since he'd done exactly that.

When Kit made it to the top, she ran the length the rope would give her. She seemed to fly. She stayed up there a long time and then, much faster than he had, bounced to the bottom.

"Allen would love this," James said.

"Who's that?"

"My best friend."

"Is he a cop, too?"

"No, he's a computer nerd."

Whitney had just come down from her climb. "So what made you become a cop?" she asked, a little out of breath.

"I don't know. Seemed like a noble profession, honorable. Never got enough of cops and robbers as a kid, I guess."

"Cool." She looked over to Gary and her little brother arranging the rope. "My brother didn't either, but on the other end of the spectrum," she said with a wink.

"What do you mean? He just got off his mission," James defended. "I've never heard such a spiritual talk."

"Oh, it was all before his mission. He's a changed man;

repented and all that. The kid got into some serious trouble."

James smiled. "Didn't we all?"

"What have you done?" Kit asked James.

"You'll have to ask my friend, Allen. He is the keeper of all my confessions."

"I'll remember that," Kit said.

Gary and Dawn had finished coiling the rope and putting it back in the bag and, along with Whitney's brother, joined the little circle of James, Kit, and Whitney. "What plans do you have today, Katy-did?" Gary asked.

"I need to go pick up invitations and then make sure my wedding gown still fits. Six weeks of no exercise makes me wonder if it went from fitted to second skin."

"You look like you always do." Whitney said. "Thin."

"I just want to make sure it still fits is all."

Gary shrugged. "I'm going to have to drop you off home then so you can take yourself. I'm going with Dawn to play laser tag."

"But . . . Gary . . ."

"Sorry, sis."

"I have to get the invitations by noon. The store closes at noon."

"Then why didn't you bring your own car?"

She glared at him. "Because I thought you could take me."

Gary looked like he was going to cave, but James broke in. "I'll take you."

"Thanks, man, you are a life saver." Gary clapped him on the back.

"No problem. Have fun playing laser tag."

Gary and Dawn had started down the trail that led to the cars and waved acknowledgement that they would have fun. Whitney and her brother hugged Kit then started after Gary and Dawn.

"I'm sorry," Kit said.

"For what?"

"For you always having to haul me around."

"I don't have to. I like being with you." They, too, began down the trail to the cars.

"Truth or dare?" Kit said once they were on the road.

"What?"

"Truth or dare?"

"You mean like we're playing truth or dare?" James scrubbed a hand over his head. "It'll have to be truth. As a cop, I can't be getting into trouble over dares."

"What is your most embarrassing moment?"

James grunted. "Oh sure, go for the throat." He clicked his tongue while thinking. "I have so many! I just have to pick one?"

"Well you can do two if you want, but that seems like you'd be setting yourself up for mocking by me."

"True." He scratched his chin. "Hmmm . . . my most embarrassing moment . . . had to be when I got caught practicing kissing with the little girl next door. What was her name?" He snapped his fingers. "Oh yeah, Alison . . . Ali."

Kit laughed. "How old were you?"

"Sixteen."

She busted up laughing. "Sixteen?"

"Yeah. It was during a boy-girl party. Everyone else was watching a movie and we hadn't ever kissed anyone before so we thought we'd get a little practice in so we'd know how."

"Your first kiss was practice? You have got to be kidding!"

"Hey, I'm a guy! I was going to take whatever I could get where I could get it."

"Now that's pathetic," she said, composing herself.

"Guys are all pathetic."

"You get no argument here," Kit laughed.

"Okay, so my turn. Truth or dare?"

"Truth."

"I'm going to plagiarize here. What is your most embarrassing moment?" James asked.

"I was in the Marriott Hotel."

"And . . ."

"And Bradley was waiting for me in the lobby. I had just come down from my room when I realized I needed to go to the bathroom. Well, I didn't want to go all the way back up to my room, so I just hurried into the public ones off the main floor there by the lobby." She paused.

"And . . ." James prompted again.

She laughed. "Anyway, I sat down to take care of business when I heard a man's voice."

"Oh no, I see this coming," James chuckled.

"Yeah. I thought, 'Wow, some guy is in the wrong bathroom.' I felt sorry for him for making such a dumb mistake and that was when I heard the second man's voice."

"No!"

"Yep. And from then on I heard a steady stream of new male voices."

"That is great!" James was outright laughing now.

"No, it gets worse. I was wearing a dress with heels so I had to pick my feet up so no one would see my shoes under the stall and stay balanced on the seat so they didn't fall back down."

James slapped the steering wheel as Kit added, "I looked at my watch and waited for them all to clear out so I could leave. My butt was so numb and my legs were tingling from the blood supply being cut off; I thought I was going to die."

"How long were you in there?"

"Twenty-nine minutes. Then finally, I thought the coast was clear, I bolted for the door and ran right smack into some guy coming in. He said, 'I think I'm in the wrong bathroom' and I just bolted past him."

"It hurt so bad that it was hard to walk for the next hour. Bradley was furious. I had made such a dumb mistake and made us late."

"He didn't think it was funny?"

"At the time I didn't think it was either."

Following her instructions, James pulled into a little bridal boutique where Kit's wedding invitations were. "I'll wait here," he said, not wanting to go into the dainty little store with her to pick up invitations to her wedding with someone else.

"Come in with me," she said.

"Aren't you just picking them up?"

"Well, yeah, but they always make me wait."

James' fingers tapped the steering wheel while he thought a second. "Okay." They got out and at the front door, James stepped deliberately in front of her to open it for her.

"Thank you." She gave a little laugh and tucked a stray strand of dark hair behind her ear. "I don't remember the last time someone held the door open for me."

"Aren't you engaged?" The sarcasm was out before he could stop it.

"Well, yes, but . . . Bradley . . ." she shrugged.

James felt heat rise to his face. The last thing he wanted to do was attack Bradley and make Kit feel the need to defend him. He thought about apologizing, but decided to let it go.

The boutique was dominated by a white motif. It almost felt like stepping into an artist's concept of heaven with all the white. Veils trailed from pegs on the wall and silky, glittery white shoes were proudly displayed on shelves.

A woman with a cropped pageboy haircut smiled widely at Kit. James thought the sticky red lipstick on the woman clashed badly with the rest of the store.

"The Armstrong wedding," Kit said, casting a glance at James and lowering her voice.

"Oh, the invitations!" the woman sang out. "They turned out beautifully!" She pulled out a large box with a white silk ribbon band around it and handed it to Kit.

Kit took the box awkwardly. "Thank you," she said, turning to collect James and leave.

"Don't you want to see them? You are the first bride in the whole time I have worked here that hasn't ripped the box open to inspect the invitations."

Kit flushed. "I just . . . don't really have the time right now."

"Are you in a fight with your fiancé?" the woman asked, trying to whisper, but saying it loud enough for James to hear.

"Oh, no. It's nothing like that. It's just that . . ."

The woman had appeared to vault the counter to get to Kit's side. "Here honey, you let me help you." She stomped over to James and took him by the arm. "C'mon, Mr. Armstrong! You really need to come look at these invitations with your bride. They turned out exactly like they were supposed to. I swear they are perfect! You'll just love them!"

She dragged James over to Kit and the invitations. She then pushed him down into an oversized chair and led Kit to the one next to it.

"But I'm not . . ." James tried to speak.

"Oh, of course you are! No groom thinks he's interested, but once you see the finished invitation, it brings the wedding into perspective . . . into reality."

"But . . ." Kit tried as the woman snatched the box out of her hands and slipped off the white ribbon.

"No buts! You two need to see your future together. That's what the invitation is . . ." She set the box on the little oak table by the chairs, and still holding the lid, she spread her arms out, acting benevolent. "The invitation is your inviting people to witness the beginning of your future . . . of your whole lives." She put the lid down and pulled out a hand-torn crème colored paper with roses pressed into the parchment that was folded into the delicate semblance of a card. She held it out to James, who could only blink at her.

"C'mon, take it and get a glimpse into your future with this woman." James took the card.

She pulled out another for Kit. "And can't you just imagine for a moment waking up every day to this man." She flourished a wave in James' direction with the card. "And he sure is handsome!" She handed Kit the card.

Both Kit and James sat in baffled silence. Without looking at the cards, they slowly turned toward each other. "I'll just leave you two alone," the woman said as she breezed away, her feet barely skimming the white plush carpet.

"I changed my mind," James said finally.

"Changed it to what?" Kit asked.

He grinned. "This is my most embarrassing moment."

They both broke into laughter and put the invitations back in the box without looking at them.

"C'mon, honey!" James called loudly, "Let's get these invitations to our future mailed quickly!"

"That's the spirit!" the woman sang out to them.

He grabbed the boxes and hurried out.

"Wow!" James heaved a deep breath. "That was . . . well, interesting."

"Sorry about that."

"Oh, don't be. If I were going to pretend to not be a pathetic bachelor, I can't imagine anyone I'd rather pretend with."

Kit flushed and gave him directions to the dress shop.

"Maybe I should wait this one out," he suggested.

"But I need your opinion."

"On a dress? I don't know anything about dresses! I . . ." He saw her disappointment. "Okay, fine, let's go."

This shop was as white as the other had been, with the

exception of various colored formals along the side wall. The sales lady remembered Kit and clicked away in tall heels to get the gown. Kit soon disappeared into a large white dressing room.

When she re-emerged, James stopped breathing. She looked just as she had when he'd seen her that night. Everything seemed to shimmer in the dress as she moved. Her dark hair bounced lightly over her shoulders, haloed by a white veil that tumbled down her back.

She shrugged shyly. "So . . . what do you think?"

"You . . ." He took a breath to slow the heart that was certain she could hear pounding in his chest. "You look . . . just like you did." The shock was so great; he felt his extremities go numb.

She wrinkled her nose, "Like I did?"

"Beautiful. You look absolutely beautiful, Katherine."

"Do you know the last time anyone said I was beautiful?" she asked, not really expecting an answer.

"Yeah, I know," James said softly. He looked away, afraid his eyes would betray his feelings.

She smiled patiently. "Oh you do, huh?" She fussed with the skirt that rippled like sunlight off of water. "Well, anyway . . . it still fits which is the important thing." She swayed in it, making it swish with the motion. "I suppose I should go change. I'll be right back."

James scrubbed a hand over his head, pacing the floor. *What am I doing here?* he thought. Every minute was torture. He was watching the girl he wanted get prepared to give herself to someone who didn't deserve her.

Kit re-emerged, tucking in her shirt. Her shoes were still untied. She sat in a chair and bent down to start tightening up her shoeslaces.

"Dang it!" she hissed as a lace broke. She held the fringed

piece in her hand glumly. "I really ought to get new shoes." She bent again to unlace it and see if it would work even though it had been shortened. James knelt in front of her. "Let me do that." He took her foot without waiting for agreement and wrapped the lace around his finger then pulled it through. Kit started to giggle at him, but then stopped.

She tilted her head to look at him, kneeling there and babbling about the intricate design of shoelaces. She shook her head but the image that had formed there stayed. The image of James kneeling . . . concentrating, mumbling under his breath; something like a memory. She had that feeling once before. Almost like she should remember having the experience of seeing him like that before.

"There you go. Looks like you're going to be all right now."

She blinked. "What?"

"Your shoelace. It's going to work for a while longer."

"Oh." She looked at her foot still resting on James' bent knee and then back up at him. "Have you ever said that to me before?"

"Your shoelace is working?"

She shook her head again. "No . . . never mind. It's nothing."

James shrugged and gently put her foot down. She sat a moment longer and sighed. "We should be going," she said finally.

"Truth or dare," James offered once back in the car.

"That's my game."

"Don't you know the rules of plagiarism?"

"What rules?"

"The first time you repeat something, you give the original author full credit. The second time, you only have to say I heard it once said and then the third time, you own the statement."

"Is that so?"

"Absolutely. So how 'bout it; truth or dare?"

"Truth."

"What's your most humbling moment?"

"Oh. I'd have to think about that one. Hmmm. Humbling as in I thought I was cool then I did something stupid and realized I was stupid or humbling as in watching someone grow from an experience?"

"You choose your definition," James said.

Kit thought about it a few moments and finally said, "When I was in young women's, I think I was a Mia Maid or something, a girl that lived in our ward but had been inactive her whole life started coming to church. We, that had been going our whole lives, thought we were better in the gospel because we were 'seasoned' and none of us befriended her. She came every week alone and went through all the classes alone. She only had one dress and it was like two sizes too small. One day when she had come into class and the teacher wasn't there, my best friend started in on her one and only dress."

"Whitney?"

"No, another friend. She was being really horrible and I didn't stop her. Anyway, our teacher surprised us with a testimony meeting that Sunday. This girl stood and bore her testimony. She explained that she had decided to kill herself on her 15th birthday and had waited for her parents to go to lunch. She had just placed the pills in front of her when the phone rang. It was our teacher on the phone. Our teacher told her that she knew things were rough and told her she'd be by to pick her up in five minutes. She told her to wear a dress. So the girl put on the only dress she had and came to church. She said as soon as she walked in she knew the gospel was true. She felt loved and peaceful for the first time in her life. She dedicated her life to the Lord at that very moment and that even when others were unkind to her because of her past, she didn't ever plan to fail her Heavenly Father. She started to cry and my friend leaned over to me and whispered, 'It's too bad she has to cry to make me like her.' I realized then that I'd been a sheep following the crowd and that I didn't really like the people I hung out with. I started to be friends with this girl and found that not only was she a great person, but I was who I wanted to be when I was with her. Because of her example, her entire family became active in the church and went to the temple."

"So, where is she now?"

"Whitney is probably home with her kids by now." Kit looked down at her watch.

"Wow! Whitney, huh? Very cool."

"Yup. So what is your most humbling moment?"

"I had a few years of being really self righteous and when I got into the MTC, I tried to live the letter of the law. I kept every rule as it was outlined to us. Well . . . they had this one rule that any songs played on the piano needed to be church related. There was a time that some other district had a meeting with our district for some large group thing. And the other district was gathered around the piano where this one kid from their group was playing the theme music for Charlie Brown. They patted him on the back and told him what a great job he had done at playing the piano and it really ticked me off because we weren't supposed to be playing those songs and it seemed to me like they were encouraging this kid.

"So he finished playing and they all sat down . . . I was going to be the good missionary and so I went and shut the piano lid and gave them all looks like they should be ashamed of themselves for not following the rules," James sighed. "I felt really good about what I had done until the testimonies came and the kid playing the piano got up and bore his testimony—he was mentally handicapped. I felt like the biggest jerk in the whole world. I learned a lot about myself that day."

"Oh, wow. I'll bet."

He pulled into her driveway.

"Would you like to come in?" she said, unbuckling her belt.

James was surprised by the question, glad she asked, but genuinely startled she did. "Sure."

The house was quiet when they entered. "Mom?" Kit called out. "Mo-om! I'm home."

He helped carry in the invitation boxes and set them on the table in the front room.

"In here," a voice called from another room. They followed the sound to an office. Marleah was at the desk. A phone in her hand blared the off-the-hook tone. Marleah was crying.

"Mom, what's wrong? What's happened?" Kit was instantly at her mother's side, pulling the phone gently from Marleah's hand and hanging it up.

"Your grandpa . . . he's lost," she said, her voice cracking.

"Lost? Where lost?"

"I don't know. I just don't know, Katherine!" Marleah was yelling now. Kit didn't appear to notice. She took her mother's hand.

"Ssshh. It's okay. Everything is fine. What happened?"

"He told Tamara, the lady who helps with his medications, that he needed some air." Marleah was rocking back and forth. "He left and never came back."

"How long ago?"

"Four hours ago."

Kit's eyes went wide. "Did he say anything about where he was going? Anything?"

"No. Just that he needed air." Marleah broke into soft sobs. Kit pulled her into a hug and stroked her hair.

"Did you call the police?"

"Yes."

"It's okay. We'll find him. I'll go look for him." Kit pushed up off the desk.

"Can I help?" James added.

"There isn't anything you could do. I'm just going to have to drive around until I find him."

"I could drive. Then you could look without killing yourself."

Kit studied him a moment. "Thank you." She smiled, though her eyes were sagged with worry. "I feel like I'm always saying thank you to you."

James shrugged off the compliment.

Chapter 16

They drove for over an hour until Kit snapped her fingers. "The airport!" she yelled out.

"The airport?"

"Yes, Grandpa used to be a pilot. He loves airplanes. Sometimes when he's forgetful, he talks about them."

James flipped a U-turn and entered the freeway. Kit guided him to an observation area where her grandpa had taken her what seemed like a million times before.

Kit started to unbuckle her seatbelt frantically as James let out a huge sigh of relief at the sight of the lone figure crouching next to a bench chained to a hook in the cement. She jumped out of the car and walked to him carefully. "Grandpa?" The old man didn't reply. "Grandpa?"

James got out, too, in case she needed any help getting the old man back into the car.

"Get down!" he hissed. His hands twisted around each other in a dry washing motion. "We have to wait until they stop the raid." He shuddered and cowered at a plane that was flying overhead to land.

"Grandpa . . . you're home now." She knelt carefully in front of him. "It's me. Do you remember me?" Tears rolled down her cheeks. "It's me, Grandpa, Katherine. Do you know me? It's your sweet pea. Let me take you home now, okay?"

He seemed to consider her offer and then nodded ferociously. "No! If we . . ." He thumped a fist into his forehead to shake loose the words he was looking for. "We . . . we can't leave the foxhole! We'll die! Get down, girl!" He glanced at James. "What were you thinking bringing a girl into a war zone? You fool!"

James didn't know quite what to say to that. He looked to Kit for some clue, but Kit was focusing on her grandfather.

After a few moments of assurances and pleading, it was evident; the old man wasn't going to move. James stepped in closer.

"Look, soldier!" he barked loudly, making Kit jump. "We need to get this young girl back to her family! I can't do it alone. I'll need someone to cover me. You've got to come."

"But they're firing. We were given orders not to leave the foxholes," the gravelly voice insisted.

"Soldier, this girl is in danger. We need to get her out!"

Kit stared slack-jawed at James and then nodded. "Please help me," she said.

The complete clarity in her grandfather's eyes was almost frightening. James had seen the man's mind tumble for words and mumble when his mind finally found them. He hadn't stuttered or stumbled over words since their arrival.

"I'll go," he said. "We'll take her to her parents, then . . ." His face went void. Kit took his hand and led him to the car. He walked with a limp and Kit rested his arm over her shoulders to help him. She got into the back seat with the old man while James drove.

"You're hurt, Grandpa." Kit observed a tear in his pants and tore them further up to the knee so she could get a better look; it was wet with blood and the back of his leg had a jagged cut up it. "What happened?"

He considered the question for a moment. "Not outta here," he said. He had returned to the vague and failing mind. "Hurts, Katherine." He pointed to his leg and back to Kit.

"What did you do?" she asked again.

"Oh, I don't know," he shrugged.

"Where did you go?"

James wasn't sure why Kit bothered to ask. Whatever the old guy knew was locked away in a forgetful mind.

"Be magical where your senses grow," the old man said.

Kit tsked in exasperation. "Always magical, Grandpa. But where did you go? What did you do to your leg?"

"My leg hurts outta here."

"Why does it hurt?"

"Bleeding."

Kit tsked again. "Please, Grandpa."

"I see you, Katherine." He ran a withered hand over her face softly.

"I love you, too." She leaned her head back against the seat and covered her eyes with her hand. James stared at her in the rear view mirror.

"Shouldn't we tell your mom so she can call off the search?" James asked, picking up his cell phone and handing it back to Kit.

"Yes, good idea. Thank you, James; I never would have been able to get him in the car. I'm so grateful you came."

James nodded as Kit dialed her home number and explained to her mom that they had found her grandfather. They talked a few minutes until Kit finally hung up. "Will you take me back to his house? I'll spend the night with him."

"Are you sure?"

"I'm sure. I think he'd be better off with things he's familiar with, in a place he knows well."

"Okay, not a problem."

He helped Kit get her grandfather into the house and settled into his chair while Kit got a washcloth and some first aid supplies to tend to the old man's leg.

"I'm a bother," the old man lamented while Kit was gone.

"No, you're not," James said. "You're fine. You're going to be just fine."

"Outta here, if I could just get . . . dumb." He tapped his fist against his forehead and then looked up at James. "Who are you?"

"I'm Katherine's friend," James answered.

"Oh," he said agreeably, although it was evident he wasn't sure what that meant. After another moment of silence he looked up again. "Who are you?"

James smiled and ignoring the question pulled a book out of the case and opened it up. It was a huge old volume. The leather spine was starting to crumble with age. James opened to the first page and began to read.

"Call me Ishmael. Some years ago—never mind how long precisely—having little or no money in my purse, and nothing particular to interest me on shore, I thought I would sail about a little and see the watery part of the world." James' voice was clear and calm as he read the first chapter of Moby Dick.

Kit's grandfather closed his eyes to listen. At moments he mouthed along to the words he knew, had known most of his life. Kit came back with triple antibiotic ointment and bandages but stopped short when she saw the two of them. She leaned into the doorframe to study the scene in front of her.

It looked right in her eyes; the two of them cozied near Grandpa's bookcase reading together. It felt right to her soul. The doorbell rang. James stopped reading and moved to put the book down. Her grandpa's eyes flew open. She hurried to put down the armful of medical things by James' chair and waved James to sit back down and keep reading. She went to the door as the bell was ringing a second time. It was her mother and father.

"Why didn't you just come in?" Kit asked.

"You had the dead bolt locked," Mom said.

James paused his reading to listen, feeling a bit foolish for being the one who locked the dead bolt when they came in.

"I didn't lock it," Kit said simply, opening it wider to let them in.

"Dad!" Marleah rushed into the room to her father. James had to move in order to keep from being run down by her. "Dad, where did you go?"

"Just outta here . . . nowhere."

"You can't do that! You can't just go whenever you want to!"

James edged closer to the door where Kit and Ryan were still standing.

"I should go now," he whispered to Kit.

"I'll walk you out," she said softly.

Ryan clapped James on the back. "Thanks, son, for all your help."

"It's not a problem."

"It may not be, but it sure is appreciated."

James shrugged uncomfortably. "Goodnight." James and Kit left, letting the screen door close gently behind them.

"Well, thanks again. You have once more ridden up on your stallion as the knight in shining armor to save the day."

"Please, all I've done is hang around."

"Well, your hanging around has been very beneficial."

"Good . . . I'm glad. You know, Kit, I was serious when I said I'd be happy to help you juggle plates. Whenever you feel like you need a break, you could call me. I'd be right over."

"Thanks, but I couldn't turn the plates over to anyone else. I chose them. They are my own making. Now . . . now I just have to live with them."

"Or choose differently."

"What?"

"It is never too late to realize one choice or another was wrong; as long as you don't break any of God's laws, you simply 'choose' a different choice, and not live with mistakes."

"What mistakes do you think I'm making?"

James backed up from her. "I . . . I'm not saying you're making any at all. I just . . . It sounded like you were locking yourself into life. No one should live in a world they merely resigned themselves to."

"I don't feel 'resigned' to my life. I'm happy."

"Truth?"

She smiled. "Is there anything else?"

"You should work with criminals sometime. Believe me, with them there is always something else."

Kit laughed. "Is that discouraging?"

"Yeah, sometimes really bad. It's a delicate balance to keep an eternal perspective on life and do the things you know you should and . . . at the same time stay true to the badge."

"Why is it hard to balance religion with the badge?"

"Oh, you know. I'm around gutter talk and cussing all the time. Sometimes, especially while interrogating, my language is as bad as theirs and it's easy to get . . ." James smiled. "You must think you're my therapist."

"I'd say I'm cheaper than therapy, but with all the gas you've used up in running me all around town, I probably cost more."

James laughed. "Well, I'd better go. Take care of your grandpa." He touched her shoulder. "And take care of yourself, too."

"I will. I know I sound like a broken record, but thanks."

"Never a problem." He winked at her. "Serve and protect, that's what it's all about."

She smiled and watched as he got in the car and drove away. Kit stayed there a moment after James' car had turned down a different street when she realized that she was staring at nothing but empty space.

She went into the house to help her mom get her grandfather settled.

Marleah was sponging down her father's leg as he scowled and harrumphed at her. "Where's the boy?" his scratchy old voice demanded. "The one that was reading to me outta here. Where'd he go?"

"He had to go home," Kit offered.

"Is he coming back here?"

"I think that would be safe to assume," Ryan answered.

"Oh, Daddy, I know he's a nice guy and everything, but I doubt he's going to make this place a regular stop."

"You never know," Ryan shrugged.

"Well, it won't be this place he'll be coming to visit," Marleah said softly. It was then Kit and Ryan noticed that in only a few seconds, the old man had fallen asleep.

"What do you mean?" Kit asked softly.

Marleah looked tired. Kit had never seen her look so old in her entire life. "Mom?"

"He needs constant care, Katherine." Marleah said. "Your father and I discussed it on the way over here. He needs to be in a retirement facility."

Kit felt her cheeks grow hot and puff in outrage. "You're pawning him off to a nursing home?" she almost shouted, but restrained herself so as not to wake her grandfather. "Mother, how could you?"

"Listen, honey," Ryan soothed. "No one can watch him 24 hours a day."

"I can move in with him. I'll watch him," she insisted.

"You know it's more complicated that that. How many times during the day have neighbors called us up and informed us he was in their fridge making himself lunch? You can't watch him 24 hours a day. You have work and all those things you volunteer for. Besides, Kit, I very much doubt Bradley would make a sacrifice like that; and as newlyweds, it would be a mistake to ask him to." Marleah looked as though she were going to cry.

Ryan put an arm around her. "It's for the best," he whispered.

"It feels wrong," Kit was crying now. "Dad, please don't do this."

"It will be the best thing for him. He needs someone all the time. He could've been really hurt out there today. It's just a scratch on the leg now, but what if he fell and broke a hip or got mugged?"

"I understand," Kit said finally after a moment's silence, tears streaming down her face. "I still think it bites though."

Marleah hugged her. "I do, too. It's what my brother and his wife have wanted for a long time. We held out as long as we could."

"I'm still going to stay the night tonight."

"That's fine." Ryan stood up. "We should get him to bed."

It took all three of them to take the man's bulk to his bedroom and settle him in his bed. After her parents left, Kit wandered the tiny house, touching the spines of the books he'd read to her or encouraged her to read on her own. In a back room were several trunks. They'd always been there, stacked one on top of the other and to Kit's recollection, they never had been opened in all these years. He had an entire wall lined with trophies from the cinematography and photography clubs he'd belonged to. In every room there were pictures he'd taken of her mom, her uncle, and her grandmother. Black and white smiles frozen forever in gilded frames.

She touched everything, memorized each item's place in the house and finally curled up on the bed in the spare bedroom for a fitful sleep, awaking every time she heard his sheets rustle, worried he might try leaving again.

Kit finally got up at 6:00 a.m. After staring at the clock click through minutes that felt like years, she realized she was going to lose her mind if she didn't get up. Wandering the house again, she finally decided on making breakfast. She fried up some eggs and pancakes and briefly wished it wasn't Sunday so she could run to the store for some bacon. Grandpa loved bacon.

"What's all this?" the old voice rasped as he limped into the kitchen.

"Breakfast." She planted a kiss on his cheek.

"You didn't have to do here," he tried to argue.

"It's already done. Go sit down and we'll eat."

He shrugged and sat down at the table.

She brought over the fry pan to serve him when Gary came in.

"Oh cool! Breakfast! Thanks, Kit, I'm starved!"

"Like that's anything new," she observed dryly.

Gary sat down at the table. "Hey Katy-did, will you get me a plate?"

Kit sniffed at him, but pulled one out of the cupboard for him. "And a fork," he said as she put his plate on the table.

"Gary!"

"Please?"

"Oh! Fine!" She tossed the fork onto his plate.

"Thanks." Gary grinned, helping himself to the pancakes and syrup already set out. "Hey Grandpa! How you doing?"

Grandpa watched Gary load his plate up with pancakes and then drown them in syrup. "Fine . . . fine. Leg hurts, though. Don't know . . ."

"Yeah, Mom said you got hurt."

"What are you doing here?" Kit asked, trying to find a place on his plate not swimming in syrup to put an egg on.

"Mom said you might want some company, or a break. So, I'm your relief."

"Some relief," Kit muttered. "Now I have to make more pancakes."

"Cool, I'm still hungry."

"Gary!"

"Just kidding, sis."

She sat next to him and lowered her tone as she eyed her grandfather pushing the egg around in a pool of butter he'd melted there. "So did Mom tell you?" she asked quietly.

Gary cut a glance to their grandpa and back to his plate. "Yeah, she told me."

"How do you feel about that?"

"I think it sucks."

Grandpa shot a look at Gary. "Sorry, Grandpa, I meant to say, I think it stinks." The old man nodded and put a bite of pancake in his mouth.

"We'll talk about it later," Kit suggested.

After breakfast, they went into the living room. The old man fell asleep quickly and easily. "So where do you think they'll take him?" Gary asked finally.

"I don't know, but Mom wanted it done quickly. You know her. She makes a decision and it had better be done. She'll want this place packed up and moved by the end of this week."

Gary laughed. "You'd think she had enough to do with the wedding without taking on a project like this."

Kit sent him a withering look. "Don't for a moment imagine that this is her project. It will belong to all of us. There's so much to do, even that won't be enough."

They both fell quiet listening to the soft raspy snores hissing from the old man. "How do you think he'll take it?" Kit asked.

"I think he'll take it like a war zone. I worry he's going to feel like we've attacked him and hold us accountable for that."

"I agree." Kit sat up in her chair and scowled at Gary. "Why aren't you in church?"

"I went to Sacrament Meeting, but Mom said you needed help, so I skipped the other meetings. Why aren't you?" he mimicked back to her.

"Well, since you're here, I could still catch Whitney's ward. They start at 1:00 p.m."

"Then you better get out of here and get ready."

Kit stood up. "Okay," she hesitated. "Don't take any naps, Gary. It only takes him a second to disappear."

"I think I can handle it," he said dryly.

Chapter 17

"How about joining us for dinner?" Whitney asked as they filed out of the Relief Society room.

"I would love that," Kit accepted.

After dinner, Whitney's husband did the dishes so that Whitney could nurse the baby. Kit sprawled out on the plush floor of the nursery while Whitney rocked in the rocking chair.

"How was California?" she asked quietly.

"Oh, it was okay."

"Gary said you came home early. What happened?"

"Why does everyone assume something had to happen?"

Whitney sent a withering look. "C'mon Kit, it's me. Tell me what happened."

Kit blinked back tears. "I don't know, I just . . ." She sat up and wrapped her arms around her legs. "Whit, they make me feel so dumb all the time."

"How can anyone make *you* feel dumb?"

"Well, I *know* I'm *not* dumb, but his mother . . . I just feel like an infant when I'm around her. And all those horrible people they hang with . . . and she put me in a purple dress!"

Whitney snorted out a laugh. "What? She dressed you like a doll or something? Why do you let her do that to you?"

"I don't know." Kit smiled thinly. "You know that song they play on the radio at Christmas time—'The 12 Pains of Christmas'? The part where the woman says 'facing my in-laws' and then later says, 'she's a witch . . . I hate her!' I'll tell you, Whit, that is exactly how I feel."

After a moment of Whitney considering Kit, she licked her lips nervously. "Kit, I don't want to be the devil's advocate or anything, but why don't you just . . . walk away?"

"Bradley wouldn't ever sever ties with his parents and I could never ask him to do that."

Whitney sighed. "I don't mean like that. I mean . . . and I'm honestly not trying to cast doubt here, but . . . Why, Kit? Why would you marry him? You are too brilliant to be treated like some trophy, won by an undeserving snob." Whitney blew out a long breath after finally spitting out the words she'd been holding in for the previous six months.

"He doesn't treat me like that," Kit insisted although, even to her own ears, it rang false. "He just has a different way of showing his affection is all."

"It's just . . .the guy is so stuffy, a nose with a cold suffers in comparison!"

"Very funny, Whitney."

"Kit, I'm not trying to burst your bubble, but it looks to me like someone beat me to it. You look deflated, and it isn't just me that has noticed. Gary says it, too."

Kit waved a hand in dismissal. "Oh, Gary. He just says that because he doesn't like Bradley."

"And maybe that is it with him; you're just worth too much to be demoted to some business tycoon's hood ornament."

Kit looked away, picking at frays in the carpet. "It isn't like that."

Whitney sighed. She backed off. Making Kit defensive would just make her more resolute in her decision. She decided to try another angle. "What is the deal with the cop?"

"James?" Kit smiled at just saying his name. "What do you mean what's with him?"

"He's absolutely adorable!" Whitney exclaimed.

"You've said that already."

"Well, it's true. If I were single . . . I'd ask him out; I'd even pay for the dinner."

"He is nice to look at," Kit conceded. "And he wears a pair of jeans right, if you know what I mean." She grinned.

"I'll bet he looks great in a uniform. Mmm-mmm. Adorable."

"And he doesn't call me Kitty." Kit leaned back onto her haunches and stared at the ceiling. "I'm so confused."

"Over what?"

"James."

"Really?" She drawled out the word with the anticipation of juicy gossip. "Tell me."

"Tell you what? He's a knight from a fairy tale; always there to come to the rescue. He's adorable, as you so delicately put it. He's well spoken, kind hearted, generous . . ." Kit trailed off, staring absently at the ceiling. "He read Moby Dick to Grandpa . . ." The image of him kneeling again flashed in her mind. Startled, she straightened up.

"What's the matter?" Whitney asked.

"I just . . . get this feeling like I've seen him before somewhere," Kit shrugged with a laugh.

"I've heard your voice somewhere before . . ." Whitney sang the tune from *Saturday's Warrior*. Kit rolled her eyes. "It seems we've talked like this before . . ."

"Oh stop. I'm serious. He's just . . . he's something different from everyone else I've ever met."

"You've got feelings for him," Whitney declared.

"No . . . No . . . No! Not like that."

"Ya, uh-huh."

"I'm engaged."

"It's easier to break up an engagement than an eternal marriage."

"No one's talking about breaking up anything. Please, Whitney, I can't think like that."

"But you already think like that or you wouldn't have brought it up."

"I didn't bring it up—you did; and don't look at me like that. I'm not in denial."

"Look like what? I'm just looking."

"Bradley will give me a very good life," Kit insisted.

Whitney stared levelly at Kit. "Is that why you're marrying him? To give you a good life?"

"No, we have so much in common; we have common goals and . . ."

Whitney interrupted, not really wanted to hear any more. "Just do me a favor, Kit. Don't give up the great life for a good life."

Kit looked away. "I won't, I promise."

Whitney nodded, not certain at all that Kit was making a promise she was able to keep.

Chapter 18

"You are navel lint," James proclaimed to Allen as they set the table for Cindy.

"You're a scabby toenail," Allen shot back.

"You both are freaks," Cindy interjected in the middle of their insult war.

"Takes one to know us," James grinned.

"How are things going with the dead girl?"

"Oh, you know. I'm in love with her, she's engaged to the biggest creep I've ever met. The usual horrible story of my life."

"Is he a bigger creep than Damon?"

"Mountains bigger."

"Wow! You should bust 'em up."

"Oh yeah. Great plan. She's marrying a guy who can afford to buy his own country and I'm a cop."

"So what are you going to do?"

"Grow old and bitter, buy a dog and buy him a wife so I can take joy in his posterity." James gave a half smile.

"That's the beauty of dogs. You can buy them a companion and they aren't usually too picky about it."

"Cindy wasn't all that picky," Allen said.

James snorted. "That's for darn sure."

"Why don't you tell her how you feel?" Cindy put the shepherd's pie on the table and sat.

The boys sat too. "I can't tell her. How would that look?"

"It would look like a very sincere man was telling a woman how he felt before it was too late to tell her."

"But she's engaged. When someone builds a ten foot wall around them, it isn't so you can go get a ten foot ladder to climb over it."

"Maybe, but every wall has a gate; and you'll never get in by staring at the wall. Go knock on the gate." Cindy grabbed James' face to make him look at her. "Tell her, James."

"I . . . I'll try, Cin-ful."

"Great." Allen folded his arms. "Can we bless this before you two get off on more analogies?"

James sighed and folded his arms. With his head bowed, he sent up a weak prayer of his own. "Help."

Chapter 19

James scrubbed a hand over his head while waiting for Jeff to give a ticket. Sergeant Allred put him with a partner for his first day out in case he wasn't as ready as he thought he was. It was annoying to be babysat, but when they pulled over the first car, James nearly had a panic attack. The uniform was his, but felt wrong on his body. It almost felt stifling, like a strait jacket.

And he felt like he might be going a little crazy; when Jeff made him handle a call for a domestic disturbance, he felt his pulse rise dramatically as the sound of blood rushed past his ears. Sweaty hands dropped his clipboard twice as he listened to the woman as she sobbed and pointed towards the bedroom where Jeff had taken her husband.

The woman's right eye was swollen and purple. Her side had the red and purpling bruises of a steel-toed boot being kicked into it. James nearly vomited at the sight of her, and then admonished himself for his weakness. He'd seen it all before and worse when he'd worked in detectives. Why was it bothering him so much now?

She didn't want her husband arrested. She hadn't put the call into 911, but a concerned neighbor had. She had screamed when Jeff pulled her husband away from her to arrest him. "Don't hurt him! Don't arrest him! It was my fault! Please! Please don't!"

Jeff hadn't released the man and really had no intentions of doing so. Instead he asked him (without really giving him a choice) to go into the back room and discuss things. Mr. Rees didn't struggle. He just ducked his chin into his tank top that had yellowed stains under the armpits from sweat.

His wife lamented over what they may be saying, what they were doing. Why was it taking them so long?

"He's a good man," she insisted, nodding furiously. "I was stupid. I'm dumb like that. I do stupid things that make him mad. He's a good man. Please just go away. You don't understand." She took a deep breath; her shoulders shuddered with the tail end of a sob.

"I do understand, Mrs. Rees. I do understand. What I understand is that you are a good woman and no one has the right to hurt you. No one, not even your husband; not anyone has the right to touch you like that."

"He isn't bad, officer," she tried to reaffirm. "He's good . . . a good man."

"He should really consider counseling for anger management. It is wrong for him to hurt you." This statement only elicited another round of her rambling over his goodness. James wanted to pick her up and throw her in the back of his car and drive her to a safe house that would reprogram her thinking.

When Jeff came back out, Mr. Rees was in cuffs.

"No!" his wife shouted worriedly. The fear of retaliation blazed in her eyes. "You can't take him! It was my fault! Please, oh please!" She fell against James' leg, sobbing, keeping him from walking.

"He needs to get help. He can't keep hurting you like that." James bent down slowly and lifted her up. He reached out to touch her softly on the face. She flinched away. "No one has the right to blacken your eye like that," James said. He wanted to just hold her and cry with her.

Jeff let loose a string of swear words when they were outside and Mr. Rees was in the car. James agreed wholeheartedly.

The neighbor came running over in a loud flowered housecoat and flip flop sandals that made a sucking sound as the plastic left her heel. "Where is he?" she demanded. "Where is that demon? Why aren't you arresting him?"

"We are arresting him," Jeff said. "He's in the car."

She glared at the car with contempt. "Good. Not that it matters. She won't testify and the judge will let him go and then he will come back and kill her. You hear me. If they don't keep him locked up forever, he is going to kill her."

James held his stomach. He could taste bile on his tongue. It was Jeff that responded. "We arrested him. It isn't up to us to keep him in jail. It is up to the judges. We've done what we can and there's nothing more we can do."

"So what? You wait till that monster kills her? I hear her scream! I hear her crying all day and night! And you walk away and say there's nothing you can do! You could take that pretty gun you've got and put a bullet in the head of that monster! He'll kill her!"

They continued to their car under her verbal attack. "He'll kill her and it will be your fault for not shooting him when you had the chance!" she cried as they shut their doors and drove away.

James looked out his window. "He will kill her, you know," he said quietly.

Jeff ground his teeth before answering, "I know." He shot a look into the back where Mr. Rees sat sullenly. He would kill her one day, but it wouldn't ever be James' fault. He had made that conclusion years before. He had no control over the testimony of a battered spouse. If she couldn't tell the truth when she got to the stand, there was nothing more he could do except arrest the guy the next time he hit her. The choice remained hers and even if he was sick over it, he had no control over the free agency of another person.

They stayed silent while they drove after dropping Mr. Rees off, neither saying the things that they were shouting at themselves in their minds. It wasn't long after when a red Mustang breezed through a red light and Jeff flipped on the overheads. "Do you want to take it?" he asked James.

"No. Go ahead." And that was where James felt panic. Panic from waiting, from the maddening click click of the overheads flashing furiously above him. Panic from the look of the vehicle Jeff had pulled over, a '78 Mustang; old, misused and with a decidedly gang related look.

When Jeff got done issuing the ticket and they were back on the road, Jeff cast a sideways glance at James. "Are you okay?"

"Yeah, fine. Like riding a horse," James tried at a smile.

"You know, Hartman, the guys all respect you for what you did. You did the right thing, the only thing that could be done. You are a hero in our eyes. I just wanted you to know it."

"Thanks, Jeff. That means a lot to me."

Once home, he ran the water in the sink while staring at his reflection in the mirror. James felt like throwing up. He hadn't eaten anything and felt like it was doubtful he would ever want to again. The little dinner left in his fridge by his mom stayed in its storage container. He played the piano for a few minutes, but didn't feel his heart in it. He rested his forehead against the keys causing a light plinking of notes.

The phone rang. He turned his head plinking more keys to look at the phone, letting it ring twice more before deciding to pick it up. "Hello?"

"Hi, James."

He sat up instantly. "Kit?"

"Yeah, it's me."

"What's up?"

"Nothing, I just . . . wanted to call and say hi."

James smiled. "How'd you get my phone number?"

"Your brother, Brian, was at your mom's last night. He answered when I called and gave me your number."

"He isn't supposed to be handing that out; but I'm glad he gave it to you," James added quickly.

"Why is your phone number unlisted?"

"I got some death threats; these guys really wanted me gone for being the guy who put their brother in jail. So I changed my number. I'm not paranoid . . . I promise."

She laughed. James' heart rate increased at the sound. "I'm not thinking you're paranoid."

"Good."

"I have something of yours. I was wondering if I could bring it by."

"What have you got?"

"You'll see when I get there," she teased.

He closed his eyes, breathing in the sound of her voice. He gave the address and hung up. He looked around suddenly. "Oh, no!" he hissed. He hadn't bothered cleaning in the last few days. Dishes were piled in the sink and he had clothes left on the couch that he'd meant to fold earlier, but hadn't gotten around to. He hurried and pushed the clothes back into the laundry basket. He threw it into the laundry room and shut the door. He started unloading the dishwasher when a glass dropped onto the floor, the broken shards and splinters spraying everywhere. He cursed and fell to his knees to pick up the bigger pieces.

James pulled a garbage can from under the sink behind him along with a dustpan and a hand broom. Losing his balance, he caught himself by slamming a palm flat into a pile of shards. Another curse flew from his mouth along with a loud "ouch!" Upon inspecting his hand, he found there were two slivers poking into his palm along with a tiny slice near his wrist. He cursed once more for emphasis as the doorbell rang.

He got up cradling his hand to get the door. His breath caught when he saw her. "Hey."

"Hey!" She smiled, swinging an umbrella in her hand.

"How did you get that?" James asked.

"Your dad must've left it when I was in the hospital."

"Oh, that's right. It was raining that night."

A flash of rain-soaked roads reflecting light from everywhere seared through her memory like a streak of lightning. She shivered and then widened her eyes in surprise. "You're bleeding!"

"What?" He looked down noticing the blood trail from his palm down to his elbow and dripping onto the stone entryway.

"Oh, my word." He tried to catch the drips in his other hand by cupping it under his elbow. "Blast! Here, come in."

"What happened?" she asked, following him to the kitchen.

"I was doing dishes and dropped a glass. I got cut when I was picking up the pieces."

"You clean this up," she pointed to his hand. "I'll catch the glass on the floor."

"Be careful," he admonished.

"You mean like you?" she grinned. "Hey, I'm just teasing."

"I know."

"You see, the trick to picking up glass is a wet paper towel," she explained, tearing off a few towels from the roll and running the wad briefly under the faucet. She swept the bigger pieces up with the hand broom and dustpan and dumped the contents into the trashcan. She then wiped up all the little slivers with the wet paper towel and dumped that in the trash as James wrapped his hand in a dishtowel.

"So truth or dare?"

James grinned. "Truth."

"Are you always clumsy in the kitchen?"

He laughed. "No, I was just trying to hurry to get the dishes done."

"Why? Because I was coming over?"

He flushed at her teasing. "Probably."

"What, you afraid I might find out you eat off of dishes?"

"Yeah, I guess it's a little silly." James scrubbed a hand over his head.

"Naw, I do it all the time. I just think it's fun you do too."

His insides were melting down and puddling in his shoes. How she could humiliate him and then reassure him was amazing. His desire to reach over and hug her was intense. He pulled the towel off his hand. "I got a sliver," he shrugged. "I'll be right back."

He went to the bathroom to pull the tweezers out of his first aid kit. She had followed him. "Need help?"

"I think I'll be okay." He smiled, squinting to see the glint of glass in his palm. After a few minutes of trying, she finally took the tweezers from him.

In resignation, he held his palm out for her, trying not to shiver as she ran a finger over his hand. She delicately held his hand in hers and pulled the sliver free of his palm. When Kit didn't let go of his hand right away, he felt himself leaning in closer. He felt her lean in slightly too, and his eyes closed briefly imagining . . .

She abruptly pulled away. "You . . . ummm . . . have a piano." She turned her head away from him.

James inhaled deeply. "Yes, I do."

"Do you play?" she asked as she put a bandage on his hand.

"Heck no, it just looks nice sitting there; came with the house." He grinned. "Yeah, I play."

"Play me something." She stood up.

Following her to the living room, he wondered if she felt her nerve endings tingling like his were. *I'm an idiot,* James thought. *Bona fide, complete idiot.*

She stood next to the piano and waited for him to play. He sat and started in at the eighteenth variation of the piece in front of him. He knew it by heart and was able to look over at her standing there watching his fingers fly over the keys.

"Bravo!" She clapped her hands like an excited child. "That

was wonderful! You play beautifully!"

"Thanks." He hesitated. "Want to hear something I wrote?"

"Of course. Play me a song; you're the piano man."

With a half smile, he placed his fingers on the keyboard. With her standing right there, it was like a floodgate of emotion opened into his soul as he played.

Her smile slowly thinned to something he couldn't read. He finished and didn't look up. She sat next to him on the piano bench and placed a hand gently over his. Biting the side of his cheek, he could only look at their hands now linked by touch.

"James?" Kit's wonderfully clear voice said his name.

"Yes?" He turned his head finally, enough to look at her.

"That was the most beautiful thing I've ever heard. It was like it spoke to my soul."

"It was meant to speak to your soul."

She smiled, not knowing he meant her soul specifically. "Well then, it does as it should. Will you play it again?"

He nodded, relieved and grateful she liked it enough to hear it again. When he finished the second time, she stared at him. "This may sound strange to you . . . it certainly does to me. When I hear that song, it's like touching a memory; not embracing the memory but more like brushing up against it from time to time." She hesitated. "What is it titled?"

He considered this a moment, thinking of the loves of people he know; people whose love was more eternal than stars in a nighttime sky. He wanted to have what they had. "Loved Like That," he said finally.

Their eyes locked. "Loved Like That," she repeated. "What does that mean to you?"

"It means someday, I want to be loved like my parents love each other, like my grandparents loved each other. Someday." He gave a self-depreciative laugh. "I hate that word."

"I understand exactly what you mean. Someday is the abyss

of not today. When you're 14, it's someday you'll get your braces off. When you're 16, it's someday you'll be asked to Prom. When you're 18, it's someday you'll get those wonderful feelings and get married."

James tilted his head to the side. "Well, from seeing your perfect straight teeth free of wire, you got the braces off. Did you go to Prom ever?"

"Yep. My senior year."

"No more braces, you went to Prom and now you're getting married, so you've probably got those wonderful feelings."

She leaned in slightly. "I do have those feelings . . . I just—I should be going now." She stood quickly.

He closed the lid to the piano and stood too. He felt like he'd been denied something and it made him a little angry. He walked her to the door. "So I guess I'll see you around then."

"Of course, you've become such a good friend, I'm certain we'll be keeping in touch."

"Yeah, of course."

"Well . . . then I should be going. Bye, James."

"Goodbye, Katherine."

She hesitated another moment before leaving. "Bye then."

James shook his head watching her walk away. He went back to the piano, but he still felt angry. Angry for having all these feelings. Angry she was engaged. Angry he didn't have the guts to tell her how he felt like Cindy had told him to. Big strong cop . . . the biggest coward in the world. He should have told her. His fingers pounded to Rachmaninov's piano concerto #2 and finally he slammed his hand down on the keys and smacked the lid down.

Why am I angry? he thought. *Why?* She was engaged! *How wrong is it for me to be angry that her feelings aren't the same as mine?* He picked up a book to throw it and saw he held the Book of Mormon in his hands. Instead of throwing it, he opened it and began reading.

Chapter 20

"Kit! Phone!" Gary called down the hallway. She had just got home from work and was changing into jeans.

"Who is it?"

"The old Bean Pole!" Gary mocked an accent.

"Oh." She bit back the disappointment and went out to get the phone while doing up the last button on her pants.

"Hello?"

"Hello, Kitty darling. How've you been?"

"Fine, Bradley. How was the party?" She wanted to yell at him for not calling sooner to apologize but realized she was grateful he hadn't.

"Kitty, you shouldn't have left. We've only a short time until the wedding and we should really have taken that time to celebrate with my family."

"You mean your mother and her friends."

"Don't be like that, Kitty. She did it all for you."

"Sure she did. So how did your dad's trip go?" She changed the subject, not wanting to fight.

"Oh, perfect! It went absolutely perfect. This is going to make our company among the strongest in the industry."

"Good for you!"

"No. It's good for us. You'll be able to quit your job."

"Why would I do that?"

"Kitty, how would it look if I had my wife working?"

"It would look like you married an intelligent, modern woman with high ideals."

"Be serious."

"I am. I mean naturally, I wouldn't work after we had kids, but before children . . . I'd be bored all day without my job."

"Darling, I need to go; we'll discuss this later."

"Fine," Kit said flatly.

"Bye."

"Bye." She sat down at the table and stared glumly at the phone. "Welcome back," she whispered bitterly.

Chapter 21

Sergeant Allred finally decided James was ready after a week of being baby-sat by Jeff, and moved him to a graveyard shift by himself. James assured him he could handle it ten times when he was in the office and ten more while Steve followed him to his desk.

"Look, Sarge, I really am better, good as absolute new. I can shoot a gun without flinching, a day on the range has proven my skills are better than ever and . . . and I didn't succumb to eating donuts when I was depressed."

Sergeant Allred laughed. "Wish I could say that." He patted his belly. "Okay fine, James, you think you're good. I'm okay with you getting back into work. But if you have any problems or situations, then I expect you to call in and get back up."

"I will, but I won't need to. I am fine."

"Okay. Well then get going." He turned to leave.

"Hey, Sarge, got you a present. I heard your wife is trying to make you eat soy burgers and drink only water. Thought you could use a pick-me-up." James tossed him a Diet Coke.

"Thanks, Hartman. You have no idea how much I need this." Sergeant Allred held it to his forehead and walked away.

James' legs did feel a little shaky going out to his car, but once inside and driving, he felt relief. He was definitely better. The shift went well. He gave out tickets, went to a burglary and checked on a few reports of prowlers; one which turned up nothing and the other which turned out to be the teenage daughter's boyfriend who was trying to sneak out.

The next evening before work, his mom had invited James and Brian with his family over for an early dinner. Annette whispered, "I figured out why some animals eat their young." She pointed at Brett who was mimicking everything Brianna said. To her credit, Brianna was trying to ignore him, but he seemed to pop up everywhere she went. She finally punched him hard in the arm to which he popped her right back.

"Hey, guys!" Annette sent the warning.

They stopped punching and mimicking and went straight to glaring.

They were dishing up their plates when Brian looked up. "So how are things going with the dead girl?"

"I don't know how things are going. We get along great, but I haven't seen her for a week." James took a bite of food and chewed thoughtfully. "This is crazy, though. I was with Jeff the other day and while we were patrolling a neighborhood, a kid fell off his bike. We stopped to help him out and Jeff said, 'Did you get the kit?' And I thought he was talking about her and started lamenting like a Shakespeare tragedy, about how unfair my life was when he stopped me and said, 'Hartman, focus! I meant the first aid kit!'" James closed his eyes and rubbed his temples. "I feel so stupid for making such a dumb mistake."

"It's not stupid. You are just in love with someone who has overridden your ability to think about anything else."

"Yeah, it's really stupid," James said.

Brian laughed at him. "Why don't you go see her? It's been a little while and after having had that bit of distance, you can see if she's as perfect as you remember her to be."

"Of course she's still perfect."

"Then go see her. What would that hurt?"

"Okay, I will tomorrow before work. I'm pulling a grave shift."

"How's work going?" Caroline asked.

"Great, Ma. Things are better than I imagined." James hurried to take a bite of the chicken enchilada before he was asked any more questions.

I can't do this, he thought to himself while looking in the mirror the next day. He had spent the morning mowing the lawn and weeding the flower garden. He smelled like clipped lawn and gas fumes when he was done, and decided he'd better shower before going to see Kit.

While showering, he talked himself out of going to see her three times and was working on talking himself out of it a fourth while shaving. He wanted to forget it and just go into work early. Overtime was available and the money would be good in helping him reach his goal to pay off the house.

"Look," he told his image in the mirror, "if you go, you are going to get your heart broken because she is only two weeks from belonging to someone else."

That was something to think about while putting on his deodorant. "But . . .," he continued, finishing up, "if you don't go and get your heart broken, you'll never have that closure and you'll spend the rest of your life pining for a chance you didn't take when you had it."

He nodded at himself. "That makes sense." He sighed in frustration. "I'm talking to a mirror . . . I'm losing it."

Kit got up early Friday morning to find the house empty. After foraging through the fridge, she finally found a yogurt Gary had hidden in the back. She popped off the top and sprinkled Grape Nuts into it. Sitting on a kitchen barstool, she ate Gary's yogurt. The phone rang, nearly knocking her out of her chair from being startled.

"Hello?"

"Katherine." It was her mom and being called Katherine meant something was wrong.

"What's the matter, Mom?"

"I need you to finish packing up Grandpa's house."

"Finish??"

"The house needs to be cleaned up by next Friday. Your wedding is in two weeks. What other time is there aside from today?"

"What about everyone else?"

"Gary and your dad are working on a foundation today. It had to be done. I'm settling your grandfather into his new house. I can't just leave him here alone."

"His new home?" Kit replied bitterly. "Why don't you say room? He has been downsized to a room, Mom."

"Kit . . ." The tired age in Marleah's voice was pleading. "Please don't. You know I'm as against this as you are." Her mother's voice cracked. Kit instantly felt bad. "I know, Mom. I'm sorry."

"I can't leave him alone. I just . . . please help with the house."

"I will. I'll go over right after work. I get off at noon today since it's Friday." Kit stood while scooping the remnants of yogurt into her mouth and hurried off to work.

Once work was done and she had arrived at her grandfather's, she had a panic attack and a meltdown in the first five minutes. Half-filled boxes were everywhere. Food was still in the fridge and freezer as well as the cupboards and pantry. Pictures were pulled off the wall, but only left on the floor once taken down.

Everything was done haphazardly and only halfway. The size of the task was so overwhelming she could only think to cry for a few minutes before steeling herself against the task.

She truly wondered if she was losing a grip on reality. Kit

felt like the world weighed on her shoulders and no one was in sight to ease the load.

With Gary and her dad working and her mom at the hospital, there would be no cavalry to pull her out of the mess she was now standing in.

Chapter 22

James pulled up to their house at the same time Gary did. "Hey there, Gary!" he greeted him, genuinely happy to see him there. "Where's Kit?"

"Dad mentioned she was going to pack up Grandpa's house. She's probably there."

James followed Gary inside. "Pack up?"

"Oh, you didn't know?"

"Know what?"

Gary clenched his fists, his face hardening. "They are putting my grandpa in . . . a home."

"Why?"

"Because he wandered off the other night and got hurt and because of all the other times he wandered off and neighbors found him . . . . So . . . now they're locking him away."

"I'm so sorry to hear that. I'll bet Kit is devastated."

Gary shrugged. "She should be. She was told she had to pack up the house and she's stuck doing it alone."

James looked at Gary with an eyebrow raised. Gary frowned. "Now, don't go looking at me like that! I have to help my dad. I just came home to get some drinks to fill the cooler and then I have to go right back."

"She has to pack the entire house up?"

"My parents started some of it the other day, but essentially . . . yes. The realtor wants it done soon so she can sell it and with Kit's wedding and everything—"

"Kit shouldn't have to worry about this too with the

wedding and everything," James cut in.

Gary looked down. "I know, but there isn't anybody else."

"Hey thanks, Gary. I gotta go."

"James?"

"Yeah?"

"Thanks."

"For what?"

Gary hesitated not sure if he should say what he was thinking. "For going to do what you're going to do. For . . . well, for being her friend."

James smiled. "I should be thanking her. She has made a huge difference in my life."

Gary grinned. "Yeah, well, we're all hoping you'll do the same for her."

James laughed. "I'm not sure how to take that."

"Take it and run with it, but don't tell her I said it."

James shook his head. "I'll see you later, Gary."

"Bye, James."

Kit was in the back room with the trunks. She had opened each one and cried over the contents. In the top trunk were all her grandfather's belongings from World War II. Drilled out German hand grenades, letters from his parents sent while he was away, uniforms, medals, guns, and a journal. The journal had a page marked by his dog tags. The spine of the book was permanently creased by the thickness of the chain left there all these years. When she picked it up, she could almost taste the sulfur of gunfire and hear the screams of sirens indicating another raid and the whine of bombs falling from the sky and exploding once they hit the ground.

Kit ran the metal chain of the tags through her fingers, the tags tinkling as they clinked into each other. She shivered. Her grandfather, as dementia slowly took over him, had been visiting this part of his past frequently. The things that happened there permanently seared into his clouded mind.

When he got like that, he said things that scared Kit, things that made her want to weep. She read the page the dog tags marked in the journal.

December 18, 1942.

It's freezing today. It's freezing every day. I haven't felt my feet for so long, I wonder at them when I look down to see they are still there. Henderson is sick. I think he's dying. Everybody else does too, but they don't admit it. His cough gets worse by the minute. I wish I could either die or go home. The limbo of in between is eating at my mind. I met a German family a week ago. They are LDS. I think it was the first time I saw Germans as people. Just people. How many have I killed? How many have tried to kill me? I don't care. Sam played his harmonica last night. He played "She'll be comin round the mountain." Joe and Thompson sang along. I didn't. Am I so dead inside, I can't sing? I still can't get over Walter being gone. I wonder if his wife got the telegram yet. If I get home, I'm going to see her. I'll tell her he talked about her every minute. I'll tell her he was a swell friend. Maybe I won't get to see her. Maybe I'll see him instead. Either way I won't be here in snow and frozen earth. What is God thinking? I wish Henderson would stop coughing. The noise is so horrible it makes me want to cough too. I'm going to try to write more often. Maybe, if I write down everything, it'll take it out of my head and I won't have to remember if I get home.

Kit clutched the tags into her fist as she sobbed. Forgetting was the one thing he couldn't do . . . even now.

"Hello?"

Kit looked up, startled. Someone was in the house. She tried to stand to see who it was, but she had piles of books and military papers resting on her lap. She finally cleared it all to the side when James came in.

"Hello? Is anyone here?" His eyes fell on her and he smiled. "Oh, there you are." Upon seeing her, his smile faded. "What's wrong?" He sidestepped the debris stuck all over the room to reach her. "Why are you crying?"

She held up the journal and the dog tags and then shot a quick survey around the room. "They're putting him in a home," she finally said, breaking into more sobs. She fell into his arms, burying her face into the soft cotton T-shirt he was wearing.

James blinked in surprise, but carefully wrapped his arms around her as she shook softly from crying. He smoothed a hand over her dark hair. "Hey, it's okay."

"I have to get everything packed away and I just . . . I just can't! I can't! I don't even know where to begin." She lifted her face to look at him. "Where do I begin?"

James took a quick inventory of the room and smiled as he swept a finger over her cheek to wipe away the tears. "Start at the beginning . . . and when you get to the end—stop."

Kit blinked. "Lewis Carroll."

James laughed. "No, I got that from *Alice in Wonderland* . . . Disney. Brianna watched it a million times when she was little and I used to baby sit a lot."

Kit smiled. "Lewis Carroll wrote Alice in Wonderland."

"Oh. Really? Well, it's good advice for anyone no matter who said it. And it just so happens . . . I have excellent organizational skills. I know that's hard to believe when you've seen my house, but it's true. I'll help you."

He pulled away and picked up a box. "Organization is key. All like items together." He started boxing up things in the desk; desk supplies of tape, pens, sticky pads, and pushpins went into the box. He had the entire desk cleared, boxed and labeled in less than five minutes. Kit just watched.

He sighed, turning to her. "It's going to be okay. It really is."

She continued to just stare at him and finally nodded with a quick shrug. "I believe you." She picked up a long leather scabbard lying beside the trunk she'd emptied. From it she pulled a silver sword. Kit then pulled the blade free of a silver sheath, metal grinding on metal.

The blade had elaborate filigree work on it and her grandfather's name etched into one side along with the letters U.S. On the other side was the military seal of the army. She held the blade tip to his throat.

"Truth or Dare?" she said.

James swallowed, his Adam's apple brushing the blade tip. "Uh, Kit . . . You should never point a sword at someone unless you intend to impale them."

"Truth or dare?" she asked again.

"Truth." James wondered briefly if Kit might not be unhinged just a little bit.

"How many times have you been in love?"

"I can't really say."

"Tell me or I will run you through." She giggled and let the blade drop. "I have always wanted to say that."

"Glad to be of use to you." James breathed touching his Adam's apple to check for stray blood. "Would you point a blade at Bradley?"

She paused sheathing the blade back into the scabbard. "Probably not."

"Why not?"

She gave a little laugh. "Sometimes it would be too tempting to follow through."

James laughed. “Then I’d have to write you a ticket.”

“Just a ticket?”

“Well it was justifiable. A ticket, pay a fine, and free to go to dinner.”

“Ha! I think not. You go to Hell for killing people.” Her face went white. “I am so sorry! I only meant . . . I didn’t mean that you . . .”

James had paled visibly too, but shrugged. “I know you didn’t. It’s okay.”

She carefully piled all the stuff she had pulled out back into the trunk and closed the lid. James had boxed a bunch of collector’s edition model cars and was working on pictures.

“You never answered my question,” Kit said after a minute.

“What question?”

“How many times have you been in love?”

James let out a laugh. “That question, lemme think . . .” He stared at her levelly. “Only once.” He looked away, hoping she didn’t see the fire he felt burning in his heart. And then . . . in a way . . . hoping she had.

“Once?”

James kept on boxing things. “Oh you know, there are the times you imagine yourself to be in love and then when you get down to it you find you don’t really love the person. You’re in love with the concept of being in love.”

She considered this. “So how many times have you imagined yourself being in love?”

“Three,” he replied. “What about you?”

“Three also.”

“Three really in love or three you just imagined it?”

“Imagined.”

“What about reality?”

She shook her head and shrugged. “I don’t know. It’s hard to say.”

James pursed his lips. "Well, at least once."

"What?"

"I would hope at least once. You are getting married after all." The word "married" tasted bitter on his tongue.

She smiled. "Oh my gosh! Look at this!" She held up a picture done in crayon. A rainbow over a hill with a sun and flowers; the sun had a happy face in it. The letters were scratchy and crooked, but the message on the paper said:

"Grannpa, you ar swet shugar candee." The phonetic spelling scrawled out in different colors.

"Cute," James said, not noticing she never answered his question. They finished that room and moved onto her grandfather's bedroom. This room was mostly done as Marleah had to get those things he needed to the nursing home with him. They moved from room to room, organizing boxes into piles of things Kit wanted for herself, Gary might want, Mom and Dad might want and Kit's uncle's family. There was another stack for Deseret Industries and another for the dumpster.

James salivated over the gun collection kept in a large cabinet by the bookshelves. Kit pulled out a Red Hawk Ruger and set it in a box of things she was keeping.

"Do you know what you just claimed?" James asked.

"Yup," she said, while sifting through the rifles.

"That's a Red Hawk Ruger," he announced incredulously.

"I know."

"Do you have any idea how rare that is or what the value of it would be?"

She looked at him. "I do, but that isn't why I want it."

"Why do you want it?"

"It was the first gun I ever shot. I hit the bulls-eye Grandpa painted on a can on the third shot. That gun has excellent sights, no kick, and it meant a lot to my grandpa. One of his best friends from the war gave it to him when he came to Utah to visit."

"You go shooting?"

"Not so much anymore. I don't really have the time, but I used to go a lot."

James could've kissed her. Not only was she not afraid of or intimidated by the emblem of his livelihood, she could use it and liked to.

"Truth or dare?" James said after a moment, wondering what he'd say if she said dare.

"Truth."

"If you could live in any century, which would it be and why?"

"Oh, now that is a good question. I would have to say this one that we're in."

James closed up a box and sealed it with tape. "Why?"

"Because in every century, and even for part of the last one, women were not free to do anything. They were shadows of the man they married. They couldn't own land or vote . . ."

"Yeah, I still don't know why we let that one go." James grinned at her widened eyes. "For so long without letting you do that, was what I was saying. Geesh, you could at least let me finish."

"Which century would you live in?" she asked after scowling a second longer.

"I think I would choose this one, too."

"Why?"

It's where you are, he thought. "I like modern convenience. I think I may have liked the renaissance too. I think the clothes were pretty cool and I would have made a great lord."

"You may have been a peasant," she said.

James laughed. "True. I would've been a cool peasant, too. 'Course, according to some I'm a peasant here and now."

She winced, and let it slide. She felt he may have meant Bradley, but didn't want to incriminate in case he meant someone else. "Yeah, well, I will never get rich with my job either," she said.

"With your education and experience, you could go elsewhere and make more."

"More isn't everything. I used to work for an ad agency here in Utah and then got transferred to their California location. That was where I met Bradley the first time. After I worked there a while, I just really wanted to come home and get away from all the glitter and glitz of starlets and advertising. I decided I could put my education to being useful to the world instead. That was when I went to work for March of Dimes."

"Do you like it?"

"Yeah, it's been the most fulfilling job I've had. I feel like I'm accomplishing something."

"That is very cool to do what makes you happy." He hefted a box to the D.I. pile. Kit took the box she had to her pile.

"What about you?" she asked hesitantly, afraid to offend him after she'd already put her foot in her mouth about killing people.

"What about me?"

"What made you decide to become a cop?"

"It's a long story."

"We still have a lot of packing to do. I'm sure we'll have time." She smiled encouragingly.

"When I was a kid . . . a teenager really, my parents were out of town and a burglar came into the house. I heard a noise in the hall closet. So . . . thinking my parents were home, I opened the door to say hi and he was standing there. He had one of my dad's guns pointed at my head."

Kit dropped the book she had meant to put in the box. Her eyes wide, mouth hung open. "No!"

"Yep. He shot me, but only in the shoulder. School was hard to deal with after that. Rumors were spread about me trying to commit suicide or me being careless when I went shooting or me involved in a robbery where I was the criminal and got shot while trying to get away."

"Kids can be so horrible," Kit said, sympathetically.

"So can teachers and ward leaders," he said with an edge of bitterness.

"I'm sorry," she said, her eyes tearing up.

"Oh, it's okay. I made my peace a long time ago. I just need to remind myself I did every once in a while." He shrugged. "Anyway, I joined the military and was discharged because I couldn't take my arm far enough behind my back during the physical, so I got a medical discharge and became a cop instead. I guess I had a need to be . . . I don't now, I just wanted to be useful," he said.

She smiled at his response. "So does it still hurt?"

"What?"

"The gunshot wound."

"Sometimes."

"Do you have a scar?"

"Yep."

"Can I see it?"

"Why would you want to see it?"

She shrugged. "Curious."

He grinned. "If I show you, what will I get?"

"My respect." She smiled playfully.

"Oh, well then. That's worth it." He stretched his neck and tilted his head to the side while pulling the collar of his T-shirt down and to the right of his right arm.

She moved her hand towards him as if to touch it but pulled away and shivered. "I'm sorry," she repeated.

James put another box in the dumpster pile. The day was ending with the sun hanging low in the western horizon. He checked his watch. "We're done," he commented. "Now, you just need some movers with trucks to load it all up and haul it where it all needs to go."

She tucked a stray strand of hair behind her ear. "I could never have done it without you."

"Sure you could have. It would have just taken longer. Hey, I've got to get to work. Mind if I change here? I've got my uniform in the car."

"No, I don't mind at all."

"Thanks." James went out to his car and came back with his uniform. He changed quickly and came out of the bathroom to find Kit waiting for him.

"I just realized; we've worked all day and not eaten. Do you have time? I could take you to dinner."

He checked his watch again. "No, as it is, I'll be just on time. I am so tired." He laughed. "Pulling a grave shift when you start out tired is a bad idea."

She frowned slightly. "I wish there was something I could do."

James chewed the inside of his cheek a minute. "You know, there is something you could do for me."

She tucked the strand of hair that had found its way back in her eyes behind her ear again. "Name it."

"How tired are you?"

"Not at all. Why?"

"You could join me on my shift and talk to me to keep me awake."

"Can you do that?"

"Sure. Ride alongs are okay as long as we don't make habits of them."

"Are you serious?"

"You don't have to if you don't want to . . ."

"No! No. I do want to. I think that could be fun. Am I okay in what I'm wearing or—"

James laughed outright at her. "It's not a black tie affair. You'll be fine. I'll take you up on the dinner offer during my lunch break."

"Okay. I'm in. I have some things to finish up here. Can I meet you in like an hour?"

"Sure. Sounds great." They arranged the meeting place and James left. The hour passed very slowly for him and when he finally pulled his patrol car into the parking lot of the grocery store they were meeting at, he stared for a moment. Her head was bent over a computer screen balanced against the steering wheel and she seemed to be concentrating on something important.

He pulled out the radio and flipped a switch, at the same time flipping on the overheads. "We have your car surrounded. Please get out with your hands up." The radio went to a loud speaker that seemed to echo and bounce his voice off every car in the parking lot. Kit looked up, startled, and then she grinned. Her face washed with the blue, red, and white flicker of the overheads.

She grabbed her bag and sweatshirt, got out with her hands up, and stood there in the light like a criminal looking repentant. James laughed at her and got out to open her door.

"Tell me something good in your life. What's your best favorite memory?" she said once settled into his car and on the road.

"Oh just one? I have too many to pick one."

"Just pick one."

"You mean like a day of fun, a spiritual day, a memorable day . . . what?

"I don't know . . . a fun day."

"Fun . . . well, at the risk of sounding ridiculous, every day I've gotten to spend with you have been extremely fun."

"Doesn't sound ridiculous at all. I've truly enjoyed your company too."

James smiled. "But off the top of my head, I think the funnest day I've had was when I just got home from my mission and Allen's family invited me to go to Disneyland. I had never been to Disneyland before and the night we got to California I was so excited I couldn't sleep. I made Allen go out with me to inspect the park. We walked all over the place. The Disneyland Hotel had fountains and gazebos everywhere and I was just coming off my mission and finally allowed to think about girls. I couldn't help but think about how great it would be to take a girl walking through all that."

James laughed. "There was this wishing well and Allen yanked off my shoe and pretended like he was going to throw it in and tripped. He ended up actually accidentally dropping it in there. I could have killed him. So I had to hobble around the rest of the way, which was really annoying. We then wandered around to the gate where you buy the tickets and caught a tram to take us back to the other end of the parking lot, which was closer to our hotel. That was when I noticed that we were going the wrong way so I told Allen we'd have to jump for it. Keep in mind the tram was going like ten miles an hour. Anyway, I jumped first which really hurt my foot without the shoe and I hit the ground running, slowed myself down and turned in time to watch Allen jump. Instead of running, he just jumped and landed face first into the asphalt."

"Oh no!" Kit said.

"Oh yeah. He looked a little like you did after your wreck."

"Poor guy."

"Yeah," James laughed. "I guess no one taught him the whole law of physics; that an object in motion wants to stay in motion. The tram driver stopped, panicked that Allen had died or something and everyone on the tram had to turn and stare at the shoeless boy with his friend the klutz. It was so funny, although I don't know why. We were just young and insane and it felt good to act like a couple of teenagers even though we were both over 21."

"Have you ever been back?"

"To where? Disneyland? No. I was going to tag along with Brian's family, but had to work."

"Don't you get vacations?

"I do now, but back then, I didn't." James turned into a school parking lot and flipped on a sidelight to inspect the dark corners where a person could hide.

"Why do you check the school?"

"Vandalism mostly because it's a familiar place for kids. They seem to return to it at night when they feel like getting into trouble."

He pulled out again. Kit lightly touched the switches between the seats. "What do these do?"

"Work the lights. These are the overheads, this goes to the lights inside, and this one here releases the shot gun behind your head." Kit swiveled to look at the gun hanging in the back window.

"You know you're a redneck when . . ."

"Oh no. No redneck jokes." He laughed. He stopped to consider her a moment. "So what was your most fun day?" he finally asked.

"Mine? Oh, I don't know. Do you want a recent one?"

"Just pick any that stand out."

"Hmmm, well, I went motorcycling up the canyon with Gary and one of his little stalkers."

"Did you have a date?"

"Yeah, I was with some guy from college . . . . Anyway we went up over Guardsman's Pass to Park City and Gary drove through a stream of cold water and got stuck. The bike stalled in the stream which cracked the engine head. His little girl-friend threw a tantrum because she had to get to work, so we agreed that my date would take Gary's back with him and then bring back a truck and trailer for Gary and I. Well, we waited and waited and waited and finally, when we ran out of food from my backpack and knock knock jokes and riddles, we'd had enough. We got on his bike and coasted it down where it would coast and pushed it when we had to go up hill. It took forever!"

"What happened to your date?"

"Oh, you won't believe it. The guy got lost after taking Gary's girlfriend home. He couldn't figure out how to get back to us. Gary almost killed him when we asked why he didn't go ask our dad to help because our dad knew right where we were going and could've found us without any troubles at all."

"Why didn't he?" James asked, heading into a neighborhood.

"He said he didn't want my dad to think he was dumb."

"Oh, so instead, he proved it to him . . . I get it." James grinned and Kit laughed. "Something like that. We were so tired and dirty when we got back to civilization we could've gone to bed, but instead went and saw a movie and ended up falling asleep in the theater. Some 16 year-old usher had to wake us up to boot us out so they could clean the theater."

James laughed. "Poor kid. Probably didn't make enough an hour to have to do wake up call. Must've been a really bad movie."

"I honestly cannot remember what it was. Could have been anything."

"So, what makes that a best memory?" James asked, coasting slowly through a neighborhood that wasn't finished being built yet. He shined his lights over the fields and into the skeletal forms of houses.

"It was a beautiful day. Perfect weather. We had good conversations, good scenery and good exercise while being serenaded by birds."

"I understand that." He paused. "So, truth or dare?"

"Truth," she replied promptly.

"Hey, wait a second . . . you like motorcycles?" he asked, the obvious just dawning on him.

"Sure I do. Love them. I like the kind of bikes you have to pedal too. Mountain biking is a lot of fun."

"I have a motorcycle," he said proudly.

"Really? What kind?"

"Street bike, Harley deuce soft tail."

Kit whistled. "Wow, that's very cool. Do you wear a helmet?"

"I do now," James laughed.

"What does that mean?"

"I nearly killed myself not wearing a helmet in a wreck I was once in."

"You should always wear a helmet," she declared indignantly. "Even mountain biking, I always wear a helmet."

James tsked. "Sounds awfully judgmental coming from a girl who doesn't wear a seatbelt."

Kit blushed. "Touché' . . . So was that my truth or dare question? Do I like motorcycles?"

"Ummmm . . . no. That was an afterthought question."

"So what was the question?" They were driving upward onto the benches of the city towards the mountains. James drove up 3900 South past the belt loop and down a road called Zarahemla. He parked the car at the dead end where it circled into an overview of the entire city.

"Oh wow!" Kit exclaimed. "I never knew a view like this existed."

"Get out. It's time for my break anyway."

She complied and sat on the hood of his car. He leaned against it next to her. They were quiet a moment before he said, "Truth, but this question is a little more personal than the others."

"Shoot. I can handle the truth. I never lie."

"Why are you marrying . . . Bradley?" He almost said that guy, but caught himself and forced himself to use Bradley's name.

"We've been together a long time," she said stiffly.

James waited. Surely there was more than that. She never finished.

"Look how clear downtown is! The capitol practically glows!"

James looked but it didn't glow nearly as bright as she did when he looked at her.

"So tell me something about yourself," Kit said.

"Tell you what? You already know my deepest secrets . . . What else is there?"

"How many girls have you kissed?"

"Gentlemen never kiss and tell."

"No, I'm serious. Tell me."

"How many have you kissed?" he countered.

"I asked first."

"But I asked second; two is a bigger number."

"Oh fine. Let me think." She looked away as if adding up some insurmountable numbers.

"Oh brother," James muttered.

"Twelve." She finally spit out.

"Twelve? You had to deliberate that long over just twelve?"

"Well, I had to sift through all those that tried, but failed since I dodge pretty well. So . . . how about you?"

"Oh yeah, I dodge real well, too."

She lightly punched his arm. "Kisses, silly! How many girls have you kissed?"

"I'm not telling," he said after a brief pause.

"Why not, I told you."

"You would laugh at me."

"I won't. I promise."

James scrubbed a hand over his head. "Three," he said finally.

"Three?"

"Yep. Each girl I thought I was in love with was graced with kissing. I didn't kiss them unless I meant it. Well, except for Alison for practice. I guess she would make it four if we counted her."

She tilted her head catching the moonlight in her dark hair. "You are not like anyone I've ever met," she said with a furrow on her brow.

"What do you mean by that?"

"You have honor." She shook her head, the dark hair bouncing over her shoulders, the light haloing her head.

James looked away. "Honor," he said shaking his head, too.

"No, I mean it," she said firmly. "It's there . . . honor in your job, in the badge you wear, in the priesthood you hold, in the person you are."

She paused, then added, "You wear it like a skin and walk about in it as comfortably as your would a casual sweat suit, never noticing it is very much like a tuxedo to everyone else." She smiled softly. "Your honor is what I love best about you."

He picked up a few bits of gravel, and tossed them over the edge. "What do you like least about me?"

The words "when you're not with me" stuck in Kit's throat. She cleared it. "I suppose I don't know you well enough to see your faults."

"Now see, that's wrong," James faced her.

"What is?"

"It's when you know someone least that their faults should be apparent and then as you grow to know and love them, their faults shouldn't seem so obvious."

"Okay, so what are my faults?" Kit asked.

"I don't know. I think I've grown to know you well enough I don't see them."

She grinned. "So, what were they?"

"You take the whole world on your shoulders and then imagine you have to carry it alone."

"I don't do that," she said.

"Yes, you do. You do it everyday."

"So what do you like best about me?"

"You breathe life into everything around you. You are selfless and giving. You aren't afraid of anything new and shine when a task is in front of you."

"Ha! You are nuts."

James shrugged. "Maybe . . . maybe." He gave her a lopsided smile. "I'll be in the loony hospital in the padded cell next to yours."

She grinned. "We would have a blast! We could play ping pong on community time!"

"Oh yeah and tap out Morse code through our walls and yell out at the nurses just to be horrible."

Kit clasped her hands together. "And dominate the television, and change the channels just as everyone else is getting into the shows!"

"And complain when they feed us meat that we are vegetarians and then whine that we don't feel we get enough iron in our diet!"

"Perfect, it'll be loony bin bliss!" Kit laughed.

"Aahh, but first, my break's over."

"Rats." She scrambled down from the hood.

He opened her door for her and then they continued on the streets he was to monitor. "Look at that," James pointed.

Kit squinted to see people in a parked car at another view overlook. "What about them?"

"Nothing special . . . just that . . ." He picked up the radio. "18-J-5."

"18-J-5, go ahead."

"Mazda license is Bravo Lima Alpha 783."

James waited while dispatch gathered the information. "18-J-5, I've got a blue Mazda 626, 1998 registered to Frank Nessle. Insurance and registration are current."

"Copy that." James put the radio down picked up a Maglight and a metal clipboard.

"Are you going to bug them?" Kit asked.

"Yep."

"Why? They look like things might be getting cozy."

"Exactly the reason to send them home."

James got out, slid his finger along the trunk to find it firmly closed and rapped on the window. Kit watched curiously from the car. The radio would make noise of other calls to other places every once in a while.

James came back carrying two licenses and got back in. "He's 26. She is 16, almost 17."

"Oops," Kit commented.

"Yep, oops. I wonder if her parents know where their little girl is."

He called in the license numbers to dispatch and said a string of numbers and words that made no sense to Kit.

He finally got back out and went to the man and girl. James talked to them for a long time before returning to Kit.

The car started up and drove away. "What did you tell them?" Kit asked.

"I told them she needed to go home. She looked panicked too. He must've said nothing was going on a dozen times."

Kit laughed. "I'd beat my daughter for being so stupid."

"I'd beat my son for not knowing better."

"Honor," she murmured to herself.

He rolled his eyes at her, but felt his face grow warm with the words of the highest compliment he'd been given.

"Would you look at that?" James pointed to the car in front of them as they got rolling again.

"What?"

"Registration is expired."

He flipped on his lights. The car was slow to pull over. It was as though the driver was undecided as to what to do. Finally the car pulled onto the shoulder and stopped.

James called in the plates, received his response and had turned on a monitor of some sort. "Sshhh." He put a finger to his lips and pointed at the monitor. Kit nodded and settled back listening to the click, click of the overheads. James received his response from dispatch and got out.

Kit admired his form as he sauntered to the car. After a few moments James had the driver out of the car. The man looked unhappy, but compliant. James flashed a light in the man's eyes.

"You been drinking tonight, Chris?" he asked, checking the license to be sure he got the name right.

"Just a little. I only had one. To toast my friend's wedding. It was just a social drink."

James refrained from mentioning the guy's tattered jeans and tank top didn't look much like wedding attire. "Put your arms out, Chris, to the side. Yep . . . just like that. Now tilt your head back and walk heel to toe towards me.

As soon as the guy dropped his head back he curved and stumbled to the right. "Lost my balance," he muttered as he tried again. He focused and took a deep breath as he moved forward. After two steps that were fairly wobbly, he stumbled again.

"I can do this, just give me minute." Chris put his arms out a third time, but James gently shook his head and moved the man's arms back to his side.

"That won't be necessary. Mind if I do a breath test?"

"Of course not," he slurred. "I have nothing to hide."

"Uh-huh," James said. "I'm sure you don't." James walked Chris back to the patrol car where the portable breathalyzer was. After administering the test, James shook his head at Chris, tsking softly.

"Chris, I think you need a ride."

"No, no. See, I have my own car. I'm fine."

"Well, you may feel fine, but you're drunk and you can't drive like that." James put Chris's arms behind his back.

"I only had one. It was a social drink."

"I know . . . social every night." James rolled his eyes and read Chris his rights as he patted him down and then put him into the back seat. Kit stared straight ahead, her face white, not once looking back to the man now seated there.

Chapter 23

"Are you okay?" James asked, patting her hand softly after they had dropped off Chris at the station and seen that the car had been towed.

"I'm fine. Did you think you'd find that, a drunk, when you pulled him over? I mean, it just looked like a routine stop to me."

"There are no routine stops. When a cop gets complacent and starts treating the job as routine . . . that's when he makes a mistake; that's when he doesn't get to go home that night."

"Do you wear a bulletproof vest?"

"Always. That is as important as wearing your seat belt."

Kit snorted in derision. "Let it go, would you? I learned my lesson."

"Good. Hey, Kit?"

"Hmmm?"

"You look tired and I now have reports to write. Is it okay if I drop you off at your car?"

"Sure. I am tired . . . a little bit."

"I appreciate your company. It helped me a lot."

"I appreciate you, too." She smiled. "Truth or dare?"

"Truth."

"What would you do if you had ten million dollars?"

James laughed. "Wow! That's a wad of change! Well, I'd pay tithing, pay off my debts, pay off the debts of my family, I'd buy another Harley and I'd hang out at the mall more often."

"You don't seem like the shopping type," she said cynically.

"Well, I wouldn't be shopping for me . . . I'd listen, listen to hear someone want something really bad, but not get it because they couldn't afford it. Then I'd buy it and take it to them."

"Wow . . . I mean really, wow! That's the nicest thing I've ever heard."

"Don't give me the credit. My mom did it once when I was with her. She heard a woman talking who had just tried on a dress. It was Easter and the woman had never had an Easter dress before. She tried the dress on and admired herself in it, but didn't buy it because she didn't have the money to spend on such foolish things for herself. My mom bought it and caught up with her in the parking lot to give it to the woman. I never forgot that—how happy it made the woman and how happy it made my mom."

"Thanks for telling me that. I can't tell you how incredible I think your mom is."

"Yeah, she is. She is the kindest person alive." He stole a glance at Kit. "So what would you do with ten million dollars?"

"Oh, I'm a lot more selfish than you. I'd pay off my debts, pay off my family's debts, buy me a nice house in the Harvard Avenue area . . . one with streams running through the back yard, put a million dollars in a trust fund for March of Dimes, where they could only spend the interest; then that way they would always have that money coming in, and I'd go places like the Ice Capades. I'd buy snow cones and cotton candy for everyone within twenty feet of me."

"You'd buy the world snow cones . . . that is so cute."

Kit grinned. "Oh yeah, I'd travel. I'd go shark diving off the coast of Australia. I would go hang gliding and hiking all the time."

"You will likely be able to do all that being married to Bradley. He seems to do all right for himself," James said flippantly.

Kit shifted uncomfortably. "I sincerely doubt that he'd have the time . . ." She fell silent, unsure what to say.

"Here we are," James announced back at her car.

Kit sighed. "Thanks again for all your help today." She didn't look at James.

"You okay?"

"Yeah, of course . . . I'm fine." She hesitated. "I'm not marrying Bradley for his money. I just wanted you to know that. I mean it's likely he'll have me sign a prenuptial agreement or whatever." She tried a little laugh and then frowned.

"I know you're not. You aren't the type to do something like that."

"I just wanted you to know." She got out. "Goodnight, James."

"Goodnight, Katherine."

She stopped upon hearing her name, smiled slightly with a little shrug, and closed the door to the car.

"Idiot!" he hissed at himself as her car drove away. "Why do I do that?" He thumped his hand on the steering wheel. He had made Kit feel bad, feel like she needed to excuse her relationship with that guy. He looked down and saw she had left her sweatshirt on the floor of the passenger side. He picked it up and breathed it in. It smelled like her. *What am I doing?* he wondered. James leaned his head on the steering wheel a moment before pulling away to finish his shift.

Chapter 24

James awoke the next morning to the ringing of his phone. He almost rolled over and let it ring, but finally with a growl scooped it up. “Hello?”

“Hey, Jamie!”

He leaned back into his pillow. “Hey, Cin-ful. Wassup?”

“Oh nothing much. I was wondering the same about you.”

“You mean, you are wondering if I have taken the plunge and finally committed myself to the institutions of white lab coats and strait jackets? I'm thinking about putting it on today's to-do list.”

She laughed. “Jamie, is it that bad?”

“It's worse. She's getting married in less than two weeks.”

“I'm sorry, but I have something to take your mind off it.”

James rolled over and threw the sheet up over his head. “No!”

“No?”

“No, Cin-ful.”

“I haven't said anything yet.”

“But you will and I can't. I am so tired of being set up. Don't make me . . . please.”

“Look, James. This one is different.”

“Different how? Don't tell me . . . . She believes in reincarnation and thinks she was once a queen in ancient Egypt. Or no, no . . . she's a botanist and has a cornfield growing in her living room and algae in her bathroom. Or wait no, I got it; she's a confirmed atheist but practices witchcraft on the weekends.”

"Don't be stupid," Cindy scoffed. "I've never set you up with a witch before."

"That's debatable!" James shot back.

She sighed in exasperation. "Look, she is really great. Just one more date and I swear, I will never set you up again."

"Why?" James whined.

"She is great, I tell you; pretty, funny, loves cops—you'll like her, I promise. Besides, I already told her you'd take her out."

"Cindy!"

"What?" Her voice oozed all the innocence she could muster, which wasn't much by James' accounting.

"Fine. I'll go out with her. When?"

"Tonight."

"Tonight?"

"Sure. You have the night off; so does she. It made sense."

"Did you tell her I would take her out tonight?"

"Ummm . . . I might have, yeah."

"You owe me," he grumbled.

"Oh, I'll be saying that to you after you meet her."

"Based on our past experience, I seriously doubt it." James hung up the phone after getting all the information on picking this girl up and when. He looked at the clock and cursed. Ten-thirty. Since he'd been up all night working and this was still his middle of the night, he pulled a pillow over his head and tried to go back to sleep. He rolled over to one side then the other side, curling up into his comforter and then stretching out completely flat.

James cursed again. He picked up the phone and dialed Allen and Cindy's phone number. "You stink for waking me up in the middle of the night," he said when she answered and hung up again. He knew she'd be laughing. Cindy was like that.

He stretched and got up. What else was there to do?

He tinkered around the house, read scriptures, played the

piano, and realized he was bored to tears. It was 3:30 p.m. He was supposed to pick up his date at 6:00 p.m. There was time to go visit his mom and see if she needed any help with anything.

When he got there, no one was in the house, but he could hear a saw humming from the back yard.

"Hey, Dad," James said, leaning against the doorframe to the shop.

"Hey, son. What are you up to?"

"Nothing." James laughed. "What are you doing?"

"Building a dog feeder."

"A dog feeder, dad?"

"Yep. Neighbor hates the way dog food bags look in her kitchen. She wants a nice wooden one that matches her cabinets. I told her I could do it. Since you're here, why don't you come help me?"

James moved over to hold the piece of lumber while his dad ran the saw through it. "It's good to have someone hold it. It helps to keep it from pinching the blade when the pieces fall away from each other." Sawdust floated to the floor and the smell of cut wood filled James' senses.

"I have a date tonight," James said after a minute.

"Really, with Katherine?"

"No, a blind date."

"What about Katherine?"

"What about her? She's engaged."

"I see your point, son. But I just can't help but think that experience you had was . . . well . . . inspired some way."

"I thought so too and it isn't like I don't care about her . . . I do. But how do I compete with a guy when she's wearing his ring? It seems wrong. Plus, he's wealthy and, truth be told, a cop will never be wealthy."

"You are not poor. You almost own your home completely,

and you don't have any other debt. Besides, Katherine isn't the type of woman to be concerned about things like that."

"But she is taken, Dad. The sooner I figure that out, the better off I'll be."

Gerald chewed the inside of his cheek thoughtfully. "Wasn't it Brian who said, 'It isn't over 'til the girl in white says 'I do'?" Gerald smiled warmly while running a bead of wood glue along a groove. "I'm not trying to confuse you, or complicate things; it's just, I'd hate to see a nice girl like Katherine divorced five years from now because she couldn't see any other options when she had them."

"I know what you're saying." James held the two pieces of wood together where they had been glued while Gerald fastened them that way with a C-clamp.

"As a bishop, I've seen lots of terrible things. Good people with bad secrets eating at them. Promise me something, James."

"What?"

"Promise me that if our Katherine doesn't find the courage to walk away from this situation she has gotten herself into, that you will have the ability to not think about her at all. It's one thing to pine over a single woman's love, and another thing entirely to pine for one that is married to another man."

"I know, Dad. I won't. That's why I have to go on this date tonight. I need to take my mind off things for a bit."

"I agree with you. I agree." Gerald sighed. "Your mother is going to shoot me if I don't get this all cleaned up before she gets back. Help me out, would you?"

"Sure."

They got things put together, with wood shavings and curls swept and tools cleaned and put away. His dad went to shower and clean up so as to take his mother out to dinner when she got home.

James left to go home to get his motorcycle. The day's weather was warm and the night promised to retain the heat. Kit's sweatshirt was at the front door. There was still an hour left before he had to pick up his date. He stared at her sweatshirt, debating and arguing in his mind.

He finally picked it up and threw it into the saddlebag on the side of his bike. He kicked the stand up and drove to Kit's, scolding himself for his weakness the whole way.

Once at the front porch, his hand hung mid air in front of the doorbell. He closed his eyes and moved to press the button when a car pulled into the driveway. James turned to see Bradley's sports car pull up next to his bike. Bradley stepped out of the car, pulling off sunglasses and tossing them carelessly to the seat.

He gazed lazily at James as he walked to the porch and stood a moment, taking him in before speaking.

"Hello, James. To what do we owe the pleasure of your visit today?"

"Just dropping something by," James said counting slowly back from ten to calm down enough to just not punch the guy.

"How nice of you." Bradley stepped past James and opened the door to let himself in. "Come on in. I'll get Kitty for you."

Gary was on his cell phone while flipping channels in the family room. His jaw fell slack as he watched Bradley and James come in together. James stayed there while Bradley made his way down the hall to knock on Kit's door. James felt his eye twitch. Gary looked at him. "What's going on?" he whispered as he moved the phone away from his mouth.

"Nothing," James cleared his throat. "Just wanted to give Kit her sweatshirt back. He showed up when I did." James shrugged stiffly as he stood there.

"I gotta go," Gary said into his phone. "I'll call you in a bit." He hung up and stood.

Kit and Bradley were coming down the hall talking quietly but obviously arguing over something. "James," she said with a genuine smile, "It's nice to see you."

"Isn't it though?" Bradley grinned, showing too many teeth. "It's a good thing you caught us. We were just going out."

"Well . . . I just wanted to give this back." He handed Kit the sweatshirt and then a small smile played over his own lips. He cleared his throat. "You left that in my car last night."

Kit's eyes went wide at the same time Bradley's narrowed. Gary snickered but hid it in a cough. "Thank you . . . for bringing it back."

"Anytime," James shrugged, feeling more comfortable by the minute. "So where are you two lovebirds going off to?" James asked, emphasizing the word "lovebirds."

"Dinner, actually. If you're not busy perhaps you'd care to join us," Bradley said.

James felt satisfaction as though someone were spooning it over his head and it was now dripping to his toes. *That's right*, he thought smugly, *keep your enemies close*. "Oh I would love to, except . . . I have a date tonight." He wanted to grin when Kit's face darkened, but kept his composure and then the stroke of brilliance hit. "I know!" James snapped his fingers for emphasis, "Why don't we make it a double date?"

Kit looked like she might throw up. Bradley relaxed, to James' surprise, and the Cheshire grin seemed toothier than ever. "What a great idea," he said over Kit's, "I don't think . . ."

"Of course, we'll have to go to a less expensive restaurant," he said. "I certainly don't want to put you out or anything."

"Don't worry about me," James said. "This girl is worth any extra. I'm sure I'll get along fine." He hoped Cindy had been right when she said this one was different.

"Can we come too?" Gary piped in, looking intrigued with the idea of whatever entertainment could come from a night like this. "I haven't been able to think of anything to do with my date tonight and it would help to have a group."

"Gary, I know you can't afford this place on your budget and I certainly do not intend to pay for you," Bradley said, exasperated.

"I'll cover you, Gary," James said, loving this more and more. "Your company would be perfect. You are bringing Dawn, right?"

"Yep. She's the one," Gary said.

"Great, sounds perfect . . . unless, of course, Bradley has any objections."

Bradley's lazy gaze swept over all of them and ended on James. "Of course not. The more the merrier."

"Cool," James said. "Hey, Gary, you've got a motorcycle don't you?"

"Yeah."

"Why don't you get your bike and we'll pick up the girls on our motorcycles. We can travel together that way, unless . . . well . . . unless this is a dress up restaurant. Is it, Bradley? I mean, should I be wearing a suit? I can change."

Bradley's composure never changed, but the eyes seemed to roll in exasperation. "Right, actually, perhaps we could tone it down for a bit tonight. Since Kitty isn't really dressed appropriately either. Where would you suggest, James?" His voice seemed to ice over James' name.

"I don't know. What's your favorite food, Kit?"

Kit rubbed a finger over her temple. "Italian," she muttered.

"I know a great Italian restaurant. It's not really nice or anything, but the food is to die for."

"How's that, old Bean?" Gary asked clapping Bradley on the back a little harder than necessary. "You prepared to slum it for a night?"

"You've no idea what I am prepared for," Bradley said.

"Very cool. So we can meet at Robintino's. It has great atmosphere. You'll love it and, hey, Bradley, since it's not a real costly meal, I'll catch the tab. You can pick it up when we go somewhere nice." James winked at him. "So are we ready, Gary?"

"You bet."

"Great, we'll catch you two there," James said.

Gary backed his bike out of the garage as James started his up. "What are you doing?" he asked.

"I don't know, but that was fun," James laughed and revved the engine a little as he backed out to say goodbye to Kit and Bradley as they stood at the doorway watching.

James picked up his date first and was surprised when he did. She wasn't wearing any makeup and didn't need to. She had a fresh scrubbed beauty that even plain looked extraordinary. Her blonde hair hung loose over her shoulders. When she saw the motorcycle, she promptly braided it back to keep it out of her face. Her name was Jami, which made James laugh. He had been so tired when Cindy called that he hadn't made the connection of their names.

"I love your bike!" she said settling in behind him after strapping on the spare helmet he kept locked on the back of the bike.

"Thanks. I—" He cut off as she wrapped her arms around his waist. "I like it, too."

The Jaguar was parked in the stall closest the door that wasn't handicapped. James was disappointed it wasn't in the handicapped stall so he could ticket it.

"I love this place!" Jami exclaimed as they locked the helmets to the bike. "They have the best, stringiest cheese on their pizza."

Gary and Dawn followed them in, holding hands. Jami took

hold of James' arm so he could escort her in. Kit and Bradley were waiting to be seated. The restaurant was busy for the evening.

Bradley's foot was tapping in time to the fingers he had drumming over his leg.

"Looks like we should have made reservations," Gary grinned.

"Bradley did, didn't you?" James looked at Bradley who in turn looked alarmed.

"I don't think they take reservations, but you never said I should—."

"No, didn't you let them know when you got here that they would be seating a party of six?"

Bradley darkened, "Yes, I did." He was catching James' angle and wasn't appreciating it.

"Your table is ready," the hostess broke in. She led them to a table in the center of the restaurant. James held the chair for Jami and settled into his own. Kit sat straight across from him.

Gary picked up the menu the hostess had placed in front of him. "Great place you picked, James."

"Yeah. Everything looks good," Dawn agreed, scanning her own menu.

"We should get a pizza and share it," Jami suggested.

James shrugged. "Sounds good to me."

Bradley touched the menu carefully at the edges as though afraid to catch some communicable disease. "I think I'll be having the vegetarian lasagna."

Kit looked disappointed. "C'mon, Kit, share a pizza with us," James said.

"I think . . ." She looked at Bradley, furrowing her brow as she looked back to the menu, "I'll just have a calzone," she said finally.

"But you love pizza," Gary said.

"Calzones taste just like pizza," Kit insisted.

Bradley puffed his chest. "Nice to have a woman who can think on her own."

James snorted at him. Gary ignored him altogether and the two girls just blinked in wonderment at Kit and Bradley.

"Oh, I get it," Gary grinned at her "It's the old 'tastes like chicken' theory. If it tastes like chicken, why not just eat chicken. If it tastes like pizza, eat pizza?"

"Lay off, Gar. If she wants a calzone, she can have a calzone," James said. He turned to Jami. "What kind of pizza do you want?"

"Anything is good. You can pick."

"Meat lovers!" Gary exclaimed. Dawn scowled at him.

"How about half and half. Meet lovers one side, vegetarian the other," James offered. Dawn looked infinitely happier.

They all agreed in time for their waitress to bring bread with ranch dip and take their orders.

"It will be two separate tickets," Bradley said indignantly. "You won't be needing to pay for mine." James rolled his eyes.

When the waitress was gone, Jami leaned in closer to James. "So tell me what it's like being a cop. Are you ever offended by the TV show 'Cops,' or is it a pretty accurate portrayal of how things really are?"

"'Cops' is pretty accurate, but they only show the exciting stuff. They never show the mundane garbage we do all day; writing reports and scanning the streets, picking up stolen bicycles and stuff."

"What kind of weapon do you pack?" she asked.

"Gloc 40. Most cops carry a Gloc."

"Ooooh, can I see it?"

"We're in a restaurant," James protested.

"C'mon, James, I'd like to see it too," Kit agreed.

James contemplated a moment and looking at Kit, he

finally said, “All right, but you guys are going to get us thrown out of here.” He pulled the gun from his fanny pack and checked the chamber before letting anyone touch it.

“Looks to be a Gloc 10,” Bradley commented importantly.

James and Gary looked up at the same time, astonishment evident with their eyes wide enough to pop right out of their heads.

“It’s a Gloc 40,” James said patiently as if explaining it to a very small child.

“It is only a 10 mm. Well, not even a 10 mm. So it couldn’t be a Gloc 40,” Bradley insisted with an edge of derision. Kit closed her eyes briefly, her face bright red.

“Forty has nothing to do with the millimeters, Bradley. It’s a 40 caliber. Hence the Gloc 40 name. Trust me on this.”

“I am certain that is a Gloc 10.” The guy just wouldn’t let it go.

Kit put her hand lightly on his shoulder. “It really is a Gloc 40.” He reddened, but backed down.

Everyone sat in a cool twelve seconds of silence before Bradley spat off, “Well it certainly looks like a Gloc 10.”

Gary started laughing. “That’s what you get for not checking to make sure your brain is loaded before you go shooting off your mouth, huh, old Bean?”

“Gary!” Dawn was about to reprimand but lost the effort of it when Jami started laughing too. She had a clear high laugh that James liked.

“Oh, c’mon, Brad,” she said, “Lighten up and laugh a little.” Bradley glanced at her. James was surprised that Bradley remained as quiet as he did. The waitress brought the food out to which Jami grinned in delight. “I love food,” she said, pulling a piece from the pan, the cheese stringing along until she broke the connection with her finger and popped it into her mouth.

“So Brad, you say you own a computer something-or-other?" she asked after taking a bite.

"It's Bradley, not Brad, and it's a graphics design corporation. We just went international."

"Interesting," she said around a mouthful of food. Although she wasn't smacking or showing off any train wrecks, it was obvious that it made Bradley uncomfortable to talk to Jami while she was chewing so enthusiastically. James put his elbow up on the table to rest his chin in his palm and watch her.

He wasn't certain why she was . . . what was the word . . . intriguing, yet she was and then he saw it. She was natural, nothing at all pretentious about her. She was very likable.

She took another bite. "So are you two married?" she asked pointing at Bradley and Kit.

"No," Kit said. "We're engaged."

"Oh, very cool. When's the big day?"

"Two weeks." Kit furrowed her brow, "A week from this Friday."

"You got everything ready?"

"I think so; invitations, decorations, reservations and any other 'tions' I can think of." Kit smiled. "A lot of work, but it is almost over."

"Or just starting. I hear marriage is a ton of work." Jami pulled off another piece of the pizza.

James stared at Kit. "I don't think it would be as long as you really love the person you are marrying." Kit looked away from him and started cutting away at her calzone. In the light with her head titled that way, the pink scar along her jaw line seemed to be highlighted.

Gary was watching Kit too, and noticed it. "Your scar seems to be getting smaller, Katy-did," he commented.

Dawn looked up. "You know it really does look better, Kit."

"What scar?" Jami asked, tilting her head to inspect Kit closer.

Kit raised her collar uncomfortably. "I was in a car accident a couple of months ago," she explained simply.

"Oh, no!" Jami exclaimed. "That's terrible."

"That little stunt postponed our marriage by two months while she healed—and lost me a really great car," Bradley remarked. "Even still . . . she has that scar. It won't look good for the pictures. We'll have to get them retouched so the scar can be removed from the photos."

James sat up straight, dropping the pizza to his plate. "Why would you do that?"

"So she looks as good as she can," Bradley said, baffled that James needed to ask.

"She does look as good as she can," James insisted. "Are you blind? She's beautiful and that scar is a part of who she is and things she's made it through. It is a sign that she is still alive when she could have died in that wreck."

Everyone was staring at James. Gary nodded as if confirming something to himself and Jami had a slight smile as if seeing something she hadn't noticed before.

"Oh, give me a break, Hartman. Don't be so dramatic. Of course she looks fine, but that scar will be shrinking further yet. It may not be there in ten years, so why have it in pictures when it is such a trivial point?"

"Can you guys stop talking around me? I'm right here, you know. Why not ask my opinion on this?" Kit glared at both of them.

"Sorry, darling. What would you like to see done?" Bradley rushed to placation.

"Nothing at all. I can tilt my head in the pictures. It won't be noticed."

"How did you get in your wreck?" Jami asked.

"I . . . I don't really remember," She shrugged. "I don't know where I was going or what I was doing in that part of town. I only remember, and even this vaguely, waking up in the hospital."

"You don't remember any of it?"

Kit shook her head and shrugged. Bradley watched Kit lazily. "You should ask Hartman, here. He seemed to be the on the spot emergency person. He probably saw the whole thing."

"Well, I did," James admitted, "but I couldn't tell very much. I wouldn't be able to guess why she was there or anything. I'm just glad I was there."

"Wow," Jami whistled. "I got into a wreck once. It was really scary, but nothing like that. You should probably be glad you don't remember."

"Maybe," Kit conceded. "But have you ever had the feeling like something was missing . . . information, I mean, and if you just had that little bit of missing information, then everything else you knew would make sense?" Kit gave a self-depreciative laugh. "That's crazy, isn't it?"

"Not at all," Jami said honestly. "It sounds like poetry, true and lovely with a melody of melancholy."

"Poetry is garbage," Gary said. "Well, except for Dr. Seuss." He grinned.

"Don't believe him, Dawn," Kit soothed at Dawn's scowl. "Gary may act like a clown, but he writes poetry. Ask him to show you some time. He's really not as shallow as he looks."

The conversation flowed easily after that. Bradley had turned to quiet skulking as he picked at his lasagna as the girls chatted along about jobs, movies, and weddings. James and Gary teased in all the appropriate places.

James took both checks and paid them. The waitress had assumed he was the head of the group and handed both of them to him. Bradley glowered at that.

When James and Jami climbed onto James' Harley to drive away, Kit seemed to be good friends with Jami. She gave Jami a hug and said she hoped to see her again. When Jami got on behind James and wrapped her arms around James' waist, Kit paled, but smiled and waved as they drove away.

"He's gone, darling . . ." Bradley said grimly. "You can close your mouth now."

"What is that supposed to mean?"

"You've been drooling all night, though I swear it buggers me that I don't know why. He isn't much to look at and has nothing to offer, not that he's offering, mind you. He looks very comfortable with his lady companion."

"You are so twisted. I'm not thinking anything and I wasn't drooling!"

"Say what you will, but I'm not worried. Jami was drooling too and she's going home with him. You are coming home with me. Those facts alone take the worry away."

"How dare you—"

"I'm not implying anything horrible would ever cross your altruistic mind. I'm just saying be careful. When you spend enough time with someone to be leaving clothing in his car, you have opened a door to feelings for him. I just don't want you confused so close to the wedding, love."

"I'm not confused." She stuck out her chin defiantly.

"Glad to hear it," he said lazily as he pushed the door unlock button on his key ring. The car beeped and lights flashed. Kit got in. *I'm not confused,* she thought. *Am I?* She looked out the window, not talking at all except to nod in the right places as Bradley droned on about the business site in the United Kingdom.

"Here we are," James announced back at Jami's house after touring her through the city from the back of his bike. Jami jumped off and waited for James to kick the stand down and get off too. She took his arm and let him lead her to the door.

James leaned against the railing to the stairs. "Do you realize you're the first blind date I've ever enjoyed being with?"

"Really?"

"Definitely. If you are willing . . . I'd like to go out again sometime."

Jami sat on the top stair and patted the spot next to her for him to sit, too. "I can't go out with you again," she said once he'd seated himself.

"What . . . but why?"

"I have a very strict rule against dating guys who are in love with other women. It cramps my style . . . makes me feel like second best, and trust me, Hartman, I am nobody's second best."

"I'm not in love with—"

"Nope . . . no. Denial is for the weak. You aren't weak. Listen, I'll make it easy on you. If your girl Kitty actually marries the corporate British Boy and you are totally over it and no longer on the rebound in six months, look me up. We'll go dancing or to a movie or something. But if you are half the man I think you are, you will not let her marry this guy." She paused. James was stunned. "Oh, I mean he's cute and the accent makes him charming and he's obviously got some green to spend or pounds or whatever they call it, but Kit isn't for him. You know it and . . . and I think she knows it, too."

James took Jami's hand in between both of his. "If I had met you three months ago . . ." he started.

"I know . . . I know. You'd be the luckiest man alive right now, but I don't know . . . I still think you could end up pretty happy."

James kissed her hand and hugged her tightly. "Cindy told me you were different from the rest."

"Well, she was right," Jami grinned. "So what are you waiting for, Romeo? Go get her!"

James hopped up and took two steps before turning. “If things don’t work out, I can still ask you out in six months then?”

“Yep.”

“What if you’re not around?”

“Then you shouldn’t ask.”

He stepped back towards her, leaned down and kissed her cheek. “Thanks.”

“Sure thing,” she said as she watched him bound down the path, jump on his bike, and drive off.

Chapter 25

"Be serious, Kitty," Bradley complained.

"I am serious." They were at Bradley's condo. He had decided not to take her home and wanted to show her the drawings for the office in England. Building would start as soon as the drawings were approved.

"How can you hate the design? It's everything we asked for and more."

"It looks so . . . I don't know . . . pushy. I would never go to your company if I needed a job done because this building looks large, impersonal, uncreative, and pushy," she said, repeating herself for the tenth time.

"Our clients won't come there for meetings until they have been properly wined and dined in other places. This is where the work will be done, papers signed, deals completed."

"So where are you going to wine and dine them? France?"

He hesitated. "I was going to wait until our wedding night to show you this as it was meant to be a gift, but . . ."

"Show me what?"

"I have other designs here that I want your opinion on."

"Okay, show them."

He pulled out a long tube with blue prints of a large house. Everything was there. Drawings of what things would look like completed. The yard would be expansive with a pool, hot tub, tennis court and stables. The house seemed equally expansive. It appeared to have the purpose of entertaining with a theater system, game room, and a dining hall. The hair on the back of Kit's neck rose.

"What is this?"

"It's our house."

"Our *house*?" Kit felt sick.

"Of course. The one we'll be living in."

"Where is this house?"

"In England, naturally."

"No! Bradley, no! There is nothing natural about England!" She swatted at the plans, causing them to roll back up into each other.

"What are you talking about? It's my homeland. I have citizenship there and the business is there. It's the next natural step to move there."

"I don't have citizenship there and it is *your* business, not my business. I have a job—one that I really love—one that I believe in. You have got to be joking!"

"Of course I'm not joking! Why in the world would I be joking about something as important as our future? This is our life we are talking about."

"*Our* life, Bradley? *Our* life? Did you not hear yourself? You should have consulted me! Should have said something!"

"I am saying something!"

"Not today, not now! You should have said something when you concocted this whole idea. Now is not soon enough!"

"What are you saying?"

"I don't know what I'm saying! Just take me home, Bradley. I need to go home now."

"But we've not discussed anything yet."

"I can't discuss something that I have not been given the opportunity to think about. Take me home!"

Bradley's face darkened but he pulled out his keys. They didn't talk while driving and when he pulled up into the driveway she simply got out without saying goodbye and walked to the front door alone.

James pulled a weed from amongst the daisies growing in his garden. He tossed it to the sidewalk with a little more force than necessary. No one was home at Kit's place when he went there. He took his bike down the street to park it and waited for an hour under the cover of trees in case Bradley was still with Kit, which James assumed he would be. James had steeled himself against the thought that he may be forced to witness an uncomfortable make-out scene. After he'd waited and waited, he worried she might not be coming home. Frustrated and confused, he had left to go home.

Now he was weeding in the dark. For all he knew, he hadn't pulled a weed at all but actually got a flower. He scrubbed a hand over his head. He would go over as soon as church was over and tell her the truth. At least then it would be out and maybe it would stop driving him crazy enough to weed the garden by moonlight.

He pulled at something else and tossed it to the sidewalk before getting up and going to bed.

Chapter 26

Church had been agony. He could honestly not recall one word said in any of the three meetings. He didn't bother to change clothes, but went straight to her house.

"She's already gone," Gary said when he'd answered the door.

"Where?" James felt panic that she wasn't there.

"She had an appointment to meet one of the coordinators for the wedding at the reception place."

"Where is that?"

"Garden Park Ward on Yale Avenue."

"She said she wanted a house around there someday," James mused.

"That would be no big surprise. Kit loves it there."

"Who's with her?"

"Today?"

"Yeah."

"Whitney, the person in charge of decorations, and my mom."

"Where's Bradley?" James felt stupid for asking, but wasn't able to stop himself.

"Who knows, and, more importantly, does anyone really care?"

"So he's not with her then?"

"Nope. The coast is clear, pal."

"Thanks, Gary."

"Over here is where I want the band." Kit pointed to a large arched wall with a little brick stage. It was beautiful. The whole place was beautiful. Even Horrible Dianna could not complain about a place like this. She probably would anyway, just out of principle. Kit contemplated reminding her mother-in-law to be who was going to be in charge of her future retirement home.

"Why are you having a real band? Why not just get a D.J.?" Whitney asked.

"Dianna will expect a real band; anything less would be demeaning."

"Then tell her to pay for it," Whitney grumbled.

"She would if I gave her half the chance, but there is no way I am giving that woman any more control over this day than I have to. Besides, since I'm living at home, I've saved up quite a bit. I can afford to pull off this wedding all by myself."

"I'm impressed! My parents asked if they could pay me to elope. They said it would be cheaper."

"Bradley wants to move to England," Kit said after a moment.

"Are you surprised?"

"Yep. A lot."

"I'm not. I expected he would eventually."

"Why?"

"He's too English. I mean seriously, he's lived here half his life and his accent is still perfect. It's like he's working on keeping it up on purpose."

"I feel like he lied to me."

"So are you going to marry him still?"

"I . . . don't know. I don't know what to do." Kit tossed a flower petal into the pond. "We've been together for so long, I just . . . I don't know."

"What about that cop?"

"James?"

"That would be the one."

"We went on a double date last night. It was horrible. Bradley was a complete jerk and James' date was great. He's probably with her right now," Kit frowned.

They wandered away from the stage around the stone railing to the pond. Kit's mother, Marleah, was with the coordinator, working out details for where the tables and chairs would be.

"I am going to float flower arrangements with candles on the pond," Kit said.

"How do you think the ducks will react to that?"

They sat on the lawn to take everything in. There were brick and stone walkways that led from the front of the church to the back and then surrounded the pond. The water inlet came from the east side of the yard down over a perfect waterfall into a smaller, deeper pond that ran out into the larger one. From there it cascaded over a few smaller falls into a little stream that ran off the church property into the neighbor's back yard. The streams were crossed by two bridges, and the entire yard was taken over by well-kept lawns and fragrant gardens. Towering oak trees bordered the west end.

"Wish I'd known about this place when I got married," Whitney commented. "It would have saved my parents a fortune."

Marleah joined them. "I feel terrible being here on the Sabbath, Katherine," she hissed.

"It was the only day she could do it and it isn't like working . . . it's like taking a lovely Sunday stroll."

"Do not try to justify our purpose here!" The scowl on Marleah's face deepened. "We only have a week and a half left. There is so much still to do. I've got to get home now. I'll see you both later." Kit watched her mom hurry off.

The coordinator was still wandering around and inspecting every inch of the yard. Kit closed her eyes and turned her face to the sun. "Hello, Kit . . . hi there, Whitney."

Both girls squinted up to see James standing there. "Hey, James!" Whitney said. "How the heck are you?"

"Doing okay, great actually."

"I'm going to go check on your coordinator. She had said she might need some ideas." Whitney stood up and bounded down the path to the other end of the yard.

"Mind if I sit down?"

"Go ahead." Kit scooted over even though there was plenty of room for him.

"This place is great!" he said, once seated.

"Yeah, it's nice. I think it'll work fine for the reception."

"It should . . ." He picked at the blades of grass.

"So how was your date?"

"My date? Oh she was great . . . fine. You were there."

"She seemed really nice."

"She was." He started throwing the blades one by one into the pond.

"Good."

"You know . . . she said something kind of interesting."

"Really, what was that?"

He took a deep breath. "She said she couldn't see you married to Bradley."

"Why not?"

"She says you're better than that."

"Bradley has a lot to offer."

James felt his chest tighten. "Kit . . ." he exhaled and tried it again. "Truth or Dare."

She blinked at him, not responding right away. "Truth." She said finally.

"Why are you marrying that guy?"

"We've been together a long time. It was the next natural step." She squirmed as she heard Bradley's words fall from her lips.

"There's nothing natural about marrying someone you don't love."

"I never said I didn't love him!"

"But you never said you did either! Do you? Can you honestly say you do? And can you honestly marry someone else when you've got feelings for me?" He held his breath; he was taking a chance, taking the chance that she did have feelings for him. Would he die if she said she didn't? His extremities went numb from the fear of her doing just that.

"I . . . I don't . . . look, I do have feelings for you, but I'm marrying him. I agreed . . . we agreed to get married. It's not something you back out of."

James' jaw clenched shut. He tossed the remaining blades of grass into the water. "Right . . . of course." He stood. "Then there's nothing left to say. Goodbye, Kit."

He was walking up the path, wondering that his limbs worked when they were so numb. He stopped and looked back. "You know, Kit, it's easier to break off an engagement than a marriage when you realize you made a mistake." He turned back to the path and kept walking.

"Wait," she whispered hoarsely. "Wait . . ." She jumped up and ran to catch up with him. He didn't slow his long stride at all. "James?"

"What?"

"Why do you think it's a mistake?" They had rounded the church and were at his motorcycle now.

He grabbed her shoulders and swiveled her to face him. "If you had ever once said 'dare' in all those little games, I would have picked you up and carried you off to marry me. *Me*, Kit, not him. He's . . . he's completely wrong for you. He's a jerk; your family can't stand him. He walks all over you and you let him!"

"That isn't true!"

"It is true! When was the last time that idiot called you beautiful?"

She pulled from his grip. "I'm sure I don't know . . . I'm sure he . . ."

"I know! The last time he called you beautiful was when you got engaged and he tried to get you to . . . to . . . anyway, it doesn't matter. You didn't and he hasn't called you beautiful since."

"How would you know that?" Tears were in her eyes. "Did he tell you that?!"

"No, Kit. *You* told me that. Don't you remember any of it?"

"Remember what?"

"The wreck, that night. You were dead, Kit. You died! I knelt down to do CPR and there you were, shining like some dark-haired angel. You told me to save you. You said, 'How will I ever get to know you if you let me die?' You can't believe that all that happened just so you could marry *him*!"

Kit faltered back. James kneeling, murmuring . . . no, counting . . . CPR. She backed away further. "I don't . . . I don't remember," she said.

"No, I guess you don't." He got on his bike, kicked up the stand and drove away.

She stood there. Her mouth hung open. The rain had been pouring that night. She had Bradley's car. She was crying. Why was she crying? She'd been to the temple earlier. She'd been fasting. For what? Kit couldn't remember. She leaned against the side of the church and tucked a stray strand of hair behind her ear.

The image of James kneeling was now coupled with the image of her own broken body next to him. She could see it as if she had been watching . . . but then she *had* been watching.

"James!" She straightened and ran to the road. He was gone.

"Kit, there you are! What's wrong? Where's the cop?"

"He's gone. Where's my coordinator?"

"She's gone, too."

"Whit, I have a huge problem."

"What's wrong? Did he say something to you? What happened?"

"He told me Bradley's all wrong for me. He told me . . ."

"C'mon, Kit, breathe. What did he tell you?"

"He said he had feelings for me and then he said he saw me that night when I got into my wreck. He saw my spirit and I was dead. He said . . . Oh no, Whitney, I have agreed to marry Bradley in less than two weeks! What should I do? Tell me what to do!"

"Calm down. Here . . . sit down here and close your eyes."

"Why?"

"Just do it," Whitney said, exasperated.

"What are you going to do?"

"Nothing, just ask you some questions."

"Why do I need to close my eyes?"

"To help you think. Now close them!"

Kit closed her eyes.

"Now, I want you to think about both guys in each of these scenarios and then think of which one better suits the picture. Okay?"

"Okay."

"You are washing dishes together and get into a water fight . . . who are you with?

"You are sitting on a couch and reading to him, no make out involved. Who are you reading to?

"You go home to make a nice dinner to tell him you are going to have a baby, knowing he is the one to help you raise it." Whitney watched Kit's expression change slightly with each question.

"Okay. Riiiiiiiiiinnnnngggg . . . the phone's ringing. It's for you, Kit. Who do you want it to be?"

Kit's eyes flew open and then she gasped. She remembered.

She had gone to the temple to quiet the doubts she had about marrying Bradley, and while there, she knew in an instant she was making a mistake. Bradley was not the right one. She remembered the feeling that someone would be brought into her life in a miraculous way so that she would not have any doubts. "Oh my gosh!"

"Yeah. That's what I thought. Now all you have to do is say goodbye to Bradley."

"But, how can I? We've already sent out invitations!"

"You'll need to make some phone calls, but I think that's a small price to pay for eternal happiness. Don't you?"

"I gotta go." Kit stood abruptly.

Chapter 27

"Kitty, I'm glad you've come back. I trust you've had time to think over everything?"

"I have." She bit her lip and tucked her hair behind her ear. "Where did you find my ring?"

"What?" His face was pinched in confusion.

"The night of the wreck, I wasn't wearing the ring."

"I don't understand what that has . . ."

"It was in my bag. I put it there before leaving the temple that night."

"So?"

"When you came in that morning before I woke up, you had to have seen I wasn't wearing it, fished it out of my bag and put it back on my finger. During all that . . . did it not once occur to you to ask why I wasn't wearing it?" She tugged at the ring on her finger, pulling it over her knuckle.

"What are you doing?" Bradley looked alarmed as Kit put the ring on the counter near him.

"I'm not going to Europe with you. I'm not going to be living in England. I'm staying here in Utah where my grandfather is and where my family is."

Bradley just stared. "What will I tell everyone? The invitations . . . what will people think?"

"You have got to be kidding me! You have a brief moment of opportunity to change my mind . . . to convince me I need you, and you're worried about what people will think?"

Bradley paled and moved to hold her. Kit stepped back.

"Darling, I didn't mean it like that. Please . . . we could have such a future together; all your dreams . . . anything you want I'd get it for you if you just gave England a chance . . . I think you'd love it."

"I am an American. It would be fun to visit, maybe even stay a month or two, but I like living in America. I don't want to live anywhere else. I don't want to be a live doll for your mom to dress and I'm tired of being called Kitty. What kind of respect could your friends or class of people give a person named Kitty? I hate that you never call me by my real name."

"No one calls you by your real name! What is the difference between one nickname and another? If you didn't like it, you should have told me. You cannot hold me accountable for things you seethe about inside, but never tell me!"

"I'm not holding you accountable . . ." She pressed a hand over her eyes. "I just . . . it's just not what I want."

Bradley slammed his fists into the counter. "I get it! It's that bloody cop, isn't it! He's put these foolish ideas into your head."

"No . . . not really. I went to the temple to get an answer and I got one. That is why I took off the ring. That is why I was rushing to get home and in my confusion and the rain and the hurry, I got off the belt route. That was how I ended up in that wreck. And in the wreck, I forgot all that. Forgot I'd ever taken off the ring . . . forgot I had my answer."

"I should never have allowed you to be friends with him!"

"Bradley, are you listening to yourself? Or to me? I'm not a puppet you can dance on your strings!"

"Kitty . . . Katherine, I'm sorry . . . I don't mean it like that. I just don't know where this is coming from out of the blue like this. We've been together for two years and now all of a sudden, I'm some evil, sinister character in the plot in your head instead of the man you're marrying."

"I'm not saying you're sinister! How you twist things!

Bradley, the time we spent together has been a facade. We are putting on a show for other people . . . for each other. When you asked me to marry you, did you really think for a minute we'd go through with it?"

"Of course I did!" His face was red and blotchy.

"Now, you're lying to me." Kit felt calm. She leaned in and kissed him on the cheek. "Tell your dad I hope the business is phenomenal. Goodbye, Bradley."

Chapter 28

Kit drove to James' house; his bike was parked out front. She couldn't help but notice how organized everything was. The flowerbeds were weed-free and the lawn mowed to the perfect height. She rang the doorbell and waited. No answer. She rang it again and stood up on tiptoe to see into the hexagonal shaped window in the door. She couldn't see anything.

Kit's heart was racing. Was he really ignoring her? She knew he had to be there since his bike was there. Firmly resolved to at least talk to him no matter what he said, she wandered around back. Nothing seemed to indicate he was home; there was no movement in the windows or anything to hint at the presence of life.

Kit sat on the bench on the front porch after making her way around the entire house. He really wasn't there. Where could he be? She got up and drove to his parents' house.

"Well, hello there!" Caroline greeted her at the front door.

"Is James here?" The sound of blood pumping furiously through her veins rushed past her ears.

"I haven't seen him, but hang on, his dad may have. You know James pops in and out regularly and it's easy to miss him. Why don't you come in?"

Kit obliged, following Caroline into the house and around to the living room. Gerald looked up from the book he was reading and smiled. "Well, if it isn't James' angel!"

Kit blushed as he stood to hug her. "What brings you here?"

"I really need to talk to James, only . . . I haven't been able to find him. He isn't answering his cell phone either."

Gerald looked at Caroline. She nodded. "You'll most likely find him at Allen's house. He spends a lot of time there."

Kit was quick to get the address and leave. The adrenaline was starting to make her feel sick and it was getting dark. She flipped on her headlights and continued to Allen's place.

"Can I help you?" The girl standing at the door looked suspiciously at Kit.

"I'm looking for James Hartman," Kit started.

"And who are you?"

"I'm Kit . . . Katherine Riley. Is he here?"

Cindy paused and then finally said, "No, he isn't. He just left to go to work. He's on the graveyard shift right now."

"Oh." Kit swallowed her disappointment. "But he was here, then?"

"Yeah, he was here."

"Did he . . . say anything?"

"Well he's been here most the evening. We didn't just stare at each other," Cindy said, sarcasm dripping from each word. She regretted it instantly when she saw Kit's face.

"I'm sorry," Cindy said softly. "He just came to talk. He has a lot on his mind right now. I didn't mean to be rude. I guess I'm just protective of my Hartman. We worry a lot about him."

"I understand, really I do. Thanks for letting me know where he went." Kit walked away, feeling dejected. He had already gone to work. She felt horrible that he had gone without talking to her first.

She drove around for almost an hour. The depression was consuming. She remembered once that Dianna had accused her of manic depression. *Wow*, she thought. *She should see me now.*

She found herself along the eastern benches of the city and followed the path James had taken to the lookout point at the end of Zarahemla street. She sat in her car not even looking at the city view in front of her. Kit simply rested her head on her steering wheel. She wanted to cry.

Rap! Rap! Rap! Startled, Kit looked up. A bright light was shining in her face. She rolled down her window. She couldn't see who held the light, but the utility belt complete with cuffs, gun and nightstick identified the holder as a policeman.

"Sorry to bother you, ma'am, but this isn't a safe place to be alone at night." The voice was gruff but familiar.

"James?" Squinting her eyes to see better, she could make out enough detail to feel confident it was him.

He opened her door. "Get out," he said softly. "It's time for my break anyway."

She got out and followed him to the front of the car. They leaned against it, standing next to each other. The silence seemed to consume the space between them.

"So, I was thinking about things today and I . . ." Kit faltered. "You're angry, aren't you?"

He let out a breath he hadn't realized he was holding. With the release of air, it occurred to him he really wasn't angry. "No, how could I be?"

She leaned over to look into his face. "Truth?"

"Truth."

She nodded. "I was trying to find you earlier so I could explain things to you."

"There isn't anything to explain, is there? You are going to get married as planned and that's it."

"Plans can change . . ."

"Can they?" He picked up some gravel to send over the edge.

"Truth or Dare?"

"Kit, I can't. No more games. I don't have the heart to play anymore."

"Just one more time, James . . . please?"

He looked down at her and tossed the remaining gravel over the edge then wiped his hands off on his uniform pants. "Truth then."

"Do you love me?"

His chest tightened. He looked away. "Does it matter?"

"That isn't the question, you see. I only ask because I love you. I really love you and since I'm not getting married in two weeks anymore, I thought . . . if you weren't busy . . . you could go out with me . . . to celebrate or maybe just so I'm not alone that day. I could help you tie your shoes and then we'll be even. We could just go out."

"You're not getting married?" He blinked at her as the reality of the words began sinking in.

She shook her head; tears fell silently down her cheeks. Her lip trembled.

"You're not getting married . . ." he repeated, then shrugged. "Since you aren't getting married, yeah, I guess we could go out." He tried to feign nonchalance but he couldn't wipe the smile from his face.

She smiled too, through her tears.

He tucked the loose strand of hair behind her ear. "Don't cry, Katherine. The answer is yes. I do love you." He pulled her to him and held her there. He started to laugh, picked her up and swung her around.

"You're not getting married!" he shouted. He pulled her to him again. "I see you." He pulled her far enough away to look into her eyes, "I see you, Katherine."

"I see you too, James. I see you now."

About the Author

Julie Wright was born the fourth out of five children in Salt Lake City, Utah, on May 13, 1972. She focused on writing at Brighton High School and continued that focus through her years of education at Brigham Young University.

She has won several awards for short stories and poetry, and has written a screenplay.

She met her husband, Scott, in high school, and sent him off on an LDS mission to Sweden. They married upon his return. She speaks, reads, and writes fluent Swedish, and loves to backpack and go rock climbing.

She has a deep appreciation for fine art, good reading, and great Italian food.

She currently resides in Oak City, Utah, where she and her husband own a small grocery store. They have three children: McKenna, Merrik, and Chandler.

Julie has also written the best-selling novel *To Catch a Falling Star*.